THE ~~STRUGGLE~~ OF MY  LIFE

SACHIN CHAUHAN

THE STRUGGLE OF MY LIFE

Author

SACHIN CHAUHAN

books

The struggle of my life (*novel*)
by Sachin Chauhan

Published By   : **Redgrab books**
942, Mutthiganj, Allahabad, 211003
Website : redgrabbooks.com
E-mail : contact@redgrabbooks.com

©   : Sachin Chauhan
Typeset by   : Shree Computers, Allahabad
Cover   : Shree Computers, Allahabad
ISBN   : 978-93-87390-34-8
Edition   : First, October 2017 (Anybook Publication)
             : Second, May 2018

The journey to write this story is about 5 years old.

Being a software engineer, writing a wide and deep Tale, at some point of time seemed almost impossible.

Further, my purpose was not just to write a story.

My goal was to give an inspiration, a message at every phase of age through a Tale.

There was a time when I felt that this story would not meet the status as the subject demands.

Then I got the guidance from my Master Mr. Kamlesh D Patel, Daaji!

He taught me the art of fulfilling the goal with the entanglements of social life.

From him, I learnt the magical heart-based mediation called Heartfulness; that eventually paved the way for both; this story and my goal.

Thank you Daaji!

This book is dedicated to every boy and girl
who once had a dream, had fallen in love and
struggled to see it home.
To the souls who had their hearts broken
and had it mended in the
warm embraces of Friendship.

This is a dedication to
'Love, Dreams and Friendship'

ACKNOWLEDGEMENTS

This book was a dream project for me, my whole life bundled inside a cocoon of this book. A project can never be accomplished without a team.

In this note I would rather replace the word Project with 'a Narrative' and the team with 'a bunch of friends'.

Whether it was a media work or a literary work, these guys and gals were just a call, a text away from me.

I would like to acknowledge the efforts and love of my extended family, my friends;

Arpan Banerjee, Lalit Adhikar, Nihar Ranjan Samant, Nikhil Pratap, Pooja Chandra(Rupal), Punit Gupta, Pavan Patel, Sagar Gohri, Shashank Mishra, Sumit Pratap, Vineet Kumar Ankit, Vijay Bohra.

Thanks a lot strugglers, dreamers; you're the real winners!

-Sachin Chauhan

CONTENTS

CHAPTER ZERO

I had heard of such phone calls and had seen people receiving such calls but never expected that I would ever get one.

It was early morning on 24th April, 2011(Sunday). I precisely remember that it was 3:00 in the morning when that call woke me up. What I heard was something I still remember, and I still feel the same chill run down my spine thinking about it even after all these years.

It was a sudden gush of sweat from my entire body; I was shaken from the roots of my very nerves. And what happened after that was something which shook many lives.

"Hello" (sleepy me)

"Am I talking to Aditya?" (A frightened voice)

"Yeah! Who is it?"

"Please rush to Agra as soon as possible. I will message you the address."

"Agra? Why? Who are you? Hello... Hello! You there?"

And the phone got disconnected.

The very next moment I received an address of some

hospital in Agra from that unknown number.

I tried calling the number back, but it was out of reach. I even tried Rahul's cell, but that too was switched off.

I knew that Rahul had gone to Agra two days ago.

I googled the address, and it was a valid address. I even tried to call that number from another cell but the number was still unreachable. I tried that number on truecaller but didn't find a match. Now I was more petrified. It was not a prank call for sure.

I was unable to understand what was happening, but one thing hammering in my head like an emergency alarm was,

"There is something wrong."

I took a deep breath and walked towards the window. It was a grave silence outside and very dark. A malfunctioning tube light which was getting on and off simultaneously on the basketball court, that's chrrr... chrrr.... scary scratching sound could be heard from my room. Except for that eerie sound, the entire hostel was quiet.

At the entrance of the college, there was warden chacha who was resting in his old armchair and near to him was Delfi, who was supposed to be sleeping at such late night hours, was alert, wagging his tail.

Everything was placid. An aghast stillness was all around; soothing winds started stinging suddenly.

There was little heaviness in my eyes, and a strange fear started making a lump in my throat, I was feeling petrified.

Like a bolt of lightning had struck me and I had no Idea what to do next. Like, I wanted to scream, Scream like anything. Heavy breaths and negative thoughts had already started their business in my mind and heart.

I turned around.

There was a photograph of Rahul in a checkered shirt and me together on the wall, seeing which I could not control but gave out a smile.

I again tried both the numbers but the status was still same.

It was the longest night.

The time between that scary night and the morning was getting elongated, as if someone had prevented even the sun from rising.

The sleep and restlessness were making me weak, and I could feel the tight slaps of all sorts of cranky questions on my red face.

This was the moment when I was standing clueless between the skies 'wrapped in clouds of danger' and the grounds of 'questions and uncertainties.'

7 Years Back

~~THE CHILDHOOD~~

I was in the 8th grade when we shifted in a 3 B.H.K. apartment, inside a famous Intermediate college of the City.

"An apartment inside an intermediate college campus."

No matter how strange does it sound, but I bet you can't imagine how exquisite it was.

In the campus of a huge college was a beautiful Teacher's colony, which had almost twenty families living in it. There were some interesting things about the colony which included a two-story building in a shape of a circle which was like a stadium, with an open area in the centre of it.

There was a park at the centre of that stadium look-alike building, which was a beautiful place. The greenery was enough to enchant people with its beauty, having no swings or swimming pool, just trees, plants with pretty flowers blossomed on them and a few benches to sit. The balconies of all the apartments faced that beautiful park.

There stood a giant Eucalyptus tree in the middle of the park, which would have been around 50 to 60 years old.

Although the beauty of the place was more than enough to take my breath away, I somehow was still disappointed about leaving our old house which I used to call home. Along with that house, I also had to leave my old friends behind, all of whom I kept on missing every day then.

However, relocating was a regular affair for us as dad had a banker's job and we had to move to different cities frequently because of periodic transfers.

By then we all were habituated of changing houses and cities, but it always took some time to accept the change; guess I never got used to it completely.

This time was a bit different; I was adjusting a little too quickly to this place because of two reasons at my new home.

First, Dad had told me that we were not going to move to a different city anymore and we'll be anchored there. Second, there were plenty of grounds in the neighbourhood. That meant I'll get plenty of time and place to play. What else could I expect; this of course was the reason for my happiness in that new city.

Right in front of our house, lived the principal of that college along with his family. Naman and Pratham were his two cute sons who became my first ever friends in that unknown city. Although I was four or maybe five years older to them but I think amongst kids, there are barely any age boundaries, there is no one who is elder or who is younger to anyone;

Kids are Kids, aren't they!

We used to play cricket every day, almost for 2 hours in the evening. We had a time slot for it, between 5 pm to 7 pm.

The evening was the time when all the men of the society would take a stroll around the park circling our playground in the center of the park, and the ladies would invest the time to discuss the entire city sitting on the benches and watching us all play.

And there was this special bench at the corner of the park, where every day sat the only elderly lady of the society. Her grey hair, sunken eyes and wrinkled face had concealed the tales of her immense losses, having lost her only son, and husband to the wars at the border. All she had to her support was a 3 feet stick that she held firmly while she walked; and all she had left to her beauty were the furrows of unuttered, unresolved questions that donned her forehead. On her aged lips she held a mild smile, almost always; the only thing that life couldn't take away from her.

There she was, an epitome of cheerfulness and mirth; the eldest kid amongst us all who had seen 70 autumns of her life,

'Jaya Amma'

The view seemed almost like an enlightening session or a spiritual gathering, where Jaya amma was the one giving a mythological discourse, the rest of the ladies were her devotees, and she was their Idol. It was amusing to look at their expressions, as it seemed that they were the ones running the entire universe sitting in that park.

Of course, after a long day, the people of our society used to come to live their lives in the park from 5 to 7 in the evening. Peace was the only thing one could find there, away from their offices and their regular lives.

For children, it was still summer vacations.

The entire view was fascinating for both eyes and soul. Adorable kids playing in the middle of a lush green ground, Uncles walking on the round trail and in the corner of the park watching kids sometimes, sometimes observing fathers of cute kids, sometimes looking at herself and most of the times following Jaya amma, there they were the respected ladies of our society.

Jango, the 50 – 60 years old tree which was right in the middle of the park, which I thought was almost of the same age as Jaya amma's; was every kid's best friend. Be it a chance missed for batting or balling, or maybe a scolding session from parents or anything for that matter, be it them being happy or sad; they would come to Jango and talk to that mute tree. They used to share every small moment of the day with it.

Jango also used to play cricket for both the sides but only as a fielder, as it used to stop the balls coming towards it because of the humongous structure.

As the time passed by, amidst all these, everything started to get normal. The new house, the new place, they weren't new to me, and I wasn't new to them anymore. That summer, the summer vacations seemed familiar, like the one I have had before; something I enjoyed just the way I used to enjoy before as well.

Although we used to go to my Grandparent's place to spend the vacations every year; but since we had moved from Indore to Moradabad, it didn't happen that year. But among everyone in this society, all the kids I played with, all the uncles and aunties who made it feel like one big family, and the quarters surrounding the field in a circle; made everything feel safe and made me feel I was home, finally.

* * *

Apart from the daily routine that we used to have, one evening the kid's gang decided to skip cricket and go to "Ram-Bagh" instead. In that city, well not really a city as such rather, it was a town to be precise. So, in that town, we had a pretty old temple went by the name of "Ram-Bagh." The temple was quite magnificent with all sorts of wondrous artworks all over the walls; a spectacle in itself to our childhood minds. I think they must be prehistoric almost 200 years or maybe 300 years old, the sculptures along with the abandoned galleries of the temple.

Apart from the beauty of the temple that it was, the place was known for something else too.

There were a lot of rumours of Paranormal Activities on a ground which was adjacent to the temple; that a lot of unexplained ghastly phenomenon had happened over the past. Once every month or so, a new story would get added to the list of unusual stories by the local newspapers.

It was almost sunset when Naman, Pratham, a few kids from other societies in the neighbourhood and I reached there. Naman came up with some scary ideas as he was the one who forced us to go to the same rumoured ground.

As soon as Naman pitched in his idea, I said,

"Ghosts come out at nights; if you want to meet them you should come here at night. Don't you watch horror movies? They sleep during the day and get back to life at night; you would not find anything at this time, dear Namani."

(The bunch of kids burst out into laughter, and it was giggles all around.) But Naman was adamant about it; he meant business. We were left with no choice. We tried, but he was not convinced at all and eventually, we all reached the "Holy Ground" by 8 PM.

The evening turned to the night; I was scared of parents more than I was of the ghosts. Being the eldest in the team I promised them to return by 8 PM, but look at us, we were waiting to meet the ghosts in a rumoured haunted ground.

It was almost half an hour of wait, but we had no signs of ghosts around, neither a toy with blood all over it nor a big dark shadow with feet turned backward.

Eventually, we started back towards home.

As we were about to approach the main road walking through the exit of the temple, I heard the sound of a pacing motorcycle, approaching us. On the bike, there were two men, faces covered with masks. They stopped by us and in a split of a second started to drag Pratham towards the bike. The situation was scary, and then all the kids started to cry. This made it even scarier. I was terrified and got stuck to the ground I was holding. I knew I had to call out for help, so I shouted my lungs out to gather people. Amidst Pratham had fallen as a result of an exchange of fists between the bikers and all of us.

They finally ran away, and we could see the taillights disappear into the darkness. I felt life coming back to me.

Thankfully Pratham was fine, and there were no scar on his body, but now it was difficult to handle the children. So, we quickly made a move and hired a rickshaw towards home. On our way back home, I told everyone to refrain from discussing the incident with their parents or in fact with anyone for that matter.

I had to do it with calm, and I hoped that kids would understand it.

Next morning what happened was opposite to my expectation. While I was dictating the kids (which according to me was the gentlest way possible.) to not disclose the matter, I missed out one fact, and that was, Pratham was just five years old, despite the name he was second child in his family.

Yes! He had told everything about last night to his dear Mom.

Now what, I could hear his Mom's voice calling out my name from their balcony,

"Rahul!Rahul!",

I ran towards my balcony making an innocent face

and said,

"Yes aunty"

"Such a terrible incident happened yesterday, and you didn't tell me anything about it."

"No, No aunty, nothing happened yesterday."

I noticed something; there they were Naman and Pratham, standing behind their mom, shivering. It seemed that they were trying to be sorry, and so I understood the entire scenario now.

"What? Nothing happened?" she asked again. "Then why is Pratham crying since last night? This is it. No cricket! No fun from tomorrow onwards. This is ending now; schools are reopening from Monday so start preparing."

She shut the balcony door with anger, and here we were left with no game, no fun, everything was over with one door bang.

This was awful; we only had 3 or 4 days left of the summer holidays. At least we could have enjoyed more, we could have rejoiced those four days, but she didn't listen, and shut the door on everything.

That was aunty, Pratham's mother who calmed down after showering her anger on me, but there was one more Mom who had her ears glued to this whole conversation and there she was, my Super-Mom.

As soon as I turned around from the balcony, I was shocked and started to shiver like a little kid, which I was.

"No Mom, nothing happened, we would not play now, we would not go anywhere, I'll start studying now..sorry mom .. sorry."

I was singing the anthem in front of her while she was talking to me with a stick in her hand.

And somehow, after a couple of days of getting an earful, this incident was behind us. We were lucky that nothing bad happened that night.

* * *

The amazing time full of fun and frolics of summer vacations had come to an end now. Eventually, things got changed, and I was enrolled in Class 9th in a new school. Pratham's family had moved to their new home, and they left their rented accommodation that was right in front of our house.

That year July was a tough one, days didn't pass. I was wading through the days in my new school away from my old friends at school and society.

New school, oh no not school precisely, it was a college now. In a 9th class; the place where you go to gain knowledge as if your entire life depends on it, that is no more a school that becomes an entry stage college for you, and when you enter in a college, the tag of being a child is removed from you.

We had stopped playing games now. Cute Naman and Pratham had left our society and had gone far away from us.

Waking up early in the morning to get ready for the 'college' then classes from 8 AM to 3 PM, a power nap after that, and then rushing towards the tuition, not one but two of them and ending the day with self-studies. I felt as if someone had snatched away my life from me, and had put me in a robotic routine.

I was a part of a weird war now. It felt that the days when we used to live our lives would return with the summer vacations only.

I was tired all the time, the pile of books, pressure of expectations, amidst all this my own desires went missing somewhere.

It made me think, "If this is the situation now, what would the future be like? What would it be like when I reach the next grades? What would happen when I'll start working, what would happen as I go through in life? When I can get breather barely for myself at this age, at this grade; how would I survive in future?"

In addition to these horrifying academics, I was getting tormented by the achievements of my cousin, who had gone to pursue engineering. And not to forget the pressure of my parents' expectations; I was told to start preparing so that I could crack the tough nut IIT-JEE, and as a result, the foundation course books were stacked on my table by the same cousin.

But the question was, how would I prepare?

Hours in a day were still 24 only, fixed… rigid!!

Classes, tuitions, home work, unproductive projects, and self-study, after all of this, I had only 6 hours at night. I had my plans to sleep during those 6 hours.

'Should I compromise on that too?'

Cricket was my passion, my dream; I could see that getting shattered right before my tired eyes.

Something was imprisoning my childhood; the dream was being crushed; it was the noise of expectations all around and that too of others.

"Expectations of your own." I believe this phrase didn't exist in that era.

Long live the man who discovered a Sunday. This was the only day when I could meet my dream. But that day too could get ruined because of relatives' and guests' unexpected arrivals. They too found Sunday, to build a healthy social relationship with my family and to give away unasked for advices. Every other Sunday either a relative or someone from my Dad's Bank would come over, and I would be busy in arranging snacks and food for the dear ones.

No, no !! The story doesn't end here; the best is yet to

come. Of course, they would kill you with their stupid questions.

Once an aunty said,

"Hey Rahul! You have grown up beta."

And I had to reply,

"Yes aunty, that's the only option I had."

Mom, Dad used to scold me for my behaviour and my body language, but you know what, anyone... I mean anyone, meddling with my once-a-week Cricket routine would be a devil for me.

This phenomenon continued.

One day, I heard some voices, yes, they were of kids, some naughty voices in the neighbourhood. Mom told me that a new family had moved into Pratham's flat and the most amazing part was that the new family was a photocopy of the previous one; two cute children Luv and Kush along with their parents.

It did sound well to me; it was indeed a happy news.

It was like things coming back to normalcy!

* * *

Every Sunday from morning till evening, I used to practice cricket on the same ground in our society. My friend Aryan and I would ball and bat alternatively for hours. From last few Sundays, I noticed a kid who must be of 8 or 9 years of age, riding his bicycle around the field. That kid would stop to watch us play for 5 to 10 minutes and would again start with his bicycle. This eventually became a ritual on every Sunday for an hour or so. I mean that kid would ride less, but watch our game more.

Noticing his repeated pattern, one day I stopped him and started interviewing the little kid.

"What is your name, bro?" I asked.

"I am Luv." the kid answered.

"Yes! I am also Love, this guy is also Love, no one is hate here, but what's your name?" I asked again.

"Hehe . Bhaiya my name is 'Luv.' "

"Oh, nice! The name is 'Luv'. If I am not wrong, you have recently moved to that flat (I pointed the finger towards their apartment)."

"Yes, bhaiya."

"Very nice! Will you be my friend?"

" You'll have to teach me cricket!"

"That's a deal mate. You have asked for a Titanic from me."

(Hehehe, we all chuckled.)

And this was how our Lagaan team began to get build. Now we were three to play on Sundays.

Earlier, during vacations, a couple of kids from other societies in the neighbourhood used to come to play in our park, but as soon as the new session started in schools, it seemed that the contract for overseas players got ended.

Slowly and steadily the studies had started to pick up the pace. It was almost three months now since the vacations ended; Midterm exams were almost a month away. The burden of books and preparation was overwhelming. It wasn't that I was not interested in studying.

I was working hard in that department too, but I guess I wanted to play as well.

While all of this was happening, I had one thought in my mind,

'If a pendulum of a clock moves equally to the left and right, then why can't things happen equally in two different departments of life too.'

For me, things meant Studies and Sports.

In order to attain that balance, I took a big decision. I

stopped one of the tuitions and set my schedule in such a way that I could play cricket too, but still, parents were a tough nut to crack again. It was really difficult for me to convince them, but I did manage somehow.

After three months of monotonous life, when I resumed my cricket during the weekdays, I saw that there were many groups of bairns playing on our ground and the most amazing part was, they all were authorized denizens of our society.

I was not even sure whether I live here, as the new picture was completely different from the weekends and vacations.

Yes, this happens to you. It happens when you keep running in life and don't realize what is happening around you. You are indulged in your hectic life in such a way that everything that surround you start to blur.

Luv, Kush, Kittu, Bittu, Nik, Jiyansh, and other kids used to play as a team on the same ground regularly.

It was a beginning of a new era; it was like my childhood was back again after a reboot. Life, which was almost killed by the books and notepads, had finally got some fresh air to breathe. Happiness was back again. I couldn't believe I gained so much just by leaving one tuition behind. I mean yes, my concentration on studies was at par, now I was much more comfortable with books as well. That was the first lesson that I taught to myself,

"You will have to take decisions at occasions; you have got the right to choose, so go with the one which makes you happy and compromise with the one which doesn't affect you anymore."

From sunrise, I used to wait for the evening. When we used to meet each other, used to laugh, used to smile, used to play cricket, used to race, used to listen to old stories from Jaya amma, used to play hide and seek, Ice-water and so on. Our games were so appealing that even newly wedded Bhabhis could not control themselves in joining us, they would leave all the so-called 'bondage of societies' in the divine feet of Jaya amma and would play every single game that we used to play. We even witnessed the days when elderly uncles, forgetting their age and concept of generation gap joined us to relive their childhood.

So, this was the story for the day, every day to wake up early to study for an hour (The punishment to leave that one tuition, here you have to trade something for another), then classes followed by a power nap, tuition and then PLAY! After that followed the night's self-study session and signing off for the day. Two hours spent on the ground were much better than rest of the activities. Hence everything else apart was in the "others" category for me.

In this way, life got divided in two halves. Though both of the parts were integral parts of my life; one of them I was not fond of and the other I loved.

The first and the biggest lie that my parents said to me was "You just have to obtain good moral in grade 9th and 10th to build the base of your career, and after that, your studies would be at a normal pace."

Unfortunately, I took it seriously. After all, parents said all of this, so I did not take the things easy.

I started to work hard, and I spent my days and nights doing that. I became passionate about obtaining good marks, just good makes. Thankfully, there were no customs in my family, like "To Top" or something, and yeah also I could not even think of being the topper of my class.

'I was an adult now, and the journey named 'Struggle' had started,' this Truth got verified and confirmed by my parents when they gave me a separate room. As I had to wake up early in the morning and sleep late at night, this was the need of the hour, and I had to accept it.

But hey! I didn't compromise with cricket, as by that time I luckily got a chance to join a Cricket Academy of the same college where our society was.

Now the academy used to call their players on weekends only, and that worked out well for me.

I had cricket kit in one corner of my closet, and the other one had fat stacks of books!

Right in front of my study table were three posters and they were of "Albert Einstein, Sachin Tendulkar, and Rahul Dravid."

Since I was inclined towards cricket more; so I majorly had idols of that particular field on my room's wall.

The uniforms were also in two distinctive sets; one pair of formals that was white for the college and the second was also white but was the sporty attire, for the academy.

I had two different lives, two roles to play, two different struggles which I could feel even at that age.

In fact, I knew that they were two different paths, these paths had different destinations and one day I would have to choose one, but the day wasn't there yet.

I often said to myself, "Till the time these two ways run parallel, let's just be with the flow. The moment I wind up at some crossroad and any of these paths would take a turn I will decide which one to follow."

With this thought in my mind, I carried on positively and happily.

THE MAGIC

It was Luv's birthday, and every kid in the block was ready in his best colourful attire to rock the celebration. They all looked so handsome and beautiful as if they were going to walk for 'Lakme's India Children Fashion Week' event.

These small parties for children are the most amazing things in this world. Which scale I am basing the term "small parties" on, could mean small to me, but for those chicks, it has always been a bonanza.

Since I was the eldest one I was responsible for everything that included decorations, cake arrangements and gathering them together, I mean everything.

Those days mobile phones were new things and quite costly to afford, basic wired phones were common in use, and we all had them at home.

The irony was, any guy whose love interest lived 10 meters away from his house in the neighbourhood, would have to go some substantial distance (Sometimes up to 10 KMs) to find a P.C.O. to talk to her, you know, Privacy mattered.

There, the phone was ringing continuously.

It was disturbing me while I was trying to tie the biggest balloon with candies inside on to the ceiling fan. I was like an acrobat standing on a chair which was placed on a table which was placed on the floor.

That unbearable phone- ring sound was irritating me, and I was unable to concentrate as my head was running between trying and balancing myself on that wobbly platform and who the heck was calling so incessantly.

"Aunty! Please answer the phone. I am swinging midair and I can't." I shouted.

Nobody was listening to my plea. Those little pennies were making too much of noise outside.

"Anybody there? Luv, Kush, Kittu... anyone for God's sake answer the bloody phone."

(I yelled again.)

Eventually, helpless me, jumped on the phone.

"Hello" I said.

"Who?" (A lovely voice replied, I thought it was kid.)

" I am Rahul."

"Rahul, who ?"

"Friend of Luv and Kush."

"Okay, will you please allow me to talk to anyone who this phone belongs to?"

"Sure why not. Would you please tell me your name?"

"Jahnavi"

"Jahnavi.., who?"

"Oh Please! Whoever you are, call Luv right now."

"Luv.. Luv .." (I shrieked)

"See Ma'am, Kids are playing outside, and it's noisy here, uncle had gone to the market and aunty is in the kitchen, please give me your message, I will let them know."

"Ohh! It's okay, thank you so much, I will call later. By the way, what was your name?"

"It's Rahul, *naam toh suna hi hoga.*"

"Ohhooo, Rahul! Bbye.. It was nice talking to you." (She giggled)

"Ummm ummm, Hello .. hey.. hello."

And the call got disconnected.

I couldn't utter even a single word further.

She was not a kid, and that was for sure.

"The voice of a Nightingale."

I had heard this phrase somewhere, but its literal meaning, I realized that day.

'Why that call got disconnected so early, why could not I get to talk to her for a few more minutes?' Being a student of 'boys only' school and having no acquaintances with any girl, I was craving to hear that mesmerizing voice again.

Suddenly that holy inner voice whispered to my conscience:

"Stay in your limits"

Now there was one more voice, in fact, many more voices around,

"Cake! Yayyy, Hurrah! Wuhooo. Let's come all."

The cake was on the table now. Those kids were now uncontrollable, and so was I because my task of decorating the room was still incomplete.

And then aunty yelled, "Rahul! Finish it fast dear. Guests have arrived, and you are running far behind. Hurry Up!!"

"5 more minutes aunty, it's almost done.", I said, hanging in the air trying again to tie that red balloon.

In a blink of an eye, the celebrations started.

Kids rocked that party; they were just perfect in the way they dressed up, the way they moved around and celebrated. Especially the dance they all did on that one peppy number that was popular to break the floor those days,

"Summer of 69"

* * *

Though it was a small event which I got to celebrate in a new town, in a new house, yet it was a beautiful memory to cherish for all of us.

I was delighted to have so many kids on my friend list. Kittu was my favorite, smallest, youngest, a student of standard 3, 7-8 years of age, lean and thin, and the cutest one.

And cute was also the voice which I heard that day, at Luv's house.

"How can I talk to her again? Whom should I ask about her?"

I kept on thinking about these questions for weeks and months. If I had asked Luv or Kush, I feared that they might customize the things and could have complained to their parents, and it might ruin my reputation with them.

"Complain? Complain about what?" I was baffled and anxious.

Everything was new; it was a new friendship a new relation.

So, caring more about that new relation, that day I compromised with my craving and forgot everything about that indelible call.

Everything felt like all the puzzles have fallen into the right place. Life started to feel more normal by the day, the struggle between studies and Cricket didn't feel much like a struggle anymore, just another run of the mill routine. I wasn't complaining anymore, everything was fine, and to add to the immaculacy of this life.

And so on, days went by, and the final terms for my 9th class were over.

Time does fly.

And now had come the hour!

That time of the year again which I loved the most, but who knew this one was going to be the best of the lot, the most memorable and remarkable one.

THE ATTRACTION

It had been two or three days since Luv and Kush didn't come to play. I thought of going to their home and bring them to the playground, but I was too lazy to do that, so I decided to call them from the balcony.

"Luv...Luv..." (I called them on the balcony.)

There was no answer to my calls. I continued screaming their names shamelessly as I was eagerly waiting for childlike appearances on the front balcony.

And then swiftly appearance happened. It was the maiden moment throughout my existence, like a bolt from the blue, struck and pierced me apart.

There she was, struggling with her beautiful wet hair, with a comb in her hand, a clip between her teeth, a pretty girl appeared on that balcony. She was untangling her long wet hair by running her fingers through them as she hurried to the balcony at my call. Most of her hairs must have been falling on her face which she was trying to get rid of, by dragging them to the side, and then she was back from the clouds of black hair shining like a Moon. Her gaze was mesmerizing and my legs were dug deep in the ground I stood on.

The moment I took a glance of her, I started to try

dodging her direct look, but I was miserably a failure in that. I must have had seen her for a fraction of second as she appeared at the balcony, and I was already star-strucked. I was hit by a thousand bolts at the sight of her, at the mere flash of her slight. It was magical as If the time had stopped, and I was the only one who moved and noticed everything about her in just that one moment of a glance I took. She must have asked me a couple of times before I broke out of the trance.

Slowly, I gathered all the confidence in my soul, I straightened my view and ....

Our eyes met for the first time.

She was staring at me.

I looked away !!Goddddd, she was damn beautiful!

I wasn't wise enough to understand what feelings had just gushed through the length and breadth of my body. I guess it was that clichéd, yet the ecstatic & inexplicable feeling of 'LOVE-AT-FIRST-SIGHT'. Till day, I could only try to describe in words how that feel was or how she looked; yet I fail miserably. As If, she was an Art that god had created with his own great hands and had left it beyond all the comprehensions, beyond all the human perceptions and beyond all the faculties to describe.

It was an awkward situation for me because she was trying to say something but I wasn't looking at her way properly. I think she was waiting for me to make an eye contact and tell what I was standing there and shouting a few moments back for. As soon as I mustered up the courage to look at her for an answer;

"Luv is taking bath!" she said with a cute child like smile on her face.

I shook my head and tried to utter, but the cat had got my tongue. All my abilities to make a communication, all of my Human senses held back. My voice didn't come out, my eyes didn't give that affirmative blink, my body didn't flinch, and I was at the paramount point in the Intertia of Rest.

Then, she smiled having said what she was there to say, just waved at me and went back inside the home. A portion of my soul just left my body that day, and followed her inside. I think, till today I am living without that missing part. I knew, I wouldn't ever be full without her.

A few days ago, I had watched Harry Potter and it felt like Emma Watson had come to Luv's home and she had brought magic in my Life, She had brought L-O-V-E.

She was so fair, so beautiful and she had innocent eyes like a kid!

Clock had passed five minutes since I had seen her for 50 seconds and yet there was a flow of such platonic feeling rushing through every inch of my soul.

I had started daydreaming already.

Then I understood the reason these kids Luv and Kush weren't coming to play. Someone had come to their home, probably some relatives; and so, the kids must have been busy with them.

I didn't think anything about it further, knew they wouldn't be able to come now; hence I kept on playing with other kids of society.

But,

With an incomplete team, other teammates were very unhappy about it. I tried to involve them in other games, but that didn't work out well.

A week passed by, Eventually, I decided to go to Luv's home to sort things out.

Their door was open, but I still knocked on the door (Etiquette you see.)

(Knock Knock!!)

"Luv … Kush… Anybody there?"

And I kept moving inside slowly calling Luv and Kush Simultaneously.

Right from the middle of the house, through their living room, almost a 5 feet tall girl walked towards me. It was her; the Emma Watson look alike. Her smile went live on seeing me. I didn't smile back; I just kept on looking at her face and her deep brown eyes. I must have looked like a complete moron then staring at her like that.

"Didi, someone is here." staring at me, she yelled.

I moved ahead quickly. "Namaste Uncle, Namaste Aunty.", I greeted.

Aunty from the kitchen and uncle out of somewhere came out.

"Oh Rahul, come... come sit." (Aunty said.)

"Can't sit, where are Luv-kush? Please call them. Kids on the ground are killing me; they want them at the playground today at any cost."

"Hehehehehe" (Chuckles!)

I turned around, that pretty girl was giggling.

(For God's sake, please introduce her to me, damn I can't ask about her directly.), I thought.

"Rahul, kids are studying. Jahnavi has given them homework."

(Now aunty took her turn to speak.)

"Homework? On vacation? That too during play time?"

(with a surprised look, I asked these questions to Emma Watson whose name was Jahnavi.)

"Hi.." (she extended her hand for a shake hand.)

"Hhhhhhh... I mean Hello..! Hello!"

We shook hands for the first time, and I started to shiver.

"Do you remember, we had a word once over the phone?" she asked.

"Over the phone? Really? When ??"

"Last year, Luv's birthday, a weird talk between us."

"Ooooh ooh yeah yeah. I got it. I got it now."

"Rahul, Jahnavi is my younger sister, Luv- Kush's Masi (aunt)."

(Jyoti aunty made everything clear with this statement.)

"Aunty! Your younger sister? I thought she is Kush's younger sister (Yes, she was so adorable)."

(Hehehehehe! It cracked a burst of laughter in the room, and suddenly Luv Kush attacked me, as they started to climb on me.)

"Masi, please please please let us go and play! It has been so many days since we have played with our team." they pleaded.

"Okay! Okay... Cool! Go and have fun."

(Emma Watson approved their request.)

The moment we reached the ground, I shot the bullets of questions at Luv-Kush.

"Who is that kid, tell me in detail? What does she do? Where did she come from?"

Luv understood everything, although he was 8 or 9 years of age he still read my desperation.

"No worries Rahul bhaiya, that girl who seems to be a kid to you, lives in Agra and is a student. She is our Masi. We will help you in your task bhaiya! "

"Oh! Shut up! Focus on your studies." I said.

I was excited and happy to see all this happening because a species known as "Girls" was extinct from my life. And shaking hand with her was like Leonardo winning Oscars in the modern days.

For a boy from a Boy's only school, who had never seen a girl properly in his life, gets a chance to talk to a bombshell, no not a bombshell, a beautiful, stunning and pretty girl; that guy ought to lose his mental peace.

From the next day, after we had had our introduction, she started to watch our game from the terrace. She never came to the ground though. Now she started to allow more free hours to Luv, Kush to play. She almost had ended her summer classes for her nephews by the evening.

I felt something, as if she herself wanted to let the kids play now.

While on the ground, my focus was less on the game and more on the terrace. As a result, I was unable to field well, started dropping the catches and was unable to score runs.

One fine day Kittu said, "What happened Rahul bhaiya? Our colony's team is losing just because of you."

I could not say anything or reply to the true lines of a seven-year-old teammate.

What excuse could have I given to him? Where was my concentration? What would he understand while I, myself was not sure of the things I was feeling those days.

Anyways whatever it was, it was happening, and it felt right in my stomach, in my guts, in the lumps of my throats and sometimes in the back of my ear. It was something nice, new and quite exhilarating thing in my boring life.

I wanted to talk to her, but how was it possible?

I was on the ground floor, and she was on the roof of the 2nd floor, she was close, yet the distance was the longest I could ever travel.

How could I have said, "Dear Jahnavi, please come down, I want to talk to you."

I was new to her, and she too was not so familiar with me.

* * *

24th May [2004], it was a Monday; I accidentally woke up at 5 in the morning. While I was walking towards the balcony rubbing my eyes, I was surprised with a view so aesthetic, so pure that I stood there fixated. I couldn't believe my eyes and my jaws dropped witnessing such serenity.

In a Cream-colored suit, with wet and untied messy hair, Jahnavi was offering water as a prayer to the rising sun. It was not that I hadn't seen someone offering prayer to rising sun before, it was who that's offering the prayer, that had struck me like the first rays of the morning, but much brighter and enlightening. I had never seen a girl as beautiful as her in my life; her face was almost wrapped in those messy wet hair as if it was the moon shining between dark clouds; sheer divinity was what I felt. That moment I understood what seeing God in someone really meant.

There was always a smile on her face. Even if she looked at someone with a poker-face without any expressions, it would seem like she was a smiling Barbie doll.

Yes! Yes, I fell in love with her that morning.

As the tag of a "Child" was finally getting removed from me, and I was slowly progressing towards adolescence, it seemed I was becoming an adult in every possible way.

Not only the body was growing physically but also mentally and emotionally; the heart also started developing it's dormant ability other than pumping blood. I could feel something inside my guts right from the stomach to my heart, must be the butterflies as the elders say. As if some unforeseeable feeling was kicking from the inside, from the outside, left-right and centre.

When I was in front of her or looking at her from a distance, I couldn't help but smile like a stupid lad. And when I was away from her I felt weak and terrified and confused.

That day I kept on thinking about Jahnavi, how simple and serene she was. In this 21st century who would wake up so early to offer prayers to the Sun? She was very humble and devoted girl with nothing but purity in her heart and that always reflected in her smile.

Although we only had the introduction by the, but I realized something; and that was that she looked like Emma Watson and traditionally she was like an actress of an Indian family drama movie.

I felt restless that night. I was unable to sleep. Was the reason Jahnavi?

I wished. As much nice it felt as to lie down and think about her all day long, I did have other things in my mind that night.

I had a bigger fish to fry!

The reason was the results of class 9th, which were supposed to be announced the next day.

I was confident though; yes, confident enough that I couldn't obtain good marks.

Although I was good in studies, worked hard for it, yet I had a substantial lacuna.

I had never attempted an entire question paper, I could never write for the entirety of 3 hours, Damn!

My hands used to cry after two hours like a baby. If I tried to write in the 121st minute, it would feel as if it was not the ink which was flowing through my pen; it was blood instead.

Like they say,

"If you haven't played the entire match, how can you expect to win?"

Such was my predicament.

With all of these thoughts in my mind, I felt more restless.

It was not the scolding of Mom or Dad that I was afraid of. It was the fear of being insulted in front of someone new, Jahnavi.

Up till now, Self-respect, Pride, Self-esteem did not exist in my life, but after meeting her software like Personality, Image, Shyness and Attitude had got installed onto my system as plug-ins.

The next day as was announced earlier, the result was out.

Unexpectedly I achieved 8% more than I expected, 68% was my score in class 9th.

Now it was my parent's turn to take things into their hands.

"Where in the hell is your mind? You studied a lot, but attained 68% only? Do you want to do something with your life or not? With this condition my boy, you will not be able to clear board exams. Why don't you get enrolled with the kids in the nursery again! Throughout the day Luv, Kush, Kittu, Nik, Bittu,Jiyansh, blah blah blah…"

It was a regular scene in my house which repeated twice a year post the results declaration. I used to score fewer marks every time, and Mom, Dad never got tired of scolding me afterwards.

After all of this, I was scared that the tale of my victory (scoring 68%) would be leaked in the society. I was so anxious about it that I told my Mom "Please scold me, mom, beat me, punish me but please don't talk about my result or share it with anyone."

"A man can give up on his body to keep his heart

pleased. "

And vice versa of the above concept,

"Error 404, page not found."

On the evening, that day, in the month of peak summer, people chastened by life and weather reached the park.

I saw another strange thing happening from my balcony (Of course I could not go to the ground, as there should be at least one day's condolence for failure, and besides I wasn't allowed to step out too). Jahnavi was sitting on the bench with Jaya amma. It was hard to believe that Jaya amma was quiet and some other lady was chattering instead. Sitting on a chair next to the bench was none other than my dear Mom, who was mad at me and was pointing towards the balcony at me from there.

The point or the issue was not that my Mom was pointing the finger at me or looking at me, but.... it was everyone else's looking at me with a face full of pity.

Jyoti aunty called me, and I had no other option but to go there.

"Rahul, how was the result?"(Jyoti aunty started to inquire.)

"Aunty! 68%" (with my head down.)

"Just 68%?"

"Hmm"

"No worries Rahul will work hard from now onwards. He would top in the board exams in his class, I am sure."

(This was Jahnavi, who showed some overconfidence on me with impious assumptions.)

"Yeah.. yeah, next year I would not let you people down.", I said.

"Work hard, yes you can." Jahnavi said.

Although every single word that she said was

inspiring, but a little girl could not command me to work hard. It was my male ego which suddenly took over my better judgment.

* * *

Eventually, that embarrassing chapter of results ended. I don't know why I was struggling with my sleep at nights; I used to stand up at the balcony most of the times in those sunny days and dark nights with a hope to see her.

My mornings used to start at the balcony and nights used to end on the same balcony. That balcony was the first place I would walk into every morning with a hope, and the last place I walked back heavy heartedly in the night.

I realized I was somehow becoming crazy about her. Sooner it was the dawn of a new person; who used to sleep till late in the morning had started to wake up too early by 5, strolled back and forth restlessly in the balcony to get a glimpse of that girl with the first light of the day.

Then she would come in front of my eyes suddenly, would say a 'hello' to me from her balcony, and I would smile at her from my balcony, this had become a regular affair for me that summer.

'Two balconies away', Hehehehe! Yes, two balconies away, it was a new unit of distance for me in my life.

Things were now quite fixed in the evening; she would sit beside Jaya amma and would watch our game. I was unsure whether she was there to watch our game or was she playing a different game all along, I surely hoped she did.

She was always in front of my eyes and in the back of my mind.

We had not had talked much by then but still, everything was just happening through eyes sometimes and in my mind mostly, yet all of it was exciting.

Although whenever I came face to face with her, I used to scrabble and the very next moment I felt like I wanted to see her more and more.

When she was around me, either on the bench sitting beside Jaya amma, or on the terrace trying to watch our game like a silent spectator, it was the best feeling in the world. The hope that her eyes were on me when I wasn't looking at her, was a feeling unlike any. I felt conscious, excited, terrified at times and ecstatic the next moment; life was at its best.

But the period of that feeling was just of 2 hours in the evenings, which felt no more than a couple of minutes long.

Nothing special was happening in the morning except us looking at each other, exchanging formal smiles and letting the eyes talk. I indeed was talking to her all day long in my mind, conversing with her about anything and everything under the sun. I used to find her beside me wherever I went, as they show in good old Bollywood movies. We had no commitments between us, still whatever was happening wasn't less than a commitment to me, and I prayed to God that she felt the same too.

* * *

In the meanwhile, one day, Jyoti aunty called me from their house's balcony and said,

"Rahul, I am giving you a roll number. Please go to a cafe to check the result and bring a printout."

"Sure aunty, anything for you." I responded.

That day the results for C.B.S.E. 10th std was declared. It was a huge rush around the cyber cafes. It was something like an exchange offer was going around, "Take your e-mark sheet in an exchange of 20 rupees and a roll number on a piece of paper."

Amidst that chaos, I somehow begged for the mark

sheet of the role number I was given. I was surprised to see that the candidate had failed the exams.

That was a boy, whose name I try to remember even today but I too fail in doing so.

So, I came back with the print of marks.

With the mark sheet in my hand, I knocked on the door of Luv's home. It was Jahnavi who appeared to open the gate for me. I had a mark sheet in my hand which had put the life of a youth in reverse gear and that too for a year. On the contrary to this, having Jahnavi standing next to me at the entrance of that house, made my heart go all sorts of crazy.

"So.., Rahul, how are you?" she said with a naughty smile.

"Wo… Wo..." I struggled to find words to finish.

"Yeah, tell me.", she enhanced the amplitude of her smile, tied her hands behind and stood firmly.

"Umm..umm !! Aunty, where is aunty?"

"She went to the park, Jaya amma just called her."

"Ohh, so..umm.. who.., Whose, whose mark-sheet is it ?", I asked.

"Hey, it's a fail and listen, the name is also wrong here. I just checked on the phone with my friend. It's 91%. She has confirmed it.", she said snatching that mark sheet from my hand, looking confused.

"Damn! How could this be possible?" I tried wrapping my head around it.

I took the paper back from her hand and jolted naively inside their home to find some light to check the details on that sheet as it was a little dark at the entrance door.

Looking at the sheet, I entered their living room which was properly lit. Now that room was witnessing something epic and monumental, Jahnavi, I and an A4 sheet between us.

I was holding that sheet from one of the corners, Jahnavi was holding it from the other, and both of us were looking at it. Our heads were closer than they ever were, and I swear I could hear her breaths and her heart beats pounding. Or probably it was me hyperventilating and hearing my own heart racing, I never knew.

"Roll Number is correct." she said with a serious look on her face.

"Are the subjects fine?" I asked.

"Absolutely!" she replied.

"Then why the hell are the name and results different?" I said in dismay.

I started to bite my nails. I was feeling so embarrassed and pained because there was just one task given to me which could be a media to impress her, and that too I couldn't complete successfully.

On the other side of the emotion, I started to sweat as she was very close to me. The corner of the sheet which I was holding started to flutter as I was shivering.

Although the temperature and pressure were well maintained in the room with the A.C. ; but I was still in discomfort. I was trying my best to touch her fingers, and with an inch that my fingers moved towards hers, it felt as if I ran miles to do that. I was firing different sorts of questions at her, and she was replying properly. With each question, I was moving towards her slowly.

Then suddenly one of my questions shattered my dream of touching her and left my jaw dropped.

"Okay! Tell me one thing, if the roll number is correct, subjects are fine, but the candidate's name is different, so what is the name of the candidate who has obtained 91%?"

"Jahnavi, It's my result." she replied.

"Really?? Oh, wait! I forgot something; I got to go. Bye." And I rushed out.

"Rahul, Listen..!"

"Later, see you at the park."

I left the place in a hurry.

She was elder to me. The girl, who I thought was a cute kid, was a year elder to me, all my calculations, the entire script had gone wrong. For a moment my ego was crushed and churned.

That day the story took a new turn.

Later that evening, I saw her celebrating her success, by distributing sweets among the society members in the park. Kids had to wait for their turn in the queue. Jaya amma was the first one to get them, and I was the last one in the line. All I wished was her making me taste that sacred sweet with her own hands, but the wish was shattered again by none other than my Mom's comment,

"Rahul, if you work hard, you can also get an opportunity to offer sweets like Jahnavi next year after 10th."

"Yeah! Definitely, I would be honoured; I will do my best now." I said.

I knew what I just had promised was next to impossible for me to achieve, even I knew my limitations.

So, in the midst of this, I gathered some words and tried to arrange them together.

"Will you come next year?" I asked her in a low voice.

"If you promise me sweets, I shall definitely come to visit." She replied.

"Promise"

With all the confidence, I just said. As if I could win the entire world for her.

My eyes were smiling while I congratulated her.

Somehow, I was sure that someone must have had cast a spell on my mother and something magical happened to her. She had brought Jahnavi to our house. I was so happy to see this. I didn't think of anything else as that act of my mother was pleasant for my eyes, heart and my soul.

In some way, I managed to leave my kids' team early and landed at home as I wanted to see her at my home, which by then I had dreamed of many times. Mom and Jahnavi were sitting in the courtyard with Cups of tea in their hands. I joined them with a glass of water in my hand (asking for tea could trigger mom to scold me for no reason).

I was ninja beaming from ear to ear while listening to their conversation; the conversation which was doing simple harmonic motion between one serial to other. But in the middle of their serious discussion when Jahnavi used to switch her view from mom's to look at me for few seconds; those were the moments for which I was ready to listen to the story of every other mortal immigrant "Saas-Bahu" Serial throughout the night.

That night the discussion continued for hours.

It was almost 9:30 in the night when mom came out with another surprise for me.

"Rahul, it's late now, go and drop Jahnavi to her place." Mom said.

"Ohk!..(my dear mom)."

"No aunty, it's okay, I will manage, it's not that far. Please don't trouble Rahul." Jahnavi said.

Someone please ask that innocent girl, which boy on this planet would feel troubled to drop a girl (who is a definition of beauty) in the night.

Mom forced her to accompany me, and she gave a life to my thoughts.

This was going to be my moment of a romantic walk,

winds blowing our hairs untidy, hands in hands, silent nothings and background music.

Of course, nothing of that sort happened, it was a windless humid evening, and definitely, her hand wasn't in mine, no background music played, and I was stupid enough to have stayed silent.

It was going to be a nice walk though, we were on foot, and the distance that we had to cover was just 200 to 300 meters.

I was holding a torch in one hand and had the other one empty. I wanted to keep moving ahead by holding her hand, my happiness was at par.

While walking the corridors, I looked at Jango and felt as if it blinked to cheer me up

"Hold her hand, man!"

Haha! I was not uttering even a single word. So "holding her hand" somehow was definitely not on cards for me.

"Do you have a girlfriend?" she broke the silence with an unexpected question.

"Hehehe! I have been a student of a Boy's school since my previous life. Wish to reconsider your question?" I chuckled.

"Your actions do not match with your statement."

"Really? So which act of mine made you feel that I have a Girlfriend?"

"Umm.. Just like that, nothing much."

"Okay. Do you have a boyfriend?" I asked almost instantly in a trembling voice.

"What?" she replied shying away.

"Do you have a boyfriend?" I asked again. Now I was bold enough to take a bullet on my chest for my nuisance.

In the meanwhile, we reached her house's gate.

She stopped, smiled, came closer, looked into my eyes and whispered,

"Good Night."

"Good night Jahan.....vi. Jahnavi!"

With a big smile on our lips, we ended our walk, and my question was left unanswered at the divine gate of her house.

Although, my walk back home from her place was no less than the walk of victory.

Thanks to her results, at least we started to talk to each other and that day had been great. She was an extrovert at times, but I was an introvert (only in front of her though).

I had to do something about this situation and move the talks further, but the question was how?

Now I had a fear in my heart that she might go back to her hometown Agra soon, it had been fifteen days since the day I noticed her, and she must have had come before that.

I had to arrange reasons to talk and get closer to her before she goes back, and give her reasons to come back next year.

But we were destined to meet only for 2 hours daily.

Even during those 2 hours, she would sit in the middle of aunties or stand on the terrace. So it was unlikely to make any moves during the evenings, hence I wanted to utilize the morning time.

Our kid's gang anyhow managed to make a schedule to play in the mornings too, by the time June arrived. Although the picture was completely different from that in the evening, like in the mornings, there were few people from our society but more from the societies from neighbours. Our park would become more of an open natural gym in the morning and less of a playground.

To move the story ahead, I had to do something.

A week passed by, but Jahnavi was nowhere to be seen at the park, on the terrace or the balcony.

* * *

It was 5:30 AM on 23rd of June 2004; a different pleasant morning. The entire city was trying to get fit and get back in a shape that people would have imagined. We were playing cricket as usual, and my eyes were swinging between the balcony and terrace.

The magic happened.

I saw someone drying her wet hair on the terrace. I could not see the face so I called Luv and inquired about the person.

"Hey Luv, who is drying hair so early in the morning." I asked Luv.

"Where?"

"Ohho, there on the terrace."

"Ohh, she is Jahnavi masi." said Luv and giggled.

"Isn't it too early to take a bath? What is so special today?"

"It's her birthday Rahul bhaiya. She has to pray and all so… go it?" Luv replied.

"Ohh, Yeah got it dude! And thanks for the info." (I was stupefied.)

In the meanwhile she turned around, and now she was facing towards us. I happily waved my hand towards her, but surprisingly she warned me with her eyes for my stupid gesture.

She wanted to urge that how could I have waved my hand at her from a packed park.

Pressing my teeth together, I immediately said sorry, and that made her burst into laughter.

That was the most pleasant scene of the day.

Jahnavi and I were in talking terms now, but

everything was happening in a sort of sign language, and there was no big deal if we both would misunderstand each other's signals and signs.

And I was so amazed to see her there in the morning. I was so happy and proud of my management skills. I thought as if all the characters and scenes of a movie are in the perfect juncture now, and the story had started to roll like a camera.

Though she was not a part of our games till then, yet she was never away from the games either.

The feeling I must tell, was a great feeling, a different one, looking at her when she didn't have her eyes on me, finding ways to look at her while she was enjoying our game was so inexplicably romantic.

Just looking at her would pump in all the energies go gushing through my veins.

I have had always seen her laughing and smiling while sitting beside Jaya amma among the ladies' brigade in the evening. I never saw her talking much to anyone though. Either she used to enjoy their company or used to suffer being a part of their discussion.

I always wanted to ask her if she was interested in leaving their company and being a part of like-minded people, which was I of course, but I couldn't muster up courage to tell her.

Now I was getting desperate to talk to her for a longer duration. I wanted to listen to her, that nightingale's voice for hours and hours.

As it was her birthday that day, it was a nice opportunity for me to go and talk to her. Thinking about it I reached their home that evening and knocked at their door.

(Knock! Knock!)

"Coming" (it was her.)

The gate opened, the heart skipped a beat, and then it started to beat like crazy.

"Hi, Happy Birthday, this is for you!" I gave her a card for her birthday; it was in style those days.

"Thank you!" said Jahnavi, she was not only happy but was surprised too.

"How did you know?" she asked as she was inquisitive.

"Ummm, guessed!" I said.

"Ohh, so you have such an amazing ability to guess, clairvoyance much, huh?" she was laughing when she said that.

"Leave it yaar. We want a party."

"Rahul, I do not celebrate."

"So, when did I ask you to celebrate?"

"Let us and the kids go somewhere. We dine together and go for a walk. Let's make this evening a memorable one to cherish for life." I peeped inside their house as I spoke.

"I will have to check with Didi."

"I will handle that." I said confidently.

Kids wanted a party, and I was keen to spend some time with her, so together we requested and with some guidelines from Jyoti aunty we got the approval to hang out.

The entire team was ready, but I was the first one to get ready, yes! Before the kids I was the one to get ready.

While we spent hours in a nearby restaurant celebrating the precious birthday, creating those kiddish nuisances, it was almost 9, and we decided to return. Now it was my turn to utilize the unique opportunity.

I said to the team, let's take a walk. They all agreed.

The night was falling dark. It was the last week of

June. It must have had rained somewhere as the wind was cold. The sky was pretty clear on a rainy season, and so the stars could witness something special in the town. It was mostly the sound of everyone walking, feet scratching against the newly laid asphalt that filled the silence of the night. And amidst that, walked the beautiful her under the moonlight and terrified me basking in her glow.

We were 8 in number; Luv, Kush, Kittu, Nik,Jiyansh, Bittu,Jahnavi and I.

Yes, I was smart about playing my cards, so I engaged the kids in some silly game and asked them to walk in the front of us, while I accompanied Jahnavi walking just behind the kids.

"Why did you do so?" She asked with a smile noticing what I had done by asking the kids to walk ahead of us.

"Kids may get spoilt listening to adults talking to each other." I chuckled.

She laughed.

I gathered all of my strength which was left in me and asked,

"You didn't answer me!"

"Answer? What?" She asked cluelessly.

"That....., If you have a boyfriend or not?"

She started laughing and said, " Rahul, in our tradition, we stay away from these things."

I was not really sure whether I should have been happy or sad listening to this statement.

"So what are the things that you stay with, in your traditions?"

"Please Rahul. Enough Yaar!" she was getting annoyed now.

Getting a hint from her behaviour, I quickly said, "Oh okay, I am sorry."

"Better" She smiled.

A moment of silence followed as we were walking together; the kids were a little quicker on feet, they were quite far off our sight now. I wished for that moment to never end.

"Jahnavi"

"Haan..!"

"Say something!"

"You say something." she said in her tender voice.

I looked at the sky and saw the stars following us, the things around us were guarding us, roads were happy to witness our steps together, and the moon was smiling upon the geniture of a blossoming relation.

I took her hands in my hands and handed over a gift to her.

"This is for you!"

"Awwww… Rahul, Thank you so much, this means a lot."

I laughed as I didn't give her any ring or something precious. I had gifted her just a small sculpture of *'Radha-Krishna.'*

Her eyes were wet as she was happy or may be extensively surprised which I could not judge.

Whatever it was, I was happy to see her happy. And yes I got my return gift. My destiny reached beyond the moon when she hugged me.

I lost my calm; I was almost mad and went crazy.

She said, "This is the first time that a boy has gifted me something."

"That too such a smart boy." I boasted hysterically.

"Yeah Yeah I know, Tom Cruise of Moradabad, Hehe.", She giggled.

Amidst the giggles and those sweetest of the moments

that we shared, we reached the entrance of our society.

We first parcelled all the kids to their homes and then moved towards Luv, Kush's house.

That epic day was coming to an end. Yes, it was a historical day; there couldn't have been anything better for a guy like me who had just started liking someone and then got a chance to spend such beautiful, memorable day with the beloved.

I was thinking about these while having Jahnavi by my side and then breaking the silence was her again, in that sweetest voice which forced my ears to dance. She said:

"Thank you for the day, Rahul!"

I had tears of joy in my eyes, a smile on my lips and a storm of mixed emotions inside my mind.

I thought, how crazy was this beautiful little girl, she gave me a lifetime of good memories in a day to cherish, and she was thanking me.

"I owed my life to her after that evening."

At that moment I opted to remain silent because if I had spoken something, she would have come to know, how weak I was at heart.

I said, "Good Night" with a smile and headed towards my home.

* * *

Contradicting what I wished for, I did not take her phone number. I wasn't even sure if she had a phone or not.

The next day mom informed us that there was a marriage in her family and we had to go there the following day.

"And when would we return?" I inquired.

"That depends on many factors. At least we should get

there first and then we would decide." She said.

"Ma, you guys go, I won't come along." I said as I didn't wish to spend a day away from Jahnavi.

After a scolding session, I was the first one to pack my bag, with a heart as heavy as my suitcase.

We all met at the park that evening, but I chose not to play.

Jahnavi called me repeatedly and was forcing me to play the game, but I was in a foul mood. I was unhappy to leave that stage and attend the marriage, I was least interested in. I did not care for anything around me anymore; I just wanted to see her, talk to her and eventually spend all my time with her.

She suddenly came to me, held my hands and brought me to the kids to play.

Without any interest in the game, I started playing with them, no one in our team was aware of the thing that we were to leave the next day.

She was the first one to notice my unusual behaviour and asked me,

"What happened? Why are you so serious today?"

"Nothing" I replied.

"Nothing what? Something is there on your face; it's most definitely the happy or lively look that you usually wear."

"We are going tomorrow." I spoke reluctantly.

"Going where?" Her voice went low.

"Delhi. It's a marriage of a relative which we have to attend."

"Ohh... How will you people travel in this steamy summer?"

I could feel the "steamy summer" concern was just a filler but the reason for her seemingly sad voice was different.

"Yeah, will have to."

"When would you come back?"

"I don't know."

At that moment I was looking down as I tried my best to not look into her eyes because I knew mine were wet. I noticed there were several questions on her innocent face and I hoped that she would have found her answers in my silence at that tensed moment.

It was dark now. We had to prepare for the early morning journey. I tried consoling myself that the marriage and staying away from her for 2, 3 days was not a big deal. The only thing frazzling me was Jahnavi's probable return to her place in those 2, 3 days. I was terrified at the thought of not being able to find her around after I return.

The river of my love (I am not sure that the word "Love" is appropriate or not at that stage but my mind froze that day.), which just started to find it's own course could be dead in those 2 , 3 days. With these thoughts in my mind, I waved my hand at the kids, turned towards Jahnavi and muttered,

"So… see you soon, hopefully."

Without uttering further, I looked into her eyes for a moment and started walking.

"Listen! Take care and come back soon!" she said.

"You just stay here; I will be back soon." I looked back and murmured.

* * *

Throughout the journey, I kept on thinking about it. Was this a short story of attraction or a new beginning of a grand tale of love? For the very first time, I was getting away from the girl; who I didn't know at all just a few weeks back. I was already feeling a kind of pain I had never experienced before. I felt as if the life was leaving my body, one ounce at a time.

But subdermally somewhere I was a little happy too. Those fairy tales which I used to listen to but never felt. Those love stories which I used to watch on the television but never liked, and all those songs with indecipherable lyrics didn't make sense until then, all had started to make perfect sense to me.

The moment I look at a girl, it felt like she was her, Jahnavi. Perhaps she was in my eyes and all over my heart by then.

I was in a blissful state now. Whatever it was, may God keep his hands of blessings on me and everything would be just fine, I prayed with hopes in the heart.

I was thinking about so many things at the same time with a constant blush on my face when my dear Mom noticed me chuckling for no reason and then she asked,

"Rahul, what happened beta, why are you smiling alone, tell me?"

(Yes, you cannot even think of her in front of your Mom. And you dare to laugh, smile or blush in front of your dear Mom.)

"Nothing Ma, I am excited for the wedding of your sister in law's niece. I couldn't control the happiness of this sacred family function; the smiling face is just because of that."

(Hahahahaha, everyone started to laugh.)

* * *

Discussions regarding travel plans to Moradabad followed the evening of the holy matrimony.

I suggested, "Let's start early morning since it's pretty hot."

We finally decided to board the first train, the next morning. Just as the trees get covered with newly sprung green leaves during the spring, the same way I was feeling a new energy around me which filled me with joy and had donned an everlasting smile on my face.

A new morning and a new beginning were ahead of me.

The journey seemed endless, making me more anxious by each passing moment. My eyes were shining with happiness and excitement, while my heartbeats skyrocketed and blood flushed through my veins; I was smiling ear to ear all by myself.

For me, the three-day excursion was on one side, and the return journey was on the other. I had never been such excited about coming back home from an outing, as I was that day. I was elated, almost as if an inexplicable ecstasy had rocked my body and my soul. I had this feeling of homecoming where the home wasn't this place for me anymore; it was more than that; it was her. She was a part of me now; she was my home now; it was impossible for me to imagine how my life was before she walked in.

As the journey was coming to its end and I could see the familiar roads that lead to my city, I looked outside and imagined Jahnavi and me in every one of those places together, She was a part of my memory now, which we never shared together but felt so much like we did; in some other time may be, in some other reality perhaps. I believed in the universe, and I believed it was talking to me, whispering in my ears that I belonged with her and she with me.

I knew it was now a matter of a few minutes before I step on the same soil that she must have dusted off of her palms after playing with the kids. Everything meant something to me and strangely associated with her. I couldn't control my heartbeats from throbbing out of my chest; neither could I make myself stop from laughing like a complete nincompoop.

It was quite a humid afternoon when we reached the destination at approximately 1 PM. The first thing which I did immediately was to head towards the balcony to get a glimpse of her.

But there was nothing!

She wasn't there, where could she be? The terrible feeling of grief overwhelmed me.

Hours passed and as the clock's hands marched slowly towards the evening, neither did I hear the Nightingale's voice nor did I see that pretty face, both of which I was yearning for over the last few days. I kept pinning for her, as an addict after withdrawal; I was going crazy.

It was 6 pm now; I ran towards the park and started waiting for Jahnavi. I was disheartened somewhere inside and that inner self-was crying,

"She's gone!"

On the contrary, somewhere I was confident too if anything like that would have had happened, the news would have reached me. Sun went down, the darkness of the night crept in and yet there was no sign of her. Moreover, I could not find Luv or Kush as well. I completely lost all the hopes. I turned to head back home.

"Kush stop, it's dark now, stop playing." , this sound resonated.

"Wuhuuuuu..."

My heart skipped a beat before I could realize that Luv had leapt over me playfully.

I pushed him away and tried to clear my view.

Jahnavi was standing there with Kush, having a beautiful bright smile on her face.

Our eyes met, and a smile spread across my face. She

raised her eyebrows, and I blinked my eyes. An unspoken conversation happened after three days. The silence had finally broken.

"So you came back?" She asked.

I couldn't utter anything, just smiled, took a deep breath , closed my eyes for a moment, and I wasn't there anymore.

"Helloo… you there?" she yelled.

"Yes, ma'am!! How are you?"

(Now I was back in form.)

"Well, so much of concern for what? You went, and so did the electricity. The city went powerless in your absence."

"Really? Wow!", I replied teasingly.

"Yeah..! The Tom Cruise of the city took power along with him, leaving us behind to struggle in this hot weather. So, enjoyed the wedding?"

"Yeah..yeah. It was really a fun over there. Getting insulted by relatives for the academics was really a fun for me. You tell how it was here without me?"

"Ohh, please! Don't ask. We Just kept fanning ourselves throughout." she remarked, and we both had a hearty laugh.

"Sounds nice. So, It's late now. Let's catch up tomorrow." I said.

"Absolutely!"

"One more thing!" she added.

"Yeah. Tell me!"

"You have to come home tomorrow. I need to learn something from you."

"Excuse me, what?" (I was little surprised, I thought, 'have we really come so close?')

"Yes, you heard it right! You have to teach me

something very important."

"Which exam you want to fail in?"

"Stop this nonsense! You better come tomorrow or face the consequences." she yelled irritably.

"Okay Ma'am, Relax! I will make sure I will be around tomorrow."

"So.... see you tomorrow", she said with a smile and started walking.

I didn't say anything I just kept on looking at her footsteps progressing towards her home.

Her presence invoked multiple emotions. Her being here filled me with ceaseless contentment and security.

I blushed like lads of seventeen (James Whitcomb Riley) and thanked the Almighty for her.

Actually, she is different of all. She is loquacious, congenial, an attractive beauty, nothing snobbish about her. So naive and innocent in her ways. She didn't get off my mind. While staring at the television, I was musing over her.

Mom suddenly remarked, "Jahnavi is blessed with a childlike innocence. She looks like a cute doll."

I was taken aback for a moment, scared that she might have read my thoughts. As it happened the second time in a week. I decided to prevent myself from thinking about her when mom was around.

I supported mom, "Yes Ma, you've got a new friend. Congratulations!"

"You shut up, turn off the TV and go to your bed."

(She lovingly admonished me and sent me to bed.)

* * *

Next morning the daily routine commenced. The children gleefully played in the park, and she was on the terrace. She instructed me to join her at 11 AM at her home to make a debut as a teacher.

"What am I supposed to teach? I will prepare myself for it. How can someone teach without knowing what to teach?" I asked Jahnavi who was at a 30 feet height from me.

"Well, this is your test! The one who teaches after learning is called a teacher, and the one who teaches without preparing in advance is called a 'Baazigar (winner)'.", She humorously replied.

"And lunatics are those who talk gibberish!" I retorted in annoyance.

"Shut up. Don't be late", she yelled.

"Fine, I will be there at 11."

The only preparation I did for one-lifetime opportunity to impress her was a long fulfilling bath which I had that morning, cleansing my mind-body-spirit. I was glad but smitten with fear of the unanticipated.

I reached her place 10 minutes before 11 to undertake my trial, Jahnavi was getting ready. I silently waited for her in Luv & Kush's study room.

Jyoti aunty asked me to have some breakfast before we start on the task for the day.

"No Di, Let's receive some profound wisdom from Guruji (teacher) before food." Jahnavi trifled.

"If the rules of the game are so defined, then the stomach of this preceptor is not filled with food, wisdom will work as food for me as well. Today I will teach you, post which you are gonna teach me.", I added.

"Whatttt?", she shocked.

"Yes, you heard it right. Once a great personality said, "Ordinary teachers need preparation before imparting knowledge but a 'Baazigar', needs no preparations.", I teasingly replied.

"Hehehehe"

(Luv-Kush chuckled from their room.)

After the humorous banter, we proceeded to the real agenda of the day.

Jahnavi - "There is an extracurricular activity in my college which I have to take part in. Final scores will be the sum of marks obtained in 10th and marks achieved in this activity. The activity involves one debate and one easy writing competition."

"Ohh, So this was the Important stuff. Okay, what are the topics?"

"Debate topic, *'Industrialization is responsible for environmental pollution.'*, and essay writing topic, *'Unity with diversity in India'.*"

"Hmm, give me a day. I will research on these topics and will come up with drafts. If they are decent enough, I will share them with you."

"Can we have a discussion right now?" she asked.

"Yes, we can, but we don't have any facts or figures to support what we discuss. Without any research, It would be just a waste of time." I suggested.

"Alright! As you suggest. I am entirely depending on you. I am really hoping for a successful outcome."

"No worries comrade...!"

In the interim aunty prepared tea and snacks for us. She had cooked many delicacies.

I thanked aunty for her generous hospitality.

"But he hasn't imparted any knowledge yet." Jahnavi quipped.

"Rahul, is it?"(Aunty thought her diligence was not worth.)

"Nothing much aunty. Winning needs preparation and hard work. We need to intensively research the topics.

Based on the collected facts, we can make an argument."

"Dear ladies, please don't trust Rahul bhaiya." Luv called out from the other room.

"I think I am going to open, and bat for the entire day today evening. I will make sure that nobody, did someone listen? Nobody gets a chance to bat today." I responded.

Pat came his jolly reply, "Rahul bhaiya is a saint, who will never break anyone's trust. Have faith ladies!"

(His passion for cricket lured him to change his statement.)

We all chucked!

* * *

I aimed to be a connoisseur in the subjects the topics were based on. I ceaselessly researched the entire night, collected information from every knowledge repository possible. From newspapers to the books and from the internet-cafe. I voraciously read every forum and article available and eventually came up with a three-page composition summarizing my research in the finest language which essentially was my only chance to win her heart.

Meanwhile, papa asked me, "what are you preparing for?"

"Nothing papa, just improving my GK.", I answered.

"This kid is getting matured."Papa said to mom.

"Yes, I too doubt if he is actually getting matured?" Ma had sensed my intentions.

Nevertheless, again I was at the same divine gate after exactly 24hours.

(knock-knock)

I confidently knocked at the door of my heaven.

"Welcome, Mr. Cruise. Let's see what you have done."

Jahnavi received me like a teacher who was about to evaluate the student's assignment.

"The soldier has arrived to prove himself." I said.

"Ahannn... Solider!!. Let me see how qualified this soldier is?"

"Don't do this drama, huh! I had to work very hard for this. And yes congratulations, you are getting first prize."

"Why? Are you appointed the judge for the event?"

"If I had been the judge, you would have to reappear in the same class next year."

"Stop it now!(She replied irritably.) Share what you have prepared."

"Sure...."

I explained her vital points and helped her to memorize the facts. Cooperatively, we composed a coherent speech, and I trained her in presenting it as well. I shared the various aspect of public speaking to instil better confidence while she speaks.

It was somewhere 12 or 1 in the noon when we were spending a kind of quality time in a shadow of an uninteresting competition.

"When is the competition?" I asked after the prolonged discussion.

"The dates are not yet finalized. We are only aware of the topics." She told me.

I advised her to read about the subject more and prepare herself thoroughly so that she can bring laurels to my name.

She agreed and said, "Alright guruji (Sir)! Now time for your Guru Dakshina (fee)."

And she called out her sister to lay the table for lunch.

I wanted to keep on discussing with her, no matter how boring the topics were. I wanted the discussion to go on just like a new lover who keeps staring at his beloved for no reason. So I insisted her that we should continue and have lunch later.

But......

She was really a kid in some matters.

The table decoration appealed me immensely.

I was amazed by what I saw. There were dishes which I had no clue about.

"Does someone have a birthday today?"

I questioned.

"No Rahul, nothing like that. Jahnavi has prepared all the dishes, and it was her idea to arrange the table in this way."

I turned to look at her. Her cheeks were flushed with Crimson. She was blushing like a school girl.

I questioned, "Is this really my Guru Dakshina ?"

"Ummm.. not exactly. But Yes, I wanted to test my cooking skills on someone."

"Hehehehe. Really?"

"No.. Virtually."

(All chuckled.)

* * *

The state's election season was ON, in the state. Having the largest premises, our colony's grounds held the party rallies to accommodate the giant crowd attending these rallies. As the sultry summers were almost over, the vacations came to an end. One of the party rallies was arranged that day. Our playground was now the rally hotspot.

People had started assembling since morning. The terraces of the tall buildings of the society overlooking the ground were almost filled by 12 in the noon.

I peeped through my window and saw Jahnavi and

other children also assembled at the terrace of the building. I decided to attend the rally too. Since the terrace was already crowded, I chose not to go there and was also hoping to see the political leader up front. On reaching the ground, I looked up in the direction of the terrace. The entire crowd was gazing at the stage. However, Jahnavi was pointing at me and trying to convey something through her actions.

"What? Anything important?" I gestured.

The exchange was impossible. Nonetheless, she wished to communicate something crucial and looked restless.

However, in the struggle to find a seat in the crowd, I didn't pay much attention to her.

The speech continued for another half an hour. Meantime I glanced towards the terrace once or twice. I could sense Jahnavi's discomfort yet couldn't comprehend what was going on.

I decided to meet her in the evening and find out what's wrong.

The speech ended, and the crowd started to disperse peacefully.

My mind was perplexed with thoughts, wondering what Jahnavi wanted to convey to me. Hence, I was desperately waiting for the evening.

I was anxious to meet her, but she didn't turn up that evening.

Just when I was about to leave, I heard her calling me from her terrace, and she asked me to join her. There was a simmering fear. I suspected bad news. I crossed my fingers and headed to the terrace. Jahnavi looked miserable and afraid.

"Why didn't you come to park today?" I asked her.

"I have something important to share."

"Important? What?" I responded with a shiver.

"I am going tomorrow."

Silence followed. None of us uttered a word. Our lips sealed in the stillest and the darkest night of the town.

"You are going means? Where?" I asked killing the silence that was killing me.

"My home, Agra. The competition is in another five days. So, I am leaving tomorrow." She retorted.

"When will you be back?"

Oh God! I wished her to say something positive, to give me some reason to hold on to faith and not break down. I prayed this was all a joke, but I knew deep down that this wasn't. My breath was stuck between my lungs, my heart had stopped beating in that very moment, everything had just ceased to exist, and all I saw was her lips, trying to utter an answer while pain screamed out of her eyes too.

She mingled her tears with few words and presented before me, where it was hidden somewhere,

"Don't know!!Maybe never..."

She managed to utter these words, and my world came falling apart.

I kept on listening to her with my head down.

I was feeling so lost. I lost track of time. Grief was pervading at that moment. I didn't know what to say or do. My mind was lost in deep anguish. I was unable to form the sentences.

"May I leave now? They must be waiting for me."

This question of her felt like it had a hidden desire of listening something magical. The magic which could give a new turn to the time that we spent so lovingly in those summer vacations. But I was not confident enough to speak further. I hadn't expected her sudden return to her hometown either. I wasn't sure of what to do, what not to do? She was staring at me with blank expressions; I was looking at her with pity face. Eventually, I somehow managed to arrange few words and said,

"If I had control over things then you would not have to ask me this question. So it's up to you now, if you want to, you can stay here, if you can't then I can't stop you."

There were a million things I wanted to ask, tell, understand, listen and hear, all at that moment. I didn't want that minute to end, but the heaviness had choked me. Words were not finding the way to the lips. I was unable to think or to act. I tried a lot and asked in broken, scattered words,

"What time will you leave tomorrow?"

"My train is at 1 pm." she murmured, followed by a silence for a few moments.

"Take care, Rahul. I will miss you."

Were her parting words.

She turned and started fading into dark. I kept on looking at her through the curtains of water in my eyes, and she slowly disappeared from my view like a diminishing star.

I felt as if life had run out of my body, and my legs were buried into the very ground I stood on. I was numb, and everything felt dead, inside and outside.

That was the most gruelling night to pass.

I kept on thinking "Why is it happening to me. Is this really just attraction or there is no age to fall in love? Will these 20-25 days which I have lived will go missing suddenly or will this story proceed further?" Apart from these facts I had to meet her next day. Who knew about the future. There was a possibility that we would never meet again and even if we were lucky enough to meet again, so much time may have passed that we even deny knowing each other.

This was it, as of now.

I started the next day from that lucky window beside balcony. I was forlorn to see her one last time, but the destiny wasn't favouring me that whammy day. The coincidences of finding her at the balcony were turning into the certainty of unavailability of her that day. When I found myself incapable of resisting the things, agitated to the core, I decided to go to see her at her place.

I was feeling jittery because at the other side of the door things could do anything to me.

Luv opened the door and greeted me, "Hi bhaiya how are you?"

I meekly replied, "Hi, I am fine. What's going on with you?"

I didn't follow what he replied. Absentmindedly, paying no heed to his words, I made my way in.

I looked around all possible dimensions and directions, but I couldn't find anyone.

"Where is everyone?" I asked Luv fiercely.

"Daddy has gone to the market. Mom, Kush and Jahnavi maasi went to Nani's place." he informed me.

"Nani's place? But I guess their train was scheduled in the afternoon, right?" I inquired.

"Yes. However, dad suggested they should leave early morning by bus since it turns really hot during the day."

"Are you telling me Jahnavi left today morning?"

"Exactly !!they did."

"At what time?

"5 AM !!"

"Ohhh….fishhhhh"

The dejected me couldn't believe it. Something broke inside. There was no noise, just stifled breathing. I wanted to see her one last time. A few seconds with her was all I craved for that instant.

The undying hope managed another question,

"So when Mom will return from Nani's house, will masi come back with her?"

"Perhaps no! I don't think that she would come. She has classes now. And she invited me to Agra instead."

"Ohh, that's great." I smiled and said to Luv.

There is a unique moment when you are extremely happy or sad, and there is one expression favouring the moment, 'Smile on lips and tears in eyes' at the same time.

I was going through that moment.

"Let's play some game as there is no one at home right now." Luv said.

I smiled and said to that lovely little kid, "Game? Hehe, definitely. But not now, Maybe later in the evening."

With many questions, with many thoughts, with many emotions, I started moving from there to nowhere.

Now the time was ripe for me to accept the truth.

" It was over"

* * *

One week had passed since she left. I used to peep through my window and fantasize her beautiful face. Her presence was very much there even in her absence. Every moment I remembered her. I would often imagine her around and have secret conversations with her.

I would recall her quarrelling with other children for a chance to bat. My day was filled with the reminiscence of her childlike innocence. Her silvery voice still resonated in my ears. She left traces of her 'larger than life' aura wherever she had gone.

Mobile phones those days were a rarity. Often, only one or two families owned a phone in a neighbourhood. All family members shared the same phone. Privacy was an alien term those days.

Who chatters with whom was no secret.

I tried to arrange her number, but it was impossible from all the angles.

I wasn't courageous enough to ask Jyoti aunty who I assumed would have her number. What could I have asked?

"Aunty! May I have Jahnavi's number?"

One tight slap would have been enough to subside the raging love in my heart. Fear was not the only reason. Our families shared a healthy relationship. I didn't want to be the reason for hurting that relationship by any means. My forwardness in this respect would just weaken the association. So my helplessness won over my love.

I gave up yet again.

The sun was set. The dark night of compromises laid ahead. To find happiness, the stars had to be shot. The vacations ended, and so did all fun and frolic.

It was time to get serious about studies.

The life was changing slowly and steadily. By the time my thinking had changed. I had assumed that I was not merely Rahul now, I had one more personality somewhere hidden inside me. Inside me, I had given a shape to the moments which I had spent with Jahnavi.

Not just an ordinary boy but I wanted to make a unique identity of mine. Not so good in studies so far, now I wanted to concentrate on my academics too.

I was calculating if Jahnavi gets to listen, she must listen good words about me, and I would we happiest person to see her happy. Somewhere I was doing it all for my happiness.

* * *

Once again, I had a hectic routine round the clock once. Waking up early morning at 4, followed by self-study sessions, morning tuition classes, college and afternoon tuition session. The days were usually long and exhausting. The only respite was the 2 hours of play in the evening. These two hours were my source of rejuvenation. It largely contributed towards my dream to become a cricketer. I practised the different shots and techniques with the young bunch of unhampered talent to improve my skill. The training at the academy on the weekends and game sessions during the week really helped me.

This is how my days started passing. Somehow this over occupied schedule of my day kept me happy. I was working hard to improve myself every day. A welcome change it was.

2 Years Later

THE ~~CRITICAL~~ BOARDS

The monthly tests had just got over. My efforts and hard work started getting reflected on the report card. My performance had improved, and I was ranked 5th in my class.

Although we all were friends in the class, but when the season of exams and results used to knock the door, every student would put on his detective hat and wear a pretentious robe. Usually, everyone during that time carried out following three tasks:

First, let nobody know how much you have studied.

Second, find out how much everybody else has prepared.

Lastly, pretend as if you know nothing, and your preparation is nil.

But the truth was; that period used to come for one or two weeks in 3-4 months.

Thankfully, the pretence was lost soon after the exams ended and we would get back to being best friends for life.

We were a group of 5 friends; Jassi, Nimit, Rehan, Aryan and me. Incidentally, we were the five top rankers of the class as well in the same order. We called ourselves

'The Killers'.

The life had started on a different track at a different pace. This was the one aspect of life that had become a regular occurrence. Company of bunch of friends gave me the certain extent of joy.

People around me whether they were well-wishers or they were just news seekers were keeping an eye on me. I toiled diligently to keep their faith in me alive. I found happiness in other's happiness. If there were studies for like 8 to 10 hours including college, then how come I could be biased against cricket? I gave equal weightage to academics and cricket. Since college took up most of my week, I would practice cricket for more than 8 hours on the weekends in the academy grounds.

My parents were amazed to see the drastic changes in my routine and personality. In fact, my mom was afraid of my seriousness and cause of change. I had heard her once asking my dad, "What happened to Rahul? Why has he become so serious?"

I also witnessed a day when dad came to my room and lovingly stroking my forehead told me,

"Beta you don't need to worry so much. We have no pressure on you."

Everybody's care towards me put me on cloud 9. There love and concern further motivated me.

I would get further inspired with these things going on around me.

I felt like the rising sun, slowly attaining its full power and shining the brightest.

* * *

After being struck with boredom and monotony of life, finally, something interesting happened.

Diwali, the grandest festival in India was around the corner.

The entire day all the children in the neighbourhood were involved in decorating every house in the locality. There isn't any 'Mine' and 'Yours' in small cities. Oneness defined the uniqueness of that place. Even though walls separated the houses, the hearts were one.

Love and unity adorned that place. For no reason, everybody stuck together. So we strived not only to make our own houses look beautiful but the entire community. People should get to know that it was the society where Luv, Kush, Jiyansh, Kittu, Nik and I were living.

After beautifying houses of own and neighbours, followed by traditional prayers and all, it was the time of bursting the crackers in that late evening. I headed to Luv & Kush's home.

They all were on the terrace with their crackers.

"Happy Diwali aunty, uncle, Luv, Kush..."

(I wished them altogether.)

"Hello, Happy Diwali to you too Rahul."

"Yaaay.. hey Rahul bhaiya, happy Diwali. Let's burn them all.. blah.. blah." (Kids.)

We together lighted flower pots, the ground spinners, rainbow-hued sparklers and rockets for almost an hour on the terrace. It was when my mom called from the balcony to get back home.

"Listen, Rahul, let's come our home first. Take prasad, and then you may go." Jyoti aunty stopped me.

"Of course aunty, you don't need to urge me. Ideas not waiting for the invitation. I, myself was coming to your home." I said.

(All chuckled.)

There we all started playing in a room. Meanwhile, I came out to inform mom through balcony that I was alive and could be found in the neighbourhood.

Aunty thought I was leaving.

She insisted me to stay, "It will take just five minutes." she added, having a mobile phone in her hand.

I told her not to worry. I was just informing mom.

She spoke to the person on the other end of the call, "Yes Rahul is here. He is playing with children."

Aunty said this on the phone. "But to whom?" I started pondering.

Probably it was Jahnavi on the line, but I had no courage to go up to her and ask, "Who is on the call? Is it Jahnavi? May I have a moment to speak to her as well?"

Keeping my ears on that call, I became the part of kiddish Antakshari again.

Then situation tilted, the phone reached to our room, and it was uncle now who wanted Luv to talk on the phone.

Now I was eager to know who the hell was on the phone. Everyone was talking to him/her one by one and that too in isolation.

I called out Luv and keeping my eyes on uncle-aunty. I asked him in a very low voice,

"Who is there on the phone?"

Giving that phone to Kush to talk, he peeped in my ears: "Jahnavi masi"

Now I was about to have a heart bust listening to these two words.

"Kush beta, say happy Diwali from my side." I interrupted.

"Maachhi Lahul Bhaiya shaying Haaa...."

"Happy Diwali..!"

I snatched the phone from Kush who was finding difficulty in repeating my words.

"Hey….Hi, happy Diwali Rahul!!"

(That lovely sweet nightingale voice after two years, and yes she recognised my voice.)

"How are you ?..It has been so looooong..!", I said.

"For me too...am good. What are you doing?" as if she was also craving to hear me.

"*Aapni kismat per naaz* (feeling proud of my luck)."

"Means you have started shayri (poetry) now?"

"You understood?"

Like always she said in a very low sweet voice,

"*Badmash, sudharjao* and take care of yourself. I will come soon to grab sweets from you."

"Umm…uuuumm.come soon !!"

I couldn't speak further. I was feeling my eyes heavy although I wanted that call to be longer but......

I gave it back to Kush. He went outside of the room with the phone.

Children were shaking me to play, but I was not there anymore. I was so lost in that call that I had become senseless by that moment. My inner happiness reflected in my smile. I conveyed Diwali wishes to the family and took leave along with the other children of the locality. I thought to myself, all these years I lighted candles and diyas and crackers, however, the real celebration actually took place today, the very first time in my life.

It felt like a flower bloomed in the midst of a dessert. As my heart danced in my bosom with happiness, I wanted to rejoice and hop and fly. I was feeling like dancing and partying.

To my great joy, one thing was established in those few minutes of that phone call that nothing had changed between us in 2 years. I was relieved that we could proceed right from where we had left.

What even more interesting was the turn of events;

How I managed a small conversation without uncle and aunty knowing. It all happened so smoothly.

* * *

Now it was the time to undertake the devious half-yearly examination. I relentlessly studied morning to night. It was not because I had to prove anything or make someone proud or win hearts.

It was all for that 'special-day' when result would be declared, luckily Jahnavi would be present here. I would be here and one reason between us that would make us happy for each other. She would be happy for my achievements, and I would be happy to see her happy.

That Reason would be,

"To score exceptionally well in final exams."

So that was it, the goal was set.

It was difficult but not impossible.

Yes, she had become so important in life by the time.

With my continuous effort, I stood second in my class this time. This was the seal of confirmation that my preparation and planning were going too well.

Appearing in the board exams, I had to take a break from cricket. I was commanded by teachers and family to act in accordance. It was not the fear of board exams that compelled me to follow these set of instructions. It was their expectations which locked my dream and passion behind the bars of imminent future. I had no clue where was I heading to. Nevertheless, I kept on running, just running as per the instructions.

I was confident and eager for the final examinations. The board announced the schedule of the examination in the cold and snowy month of January. It was like the formal declaration of war. I had to give up all sorts procrastination activities. My days were hugely comprised of dedicated hours of studying.

Pre-board examinations commenced. They were like the semi finals of the world cup.

And I was just five marks behind Jassi, who had topped the pre-board exams. I had come so close, and I was almost there.

Even though I was not the top scorer, yet my teacher had an unstated faith in me, hoping that I would bring laurels to the college. Maybe it was due to my performance graph going up in comparison to the other students in my college. I won't feel shame in admitting that it was the "Jahnavi effect" prevailing.

This is how a girl can change a boy's life.

Nature has sent women on earth with the gift of 3 superpowers;

First, they have enormous capabilities of controlling their emotions.

Second, they are not resistive to the changes. They easily get transformed from one phase of life to another phase of life.

And the vital third, their ability to completely transform a man in his entireness.

Yes, they can change this giant structure.

In my case, betterment is a more appropriate word. Yes,I was improved now. The confirmation laid in the happiness of my parents and my teachers.

* * *

There were a total of 12 examinations for 5 subjects that we had to attempt in 12th boards.

21st March 2007, the day we had the chemistry examination.

I, Jassi, Rehan, Aryan, Nimit 'The killers' would usually meet exactly 100 minutes after the commencement of the examination, near the water cooler.

In 2 quick minutes, we would exchange the summary of the entire question paper. Our conversation at that point would be so unimaginably synchronized. The rapid swap of questions and answers used to happen quietly and imperceptibly.

Chemistry was our Achilles heel as was the case with most of the boys.

I often wondered what was typical because most equations in chemistry surpassed the rationality of our small brains. Maybe that's the reason it's often associated with love by great men as reasoning often fails in love.

I knew only two, three questions in that 35 marks question paper which hardly carried 10 marks at most. That was the first time in my life I was about to cry because of an exam.

In desperate need of help, I scanned the entire classroom, hoping for a helping hand to save me from drowning. Although Jassi and I were sitting next to each other, but there was a wall separating us. As Jassi was sitting on the first bench of the next classroom. I began to scribble on the answer sheet with whatever came to mind. Then suddenly Jassi appeared at the rear gate of my classroom and hinted me to come outside.

Without a second thought, I got out of that frightening classroom.

On noticing us leave, others also joined. Breaking the regular pattern of meeting at the 100th minute, the anxious us assembled 60 minutes before the usual meeting time.

And then it began,

"The Clash of The Titans", Chaos ensued.

Our entire synchronization was thrown away in seconds. Everyone was pleading to get some answers. One after the other questions were fired. Cries of "Mine first! Mine first!" were in all directions. This was not only killing the precious time but also our hope to at least pass in the examination. Even if someone knew the answers to a few questions, he was more eager to know the answers to the questions he didn't know.

That day I practically understood,

"Rules don't work out in an emergency."

Everyone was begging for help so that they could get through that horrifying question paper.

"At least objectives?"

"What is the molecular weight of this gas?"

"What is the atomic no. of that P-block element?"

"Any ideas on 'xyz' salt's characteristics?"

"Which is the least oxidizing agent among the options?"

"Long answers?? Anyone?"

Queries like these, in puzzled hushed voices, filled the air.

And answers?? ….. nowhere!!

Anxiety was natural as a failure would result in repeat in the same class.

The falling hut caught fire when we heard an authoritative voice yelling from behind.

"What's happening there? Don't move. All of you stay there."

We had never seen him before. We wondered who he was.

"He's from the flying squad." someone screamed among us.

"Run....Run!" (All shouted, and we all ran on top of our pace.)

Jassi had the question paper, and that, made us sprint like crazy.

We all returned to the hall, banging our heads in dismay.

Now there were two reasons to be worried.

First of all, the horrifying question paper, which was still untouched. And second, the fear of being recognized by the flying squad representative.

I was sweating profusely even though the weather was cold and pleasant. So, courage was the need of the hour. I gathered myself together, revisited the corners of my brain and tried recalling the things I had studied and started to fill the answer sheet with information remotely associated with the question.

This was the only option left.

It was just 10 minutes passed when towards my right side, where Jassi used to call me from, I felt as if he had come again. I looked there properly. It wasn't an illusion. He was there for real. But this time he was not alone there he was accompanied by that government flying squad staffer.

"Yes, he is the guy!" Jassi said to him pointing at me.

"'He is the guy' means what? Who is the guy??"

I had understood everything, but I had no choice but to act fake.

Then that devil screamed at me, and we both were pulled out of the class by the representative, to suspend us to write the examination. The matter was taken to college principal, where he proposed to dismiss our candidature for the examination.

Our principal sir supported us and begged for our sovereignty. I heard him saying,

"Anyone of these two will top the city."

At this moment of time, I realized how much they were trusting on me and to what extent they had expectations from me. This meant a lot more than a prize.

I don't know whether I was bound to or got inspired by this incident; not only to perform in that just one chemistry question paper but in the entire series of coming examinations, and perhaps in the coming Life too.

So, after a long-standing debate, we were let off.

It was a close rescue from a big trouble but... the question paper was still the same.

"If God had saved us from one trouble, he shall through us from the rest too." with all my faith in him, I wrote whatever I knew. I tried my best to arrange the haphazardness of last 90 minutes through my pen.

This was how that terrible paper came to an end. Nobody discussed anything about it. The gloomy silence enveloped everyone; it was like everyone had saved the match in last over.

So finally, board examinations came to an end, with many unpredictable ups and downs.

We breathed a sigh of relief after the most terrifying one month.

* * *

The dreaded month of examinations was over. It felt as if a huge mountain of burden had been removed from our heads. I was calm and relaxed.

The sweetness of success prevails when we have really toiled for it. No matter how many setbacks we might have faced in our journey but when the goal is achieved all pain of the obstacles sparkles in our eyes and reflects a smile on our lips. We are pleased by our secret achievement and quietly rejoice over our victory, and there comes that moment when we tell ourselves,

"Yes, I did it!"

Yet I hadn't done anything special so far so that I should have cheered for myself. I had just finished the exams which almost a million of students too had done in the state.

Time and weather both were changing now, so was the mood.

A tournament had started in the cricket academy of the society. Colleges were off, but college's cricket team had to act for it's real assignment now. So there were mostly cricket matches day in and day out. I was elected as the team's captain. Just like the other boys in the country, my cricket idol was none other than the great cricket maestro Sachin Tendulkar. To share the dressing room with the legend was a childhood fantasy.

"There is only one single dream of life."

You might have aims, targets in numbers, which can vary with time and age but you have one dream in one life that we see in our childhood days.

The life was relaxed and moving at a pleasant pace now. The summers were burning us and so was the power supply, being a small town.

That era had restarted now. The park would turn into a lively place by 5:30 in the morning. Uncles and Aunties would come for jogging and morning exercises. Some would be seen discussing the headlines of the newspaper, some discussing matters of the whole universe. Beautiful and terrifying Jaya Amma occupying her favourite bench and some Aunties gossiping with her. And children playing all sorts of games.

The hustle and bustle of the morning appealed me more than the landscape beauty. It was blessing to me to be a part of this world, which was just a small colony of a small town. However, one thing was still missing,

"Jahnavi"

Indirectly I would try to gather information from Luv & Kush with questions like,

"Is somebody about to come you home?" or "Your

mom was saying that you guys wouldn't go Nani house this year, they are coming to see you, is that so?"

But Luv was no more a kid by the time I guess. He would never answer me and would keep my mouth shut with statements like: "Leave it bhaiya, you go and bowl. Whoever has to come would come, why should we be tensed for no reason?"

I too had to say sarcastically, "Yeah dude, why should we become tensed for no reason?"

I tried a lot but couldn't get any info about Jahnavi. There was nothing I could do except to wait for God's magic. I would regularly stand in the balcony or check on the window and silently pray for her to come.

If on any occasion Luv or Kush didn't come to play in the evening or the morning, an attack of collywobbles would hit me hoping the good news about her arrival.

But so far it was still a never-ending wait.

* * *

Like any usual evening, we all kids were playing in the park that day. My mom and other ladies of society including the gorgeous Jaya amma were watching our match. Luv was balling, and I was standing at non-striker's end. Nik at striker's end hit the ball to Long On, and the ball went way too far. The fielder was chasing the ball. I just ran to score runs. Meanwhile, my mom asked Luv from her place,

"Beta Luv, your mom didn't come today?"

I was still halfway during that run. I couldn't move further. I froze right where I was after listening Luv's word: "Today Jahnavi masi has arrived. So, mom had to welcome her and all."

I stopped. Looked at the sky and smiled to me. I walked out of the field (of course I got run out by that moment). I was happy to be run out. My happiness had already scored a century evident through my eyes.

I rang up Kush and asked, "Kush, any guest came to your house today?"

"Yes bhaiya, Jahnavi masi."

The way he said it was amazing, and so was the news that it conveyed. Absolute bliss. After three years, I was going to meet her, the person I wanted to meet daily to. I expeditiously headed home to peek into their window. There was an unusual tittle-tattle that could be heard. I was extremely restless and desperate at that moment and only wanted to see her at any cost.

Overwhelmed by happiness, I was rendered clueless about what should I do. Should I go to their place or go back to the park. I decided to go to the park, hoping she might come on to the terrace to call Luv, Kush or she might come to the park itself to meet me.

I was puzzled at my own happiness.

I reminisced her all through last few years, but did she?

'Does she have any memory at all?'

Three years of no communication is more than enough for anyone to forget everything.

I don't know why but my happiness was suddenly masked in the shadow of fear.

The night had fallen...

Nobody appeared on the terrace or the park to call the children. Proactively I volunteered to drop Luv and Kush to their home, hoping for an opportunity to see her that day itself.

Jyoti aunty opened the door, once we reached their place. I badly wanted to go inside when she insisted me to join them for a lemonade.

But I couldn't.

I knew nothing could've gone wrong but an unexplainable apprehension kept me a good length from the boundaries of their house.

* * *

Next morning, the sun delivered the beginning of a new era. Though, there was something different about that dawn. The melodious song of the sea's rising waves, reaching the shore was clearly audible to me in my subconscious. It was 5:45 when I reached the park to play. It was still Grey, and chilly breeze was blowing. Few drops of dew were still settled on the green leaves of the plants. Beautiful parrots were boasting their gymnastic skills on the cable lines running over the park. People were enjoying their morning walks, and almost everybody seemed happy.

The light and sound surrounding us were very subtle, very peaceful and poignant to the eyes and the heart.

My eyes were unremittingly locked in the direction of the terrace.

And after a killing wait of 40 minutes, that Monday morning with a labyrinth of her wet hair, wearing a beautiful light-yellow suit, that smiling face appeared on the terrace. Yes, lovely, tiny, beautiful, gorgeous, innocent Jahnavi was there on the terrace.

She waved from there, and I greeted her back from the park. She raised her eyebrows, instinctively I responded with a smile. She didn't wear any makeup and was nicely dressed. The moon had risen on the terrace once again.

We tried to converse with each other from the distance however it wasn't possible. Also, the entire city was witness to our wordless exchange. We didn't continue since we were little shy and more because of the restrictions of the society. But our happy faces and shining eyes were evidence of the fact that our story was still alive.

The need of the hour was to give a perfect turn to this story.

In the evening, she came down to the park and sat next to Jaya amma, her favourite spot.

Dang, Jaya amma was so lucky.

We all Luv, kush, Kittu, Jiyansh, Nik and me stopped our cricket match early that day and sat on the bench next to Jahnavi's bench. Before I could bring my restless self together to speak to her,

"Hey, remember me?" her mellifluous voice strummed the most awaited conversation of the decade.

I feigned a laugh and replied, "Didn't remember you till yesterday, but upon seeing you, glad you're a reality and not a dream now."

"You won't change, would you?" said Jahnavi nipping my arm with all the ardour in that voice.

"This is why I don't want to change. Would you ever pinch me if it were not for my mischiefs? I can't afford a change that costly now."

We were just breathing-in the love soaked in the air around us. Then suddenly children hindered our further conversation, "Let's play Rahul bhaiya, Jahnavi di, let's just play something."

Children are usually adorable, and I too love them. However, when you are talking to your love with love about love, they are better off in a corner. Ignoring that craving voice, acting as a naughty kid I asked kids, "Which game do you wanna play in the night?"

"Bhaiya Antakshari!!" Kittu said.

"No, tell some more boring games."

Hahahaha, all chuckled!!

Being the favourite game of Kiitu we had to play that game. I thought to covertly express my feelings toward her through that game. Her response would conclude our story's outcome, unravelling the fact whether she was really interested or it was just me trying to fly a kite without a string.

We were two teams now and we both were the Captains of two different teams, courtesy Kittu.

The game kicked off.

Amid the latest peppy number, when letter 'P' landed on our team, I opted to play safe.

Yes, I sang, "*Pal pal dil ke pass tum rahti ho...*"

While I was singing, I had no courage to look at her. However, I managed to grab some moments. She too was following my singing as well as the lyrics. I wanted time to stop ticking at that moment. How badly I craved to remember all the lyrics of the song so that the end of this moment is pushed further away. Somehow I dragged through the few lines I remembered till,

"*Tum rahti ho*".

Now it was her turn to sing with an 'H'. Yes, she was ahead of me in every aspect,

"*Hamne dekhi hai un aankhon ki mahakti khushboo.*" She sang this beautiful song in her honeyed voice.

I just kept staring at her without a blink.

It seemed like she had read my emotions through my eyes. She sang the full song, looking down all along.

In the night of summer, little moonlight, where there was no noise or light on the namesake of technology. Around ten kids in a greenish ground, a contemporary girl that redefined the word beauty for me was making feel all mortal, immortal things around us on the zenith of bliss by singing Lata tai's song mixed with shyness. This was the best moment of my life. If an artist could paint this scene of the park on a canvas, then this would have been the finest painting of love in this universe.

As the song got over she looked at me, and her eyes assured,

"**You** begin it; **we** will reach the destination"

And then cheer up clapping by the audience after Nightingale's show.

The power supply was restored,and all of us were commanded by our mothers to come back home. None of us wanted to leave the game unfinished. The colourful ambience and setting made it even more difficult. I wanted to ignore mom's orders as I didn't want to leave my beloved but so did the other children. As they were too involved in the game. However, the phrase that governs life,

"Helplessness is a greater power than love."

We all had to leave the stage.

We started getting up happily. Kids mischievously pinching each other, calling nicknames, all smiling faces, cute kids, two lovebirds and yelling moms.

"Jahnavi thanks", on her way back to home I said.

"You have to sing with the letter 'D' tomorrow." she turned back, smiled and said.

I laughed and replied, "Sure I will come prepared."

Her response gave me the impression that we had moved ahead of such mere formalities and wasn't required to act like a stranger to her. We all waved goodbye to everybody else with a promise to meet the next day again.

There, Jaya amma seemed a little irritated because of our increasing disobedience and not going back home even after her continuous persuasion to return home as it was her daily routine. Kittu went to Jaya amma (We were ready to witness something scary.., very scary that night) and said,

"Jaya amma, Jaya amma!"

"Haaan re Kittu bol."(Yes tell me Kittu)

"Ek baaat batao ?" (Tell me one thing)

"Pooch jaldi jaldi." (Yes, ask quickly)

"Ye Jango jayada jawan hai ya aap?" (Who's younger? You or Jango?)

"Idher aa mai batau tujhe kaun jayada jawan hai!" (Come here you naughty. I 'll tell you who is younger.)

(Hehehehehehehehhheheheehehehhee)

Everyone giggled and ran home.

* * *

We started meeting in the mornings again. She honestly used to walk her rounds on the terrace, and I used play whole heartedly with the children.

Yes, I can't deny the fact that amid these individual assignments, we used to include each other in respective activities virtually. The awareness of each other's presence was always on the hindsight.

In the evening after a usual game of an hour at the park, Jahnavi used to join us at 7. She would sit along with ladies for 15-20 minutes then would switch to our team to play. Then all the children, me and Jahnavi would assemble into a circle on green grass to play different games.

I couldn't really figure out how she managed to keep everyone of all different age groups happy. Whether it was the elder's group of the society or people of my age or the toddlers, they all seemed to be impressed by her. We played 'Antakshari' for many days.

Even though it was just the month of May and still there were many more days left for the summer vacations to end, yet I was scared that my happiness might get jinxed.

I started worrying about her return to her native place.

On a fine day, Kittu suggested we play another game, 'The dumb charades.'

Everyone happily welcomed the novelty in the evening game, and the teams were picked up.

The game started with the best Marvel comics' flicks and children favourites like Batman, Superman and so on. A few minutes later in the game Luv proposed me to give a movie name to Jahnavi so that she could act it out.

I told Luv that I was waiting for the right moment. A secret parallel game of love was also ON, which Luv wasn't aware of. The right moment arrived when Jahnavi called me to give me a movie name.

"Hey Rahul, let me give you a movie name and see if you could do justice to it." She spoke with a mischief in her smile.

"Sure", I was extremely excited.

"*Hum Dil De Chuke Sanam*"

"Really?? That's great ... that's applaudable."

"Rahullllll, Just act now...."

(She couldn't control blush in her eyes.)

Since I acted well, my team identified the movie name easily. Now it was my turn, and I went ahead with the flow.

I came close to her, very close, closer, my shivering lips were few inches away from her ears, and I went unsteadily in the mesmerizing scent of her hair.

"Hello, Movie?? Movie??" She yelled and pulled me back to my senses.

"Yea..Yea..So.., *Mujhse Shadi Karogi ?*", I whispered in her ears.

She smiled and murmured something inaudible. I didn't understand if it was a yes or an indication to stay within my limits.

Now the game was none of my concern. I was following her every expression.

I was anxious about the outcome of the game of reading between the lines.

And then suddenly, our moms also joined us. She felt shy standing alone, acting for the same movie for so long. She sat down as if she wasn't a part of the game.

Then my mom said, "Hey kids, why don't you make Jahnavi play with you?"

"Aunty, Jahnavi didi is the one who started the game. She gave up, on seeing you folks." Kittu said.

"Really? Cleaver haan, Jahnavi." Mom said.

" No aunty , I.. I was just watching their game." said Jahnavi with an illustrious smile while staring at Kittu.

"It's okay beta. It's cool. Enjoy."

Hahahaha, all started laughing and Jahnavi could be seen running behind Kittu.

She was looking so cute when she mischievously feigned not to be a part of the game. I wanted to propose her right then and engulf that beautiful moon in an overcast of my emotions. But the destination was still far away. The beginning was good. Hence I instructed myself to stop any further nuisance and enjoy the current moment.

Happily, lovingly, playfully that evening was making history. The night had fallen, and I was praying the power restoration gets delayed so that we could continue hanging out for some more time. We all could keep on sitting, keep on talking like this, this moment could become longer and loooonger.

But in the end…..

We all had to leave.

"I had a great time today." She drew closer and said.

"Ummm. Me too, Jahnavi." I was just looking into her deep eyes.

"They all must be noticing." She uttered.

"Noticing what?" I put my intellect in a corner.

"Noticing, which we are not aware of, between us."

"Are you liking this 'Unaware thing'?"

"I am living the most adorable chapters of my life."

"Then just live it and leave everything else."

"Yeah... definitely…Umm. You…"

"You...?"

"Ahh, nothing. Okay so.. Good night, see you tomorrow."

And she definitely had something for me in her heart.

"Yup, see you. Good night."

When she was going, I stayed there. I was looking at her continuously. She was about to take a turn on her way back. Before doing so, she turned back slowly, looked at me, smiled, and waved her hand from there.

That moment my existence on the planet earth found meaning.

I smiled a little, looked towards the sky and thanked HIM.

* * *

As a daily routine, I was asleep in my room on a lazy, boring May afternoon. I was woken by loud voices outside. Something unexpected happened. Tea, snacks, and sweets adorned the table; Jahnavi and her sister were home sitting around the table and watching *"Hum aapke hain kaun"*, the Bollywood classic on the television. I was surprised to see Jahnavi at our place.

While I was trying to control my emotions, aunty said,

"This girl doesn't want to go anywhere, and forcing me for long back that let's go Rahul's house, let's go Di."

I gained falcon wings upon hearing this.

My mom became a super mom when she said, "It's your house beta. You could come here anytime Jahnavi!"

This conversation of 2 minutes could never be expressed in any language by any writer. But it can only be felt by a lover when he is in front of his beloved having a curtain of shyness in between.

Where I was unable to speak anything, my mom said everything. I was a mute spectator to their eternal conversation and hoped that they would say, "Let's leave the upcoming bride and groom alone."

Just the way families meet each other for the first time during arrange marriages.

But wait, the topic which I had been ignoring for last few days and also the thing which was of utmost significance in my life at that time, came up.

"Board exam`s result", Which were to be declared the next day.

Aunty waggishly asked me, "Are you scared Rahul?"

"Yes,... now, I am afraid."

"Why are you afraid? You have worked hard. Everything will be fine."

"I am not scared of the results. I am scared that I might not be able to live up to others expectations."

"Stop all these cringy dialogues. My thrashing would ward away the evil ghost of 'Acting'." mom said pointing towards her sleepers.

We all chuckled.

I said, "Not a problem aunty. If your blessings are with me, everything will be fine."

Yes, she was still silent. She was brought to kill me

with her unceasing smile in the house.

The dusk had fallen, and the park came to life with players playing, strollers waking and chit chatters chatting.

Jahnavi came up with a thrilling idea and approached me with a naughty smile.

She said, "Let's feed everyone golgappas!"

"I am fine with it if you come with me to the market. Would you?" (Of course, I wanted to make maximum utilization of time and opportunity.)

"Yes, if you will take me on your bike I shall definitely join you.", she said with love.

"What will people think?" I said with fear.

"Let's not think about it Rahul. Let's just go. Someone had told me to live the moment and leave everything else."

"Hehehehe, Yeah."

Since she was not at all hesitant, nothing could stop me. I boldly went and told mom and aunty,

"Jahnavi and I are going to buy golgappas for everyone."

No objection was raised. After all, it was a gal-gappa party.

I ordered the shopkeeper to pack for 30 people. She asked the shopkeeper to serve us a plate right there first.

My eyes welled up with happiness as she fed me the very first piece by her own hand. I lost all my power to reason and was rendered speechless. Even I started to feed her with my hand. One after other, alternatively feeding each other. I cursed the stomach to be so small. The people around started noticing us and their expressions were like

"Abey.. aisa bhi hota hai kya??" (Ohh.. does this really happen??)

"You want more?", She asked me after 10 minutes.

"Ma'am let's leave some space in the stomach so that we can also eat some in front of the people who have granted us approval for this thrilling task."

"Oh dammit! I totally forgot." munching the last golgappa and another hand on her head, she remarked innocently.

We retreated to the park. She alone served gol-gappe to the whole society, much to everyone's joy. What a scene that was and how lucky I was to witness her diligence in completing the tasks with professionalism while carrying a child like asmile.

After the enjoyable evening with golgappa refreshments, she came to me, shook hands and assured me, "Listen, Everything will be fine tomorrow."

I smiled and softly murmured to myself, "I topped today itself."

"What?"

"Nothing, just be ready for a party tomorrow."

"Yaaaayii... Rahul bhaiya is going to treat us tomorrow."

The children started to rejoice. The happy evening came to an end.

THE RESULT DAY

The tension was brewing since morning.

In State- boardsthe marks of the students depend more upon the mood of the evaluator than the knowledge and answers of the student in the answer sheet. Good marks are a far-off dream. Students consider themselves lucky if all subjects' marks are actually printed on the mark-sheet. As innumerable answer-sheets go missing from the board office every year.

If so happens, it's more or less visiting one or the other government office. Hence, I feared board's performance more than mine.

Accordant the news the results were to be declared at 2 pm. I was accompanied by dad to a nearby internet cafe to check my results.

Yes, dad accompanied me because in our state students who go to check their board's results alone, sometimes do not return.

I secured 390/500, 78%. It was good, but I was expecting 80%.

Endless phone calls started to pour. Calls from friends and relatives. Calls from friends lasted only a minute, ending soon after the marks were conveyed and the calls of relatives could continue till next year's result until unless I hung up on them. No one in the history of my family could achieve even first division properly, and yet I was reprimanded for passing with honours.

I got to know that I was the third best scorer in the city and first among the boys. I had done something, which perhaps nobody was expecting from me.

A local newspaper had contacted me for a short interview.

I was not at all interested in that interview and was desperately waiting for it to get over. I wanted to celebrate my achievement with someone special but was unnecessarily stuck in the press office. My restlessness was getting amplified with every passing moment.

I managed to finish the interview in an hour and rushed back home.

(Knock....Knock....) I desperately waited for the doors to get opened.

Cries of congratulations filled the air as soon as they all saw me but I heard only one.

"Congratulations!"

Yes, she was there.

"Thanks. Thanks a lot."

My happy expressions changed into a surprised one when I noticed Jahnavi leaving my house.

"Why you people are leaving. I have just come home. Let's have some tea."

"No Rahul, we have been here for last one hour. It's getting late. There are other people inside who are waiting for the celebrity of our society. Go and take their blessings."

Jyoti aunty said such non-relevant things, and they

left. I cursed the interview as I missed the precious time when my love was at my place waiting for me, and I was nowhere there.

Behind the scene, there was one lady who had happy tears in her eyes.

My dear Mom.

"Ma,see your worthless child achieved it.", I sarcastically remarked.

"Beta go and serve the tea to the guests." She pulled me back to the earth. And then she lovingly hugged me.

"Ma, you please take care of these people. I want to celebrate with my team at the park. Pleeease !"

"Okay Okay. Go and enjoy". Mom gave me my reward for the day.

I happily ran towards the park.

"Let me see your mark-sheet."

Jahnavi quickly came from behind and said.

This was the moment when last time I had met Jahnavi and started working hard with the thought that next time a moment will come when I would be there, she would be infront of me and a reason between us for being happy together. I had made that reason come true.

On seeing my mark sheet, she humorously added,

"So now I know why your English is so weak. Just 63 marks?" she teased.

"Still more proficient than people from Agra." I retorted.

"Yes yes, I know how adept you are!" She said as she pinched me.

"This would have never been possible without you.", I whispered into her ears.

" What..?" she asked as she blushed crimson.

"This, here, you have my mark-sheet in your hand,

and you are happier than me. Your words "Work hard" were like inspirational quote for me."

"Thank God, At least you took my words seriously."

She was getting little romantic now.

"Let's go to the party now" she said.

"Sure let's go."

"Who all will join?" she asked.

"You and me, of course!"

"And these kids?"

"Whoever they belong to, they would care."

"Rahulllll.... anything!!"

"Okay.Okay, we will take them too."

We all proceeded to celebrate my achievement. The success party witnessed by Luv, Kush, Jiyansh, Kittu, Nik, Bittu, Jahnavi andI. A bunch of 6 very young and two older children.

We all enjoyed a lot with pizzas, burger, cold-drink, sweets, ice creams, etc.,etc. It was time to return home.

For the first time, I thought to propose her formally. That was a good day to start, but that one traditional thought interrupted,

"What If there is a 'no' in reply? I will lose a friend too."

However, I was determined to take a dig in the hustle now. I firmly decided that I had to tell her anyhow.

The night had rolled in, the skies were clear, and the landscape was drenched in milky moonlight. It was dark because of the power cut, while we walked hand in hand with the children one behind another. She was in front, and I was behind her.

"You are holding hands of the children, I am holding hands of the children, who will hold the hand of the child name Rahul." I took off.

"Ohhkay, come…You naughty boy!"

Now the sequence was; I, Jahnavi on my left, rest of the children on her left.

So the "Pre" was cleared now came the killing "Mains".

"Jahnavi, I have to say something very important."

"Important? What?", She asked lovingly.

"Ummm. I am slightly scared to express."

"If you are scared. Maybeit's not the right time!!"

I discerned that she must have inferred what I sought to tell. Girls are smart that way. She must have suspected that I might get carried away by emotion. Hence she stopped me before I crossed the line. Or just like typical girls, she was ignoring my advancements.

Okay fine, I thought I have to wait for a better opportunity and situation. It was a mighty task, and I had to be modest to crossover all barriers on the way. However, one day she would compel me to say those three magical words.

The destination was big, so how could the path be simple.

Her statement filled the air with a deafening silence. Even the children were quiet as if they recognized the tension in the atmosphere. We were slowly approaching our homes. Jahnavi was quiet, hoping that I would say something further. While my lips were gummed with the fear that my next words might turn the tables. Nevertheless, I didn't want the evening to end so sullenly, so I enthusiastically remarked:

"So, a celebrity will make headlines tomorrow in all newspapers."

"Which celebrity Rahul bhaiya? Please tell us."

The children started inquiring.

She was smiling and we were having an affectionate conversation through our eyes. She spoke in her inimitable warmth, "Don't run too much in the morning while playing with kids, otherwise Olympic staffers would kidnap you one day."

The way she spoke to me and her charming words of concern, comforted me. The prevailing tension was now pacified. I could peacefully breathe now.

"I shall keep on running, no matter if I meet my destination or not. I will cherish my struggle I endured in the journey, at least. "

I soft-steered our unending conversation towards my signature dialogue.

The memorable day came to an end. We all wished everyone else good night and proceeded to our homes.

* * *

A fresh morning with new hopes and happiness.

The children and I were eagerly waiting for the newspaper vendor.

Owing to our misfortune, the regular vendor was on leave, so another boy came to deliver the newspaper instead but later than the usual time. As soon as the boy came, the ruffled children rebuked him for being so late. The newspaper ran my success story along with my picture.

It was a rewarding moment for me to find myself acclaimed on a public forum. Jahnavi commended me with a thumbs up from the terrace. The children got so excited to see their Rahul bhaiya's photo in the newspaper that they were all over me. They were so overjoyed that they were running around sharing the happy news with the people in the park excitedly telling them,

"See our Rahul bhaiya is in the newspaper."

This was something which I had earned.

I was obviously feeling proud of myself that day.

She shouted from the terrace, "The photo is too good."

"The photo is generally good when you have a good face." I sneered.

"Ya... ya... yeah, it's your day today, I can't stop you. You have got all the rights."

I thought, 'Since today is my day, I should definitely tell her my feelings.'

However, that wasn't the right time. We weren't on the same plane as she was 30 feet above me and I was surrounded by the children who weren't leaving me.

The evening would be better, let's play the game of Rose in the evening, I thought.

That entire day I kept pursuing to prepare what I would say. I practised my speech in front of the mirror a hundred times. It had to be the perfect proposal as it was my first ever. I didn't want her to feel any discomfort by what I say and didn't wish to attract any suspicion from the people around. A perfect blend of English and Hindi. Not too desi nor too flowery. I was ready to move ahead leaving behind my shyness.

As evening approached, people started to gather. As usual, we started to play cricket, and she sat with the ladies. As the game got over, I waited for her to join us but that day she was in a great mood to talk. In her tête-à-tête with Jaya amma and group, she was the most active participant of the day. Everybody was attentively listening to her. She was speaking as the wisest among the group, often glancing in my direction as if she was aware that I was waiting for her with my proposal.

She was surely taking a tough test of my love and patience. Even I wasn't going to give up as I was a fanatic of a sort.

Once decided that I would speak to her that day, I would, by hook or by crook.

I waited her to be done with her animated talks.

"I too want to play." she suddenly appeared and said.

"Sorry, we don't let aunties play with us."

"Ohh! So only uncles are allowed to play huh." she countered.

"Okay okay, you can join! Don't get mad."

She became part of our game with weird faces.

The game was ON, and a huge storm was welling up inside me.

"What story were you telling to the ladies brigade?" I started off with my script.

"Excuse me, why should I tell you? #'Girls talks'."

"Girls talks' with Jaya amma!"

"Shut up..."

She retorted as if she knew that I wanted to say something. And she wanted me to come to the point, like a typical H.R.

I cracked a few jokes to make the mood lighter. The time was passing by quickly.

The heart was beating furiously.

The power could be restored anytime, and we would have to go back home without me saying what I had intended to. The tension was intensifying. An ongoing war of mind and heart.

'How? When? Right now? ... no..no..no not now!'

Thoughts like "Now or never", "What if it's a no", "What if she complained to my parents. I will probably be thrown out."

Amidst the storm of thoughts, I decided to hit the target thinking to face what happens.

I drew closer to her and softly murmured,

"Jahnavi, remember I wanted to say something."

"Wanted to say something ??? When and what ??"

"That result night. Something important, I was trying to tell you. Remember??"

"Result night? I can't recall." she said loudly.

"Mother Teresa cool down, Softly. They all are watching us."

"Ohh. .sorry, so what you wanted to say?"

"Ahem... um... wo ... love... love.."

"What Luv? Luv is playing there, Luv...Luv." and now she started calling Luv.

"Oho Jahnavi, for God sake, why the hell are you calling Luv?"

"I didn't understand. Please clarify."

And then the power was restored, the children started jumping on me.

She got up to leave. I just kept on trying my head down. She turned back and started moving, and while leaving the stage she said,

"Traveller travels, time changes, but destination stays right there, waiting for its true explorer."

"Ya.. Right."

I felt embarrassed.

If I found the person who laid the loving rule for a guy to approach first, I would probably strangle him. Even if the boy initiates the expression of feelings, the girl should at least be a little supportive. It takes almost all of our energy to plan and execute the proposal however girls just seem to enjoy it.

I had to finish what I had started at the earliest. I was in a deep quandary and could not sleep the entire night. In my mind, I kept analysing and replaying the events that had occurred that day.

Maybe there was no reason for what happened, or maybe she just took it as a joke. Everything was getting serious.

New challenges were waiting for me. The other two corners of my struggle triangle were gaining strength.

First, I had to go Bareilly for two days as I had to counsel for engineering. And second the most important, I had to go to play an U-19 tournament for the college team in Kanpur.

The whole tour constituted for almost a week. The month of June would get ended with these two exertions. Life would drastically change with the commencement of July.

It wouldn't have been a surprise if Jahnavi went back to her hometown in that week.

I had just two days to finish the task of life.

* * *

25th June 2007, this day could be the most memorable day of my life.

It was the first rain of the monsoons that day. It started to pour early morning.

As soon as I woke up, I rushed to the balcony to find my moon enjoying the mesmerizing weather with a blush on her face. Nature appeared to be celebrating the dawn of a new love story. The clouds were rejoicing. The sky was showering petals of roses and birds were chirping away happily.

Voices of vivacious laughter filled the neighbourhood. As if the beautiful rain was carrying the bliss with it. It was like nature had sensed the upcoming victory of an effort which was just a few moments away from its milestone.

Yes, that day, because of the rain, neither she could come to the terrace nor could I go to the park to play.

However, unlike the other days, we were face to face standing few meters apart in our respective balconies enjoying subtle raindrops plopping, this was different from the daily routine and special in its own way.

Now I was waiting for the lucky evening, with trust and confidence in myself and faith in God.

It was 6 in the evening when the shrill doorbell started to ring continuously. Everyone in the house was glued to the idiot box, and no one wanted to get up due to lethargy. Then it was Goddess-like mom who went to unlock the doors.

"Come...come....ye....yupieeeee..."

"Wow… what a pleasant surprise." said my mom.

"Hello aunty, hi aunty, namastey aunty."

Multiple voices and a noise interrupted dad and me in our movie. Jahnavi and other children had come to call me to play. Surprised to see them, I directed them to proceed to the park. The children ran out and without wasting another second I initiated the big task on our way out on the stairs.

"Today you came all the way to my place, thank you for the surprise?" I said.

"Kittu said to me, 'Jahnavi didi, let's go to the park. Rahul bhaiya is calling you for the game'."

"Hehehe, Really? Kittu said so?"

Kittu had taken a clever move for me, and I grabbed the opportunity to build on it without letting it go in vain.

"Kittu had come to me also, little earlier and was saying' Jahnavi didi is calling you at the park.'"

"Really? This Kittu is so clever.. haan!!"

Lowering my voice looking into her deep eyes I softly said, "Children are getting it."

She started to blush.

"However it's us who lack the wisdom." I finished with a pause.

As usual, the game of dumb charades started. Unusually it seemed too dragged and boring to me that day. We kept on playing, and I kept on scheming as to how to create the perfect moment, how to get rid of the children around and how to bring her closer to me to express my feelings.

With the night approaching, I had to put my plan into action.

I suggested, "Let's play Ice and water." And they all started running around.

So I became the seeker Iceman, who had the power to convert anyone he touches into 'Ice'. One after the other the children faked to be statues of ice as I ran after them and tagged them. I was covered with a layer of sweat running and chasing them. I put in all my energy to bring everyone to a standstill. In next 10 minutes, all the kids had become ice. Now I quickly headed to Jahnavi.

Finally, I tagged her, and she turned a statue.

I let my heart out.

"Jahnavi I have to tell you something very important which cannot wait."

"What ?", She asked as if she was waiting for it.

"According to me, you are a simple and beautiful girl. I don't know you believe in it or not, but I do...I just wanted to say

'I Love You'

"Ahemmmm...ahemmmm.."

.......a looking silence.......

We just kept staring into each other's eyes for a few seconds.

"You just said it. Such a big thing. Omg! I thought you

were so innocent."

I was surprised that she was surprised.

"So the innocent can't fall in love, huh? And who said that the innocent one couldn't be courageous enough to propose a girl?"

"No.. no.. I didn't mean that." she murmured.

She kept on listening, and I kept on speaking.

"Think about it. I will return after seven days."

"Where are you going?"

With a deep sigh, I replied, "Have some important things to get over with."

I felt her voice getting heavier, and her eyes welling up with something which I couldn't name, be it happiness, be it a surprise, be it the agony of separation for seven days.

But, as usual, She just smiled and assured me, "Rahul, just take care, you will get the best."

At that moment I didn't dare to know if she would be gone by the time I returned.

With little-wet eyes, I looked at her happily and said, "See you soon."

She didn't utter anything. She just shook her head and started moving. I just kept on watching her. She was going heads down. She was going further and further away. But for a moment when she stopped and looked back at me before taking a turn towards her home,

It was like I got my "Yes."

I waved her goodbye.

7 DAYS OF MY LIFE

Those were the hardest seven days of my life, constantly encircled by dilemmas. During the counseling, my mind latched onto Jahnavi's thoughts. With her on my mind I was drawn towards my dream of becoming a cricketer. In Kanpur, and seeing such extraordinary talent on the ground, I thought to myself that engineering would be the safest bet. I was stuck between pursuing my dream and taking the safer path.

"Let the things roll the way they are. Will see when something comes my way." I thought and tried my best in everything.

Compromise was inevitable. Ultimately whatever decision I would take, I would be the one to suffer, I knew.

Slowly the days were passing by. I didn't own a phone during that time so I used the public phone to contact my family.

I managed to secure a seat in an engineering college of Noida and our college cricket team emerged victorious in three out of five matches in the 'Challenger trophy' tournament. I was named the man of the match in two games overall.

Those seven days turned out to be a mixed bag for me.

I certainly felt happy at the end, but was unsure if luck was by my side or not.

As the first rays of sun hit the sky on 30th June, I boarded the train back to Moradabad. I was weirdly anxious. My heart was beating furiously. Hoping that she was still in the town. I was less concerned about Jahnavi's response to my proposal and more fretful about meeting her.

Struck with impatience, I couldn't endure waiting for the evening. As soon as the clock struck four in the evening, I ran to their home with a box of sweets.

And there she was, lavishly guzzling over the mango and her face was smeared with its juice.

"Learn how to eat first." I taunted her.

She narrowed her eyes as if she was saying, "If they were not here, she would have told me how to eat."

I handed over the box of sweets to her. Luv, Kush devoured the entire sweet-box. That box of sweets was like my wing-man. We had shed some of our shyness and were more afraid of the people around.

"How was the tour?" she asked.

"It was good."

"And..."

"And ... What? It was more of a wait."

Seeing no one around I grabbed the opportunity and asked her, "So what did you think?"

"Think? Think about what?"

"I had said something."

"You said so many things and I thought about all the aspects and...."

"and... ?"

"Jahnavi let's finish shopping today."

Aunty suddenly rapped in our conversation and I had

to leave.

For the first time in my life, I felt insulted.

She had got really busy with her family. If nothing was there, children wouldn't leave her side. It didn't matter if she stayed or left the town but I would surely leave for college or for training to Delhi in another fortnight. I kept wondering when I would get a chance to talk to her. That thought really troubled me.

* * *

Unfortunately for next few days, I couldn't speak to her for one or the other reason. I was unhappy and lost.

I asked Luv about her return. He told me that she would go back to her hometown in next two or three days.

That one day Jyoti aunty called mom and asked me to take the children out to the restaurant for dinner. This was a little unusual thing and I could sense something unhappy to occur.

I reached there well before the proposed time.

I asked Luv, "What is the occasion. How come aunty suddenly asked us to dine outside?"

Before Luv could answer, aunty said, "Actually Jahnavi is leaving for home tomorrow. I have to send huge stuff there. So me and your uncle have to go market for shopping. The dinner at home might get delayed. So it's better you people enjoy this last evening with Jahnavi."

Tears welled my eyes upon hearing those words.

I struggled to say something but I was rendered incapable to utter a single word. I just forged a smile.

Meanwhile, Jahnavi came out of her room dressed in a sky-blue Salwar Kameez. She was looking gloomy yet beautiful on that evening.

She was still looking down. Swallowing the bitter truth I asked her, "...So, have to leave now?"

Before she could speak, kids started shouting, "Let's go... Rahul bhaiya,.. Jahnavi masi, Let's go... yehhh... wohhoooo....."

We took a rickshaw. Jahnavi and I sat in front, while Luv and Kush sat behind us. For first ten minutes, none of us uttered a word. However, kids were up to some mischief.

Finally, I asked her with my voice trembling," So ... you are leaving tomorrow!"

"Hmmm..." she said without looking up.

"When will you come again?"

"Don't know."

"Ohh..!"

..A looking silence..

In the restaurant too, the mood was very heavy. She would not talk to anyone be it the kids or me. She even denied eating anything. Frustrated by her dreariness I asked her,

"Why are you not eating anything? Why do you look so sad? Please Jahnavi."

She finally burst into tears....

"I will miss you all. The kids, the evening cricket, the evening games, our late night walks, the unintended get together, Jaya amma and her stories, everything. You all are here, together doing the same things but I won't be here. I would have none of these things there."

"Hmm...." (Now I became quite.)

Seeing Jahnavi crying, Kush too started crying and said, "Masi don't go, please don't go masi.."

The exact thing that I wanted to tell her. As if Kush was playing my part there. We all three joined and started calling the same thing.

"Don't go masi, don't go"

Few people around us heard us and joined us in a sing-song tone called,

"Don't go masi, don't go."

In no time all the people in the restaurant chanted,

"Don't go masi, don't go."

The sad and depressing environment transformed into a happy and cheerful environment.

People started to clap. Sad faces turned into smiling faces, smiling faces started turning into red cheeks with happiness.

"Don't go masi don't go."

Then they all three, Jahnavi, Luv & Kush gorged the food.

I was well aware of the dreadful truth that Jahnavi was going to leave the very next day yet I put up a fake smile to keep the mood light and not let anyone get affected by my distress, especially Jahnavi. I didn't want her to cry on that last evening.

That was the day when I realized that I have grown up.

And few minutes later as we were about to leave, I asked Jahnavi, "Can we walk back home?"

I wanted to stretch the time beyond the linear space and move relatively slower for me. But I wasn't any Einstein, so I tried the best way one of my capabilities would do, walking the way back.

"Yeah, It would give us few more moments together." she replied looking away. I knew, she wanted the same I did.

Despondency loomed in the air. As we walked in silence I thought these were the most precious moments of my life which would probably never come again. The journey was about to end but the destination was still unclear. I was confident that she likes me, but the reason behind the frazzled mood was her silence.

"So at what time are you leaving tomorrow?" I asked her.

"8 am!" My heart skipped a bit!

And then the most daring question for a boy of my age then; I asked, "Phone number?"

She stopped and told softly, "There is only one phone in the family, most of the time it's with dad. You give me your number. I will give you a call whenever I could."

I was disappointed since I also didn't have a phone. I gave her my home number and told her,

"Call me on Sunday morning between 7 to 9. I would make sure that I am the one who pick it."

"Okay, Rahul." she obliged.

Then there was a moment of silence as we both walked, I guess both of us wanted to say something, and none of us knew how to.

 I broke the silence,

"You know, you have beautiful eyes."

She chuckled.

I continued, "Yes, I swear! I still remember the first time I saw you at the balcony when you came out drying your hair. Your hairs were coming on your face, it was troubling you and you were struggling to put them away from you face. That's when I saw them for the first time, your eyes. And my god, I had never seen eyes like those in my life."

I fumbled for a brief moment, I sucked in a lot of air and breathed out all of it, and I spoke again, "You looked beautiful then, the most beautiful girl in the whole wide world; and till now you look the same to me."

She looked at me and I looked at her, I couldn't understand the reaction on her face. But, I think her heart was racing at the same pace as mine was.

By then we had reached the colony's gate and there was silence, again. I asked the kids to run home and bring a bottle of water. I asked them to compete with each other in a race. Whoever gets the bottle, would win a prize.

The children ran immediately. I had the last few seconds with her alone.

She was standing with her head bending down. I sensed she was a little afraid and her lips were trembling with fear. I held her hand and said,

"Jahan….You are very different. You are so modest and simple. I will miss you ...and….and.. I am thankful to the time I met you. Tomorrow you will be gone and nothing will be same without you. But, you Jahan, you are my north star. You are my constant, you are the innocence that has kept the child in me alive, you are the light that has always guided me home. You are the best thing that has happened to me, you are my BEST FRIEND. I don't know if you feel the same way as I do, but Jahan….. I…. I LOVE YOU", I pulled her slowly in my arms. Her head was down, resting on my chest, I guessed her eyes were wet. She must have heard my heart pounding through my chest and she would have felt how much I love her.

She raised her head and brought it closer to mine. I could feel her warm breath on my face, her fingers through my hairs and her lips close to my ears. And she murmured,

"I love you too Rahul and I will miss you too."

She gave a peck on my cheek and stroked my hairs lovingly and said, " You are special Rahul. Stay the way you are. I will meet you soon."

Slowly she started to move away. She was crying and I was unable to say anything. I was in love, and she was too. Her whisper was still ringing in my ears and I was still feeling her lips on my cheek. First love and first kiss, pure bliss. I looked up in the sky, and said my thanks to the almighty above. She was a part of me now, and I of her.

Luv and Kush, the clever children, were coming slowly together hand in hand with water bottles.

"Okay ... so both of you won the gift which you guys will receive tomorrow."

Kids were happy & we were acting like we were too. And in a way we were, we were separating but we got closer too, that day.

I dropped them home, giving Jahnavi my home phone no. and bid her good night.

The walk back home was the most brutal time of my life. An unbearable pain of separation was making my heart writhe in pain. However the blooming of a new relationship brought me some solace, a memento to keep, a bookmark to resume from on this beautiful book of our LOVE STORY.

* * *

The aching agony of her departure struck me so hard that I fell sick because of not eating anything for two days. Maybe this was the consequence of love. When she was around, my heart would beat so wildly that out of anxiousness I would be rendered incapable to think or do anything. On the other extreme when she was not around, I was reduced to wreck all day in bed.

The fact is that if you feel that your life is becoming boring day by day, then you should find a nice girl and start loving her. The fun and thrill in your life will automatically be induced.

Gradually the things were falling back to regularity. Sunday was here and I was stuck on the phone from 6 o' clock even though I told her 7.

Hours passed. It became 10 o' clock. The phone didn't

ring.

It was painful. A jolt of anguish struck me.

There is a truth in human psychology. Usually, when we watch a movie, we identify ourselves as the characters of the movie, most of the times the leads. We feel emotions that they feel. We laugh, we smile and we cry with them. Once the movie ends, we emerge from the characters we had been playing in our minds to the real self.

I questioned myself if the last few months were just like a movie for Jahnavi? Was she just playing a character in the movies?

But For me, it was all real. I had no choice but to wait for next Sunday.

There, on the front screen, the time had come to make the most important choices on which my life relied on.

I had to make a career choice. Having a call letter from one of the most prestigious engineering institutions of the country in one hand and an acceptance letter from the cricket board of the city for the U-19 cricket team in another. I stood at the crossroads of two completely diverging roads and massive dilemma in my mind.

The struggle triangle was back again. The corners were so far away from each other that from one vertex, remaining two were not even visible as a dot. And the time had come to choose a corner. Love, engineering or the dream.

This decision would not solely affect only me but my family also depended on it. If it was just about me, cricket would have been a clear choice. Topping the board examination was like a curse. A mountain of expectation, achieving greater heights in academics landed on my shoulders shrouding my dream to become a cricketer. Relatives terrified me with the petrifying aspects of my dream.

One of them remarked,

"Only 11 from 1.3 billion."

I got scared and fell weak. Instead of fighting for what I wanted, my soul accepted defeat out of fear.

This is how I chose engineering.

I was well aware of the fact that **efforts of mind are doubled when it has to take care of heart and stomach together**. If I had only been in love with my dream, I would not have succumbed. However, right then it was not only the dream. My love was also there. Hence I feared failure. I feared the consequences of failure. I feared the loss of my love.

These two things can no longer go together, that was definite.

I could see that the journey of becoming a cricketer was too long and there is no guarantee of the destination. Engineering to some extent guaranteed some security to life with lesser prospects for failure.

I wasn't wise enough to foresee if the path chosen was right or wrong but I hoped to survive on the one elected. I had love; that's okay but the dream had its own value and position. It was a painful decision. This was not definitely heart. This was some different voice inside which was screaming,

"Don't go for it..."

And I was acting as unheard deliberately.

* * *

As next Monday was the joining date at my new college, I started to prepare myself for it. I was depressed and disappointed for leaving behind my childhood dream and it was the first time I was stepping outside the close comforts of house.

Jahnavi's whereabouts were still unknown. There was no call, nothing. There was not even a single mention of her name. It seemed like the last two months were an illusion and Jahnavi does not even exist. One last hope was next Sunday as I had to leave for college very next day, Monday.

That last Sunday too came but not the "call" from her.

22nd July, that whole day I kept on packing my bags with wet eyes and sealed tongue. What was happening and why? I had no idea.

I didn't want to go. Something was missing. A few days back everything was so different. We were happy. Playing, singing and dancing. The best days of my life.

In no time everything had changed. I was going somewhere for nothing.

Sooner the truth is accepted, earlier we can move away from sadness.

Blaming my destiny, I tried to sleep that night. Having no peace of mind, I couldn't sleep well. A load of memories and expectations were making my breathing heavy. Studies weren't a reason for me to worry. What bothered me were the things which were not in my control.

Monday, the day when I was going to face the harsh realities of life, embarking on a journey all by myself. The dreary feeling of leaving home and family was inexpressible. I couldn't even meet anybody's eyes as I was almost on the verge of tears.

When mom blessed me saying, "Things may or may not happen in our favour. Whatever it is, you always stay happy my child."

For a second I felt like putting my bags there and leave the idea of engineering and rethink about my decision. But,

That "fear of losing" won again.

The children of the locality assembled at my gate to bid me farewell. These small children were like flowers from god to wish me luck on the new journey. With a little smile and lots of love I said to kids, "See you soon buddies".

Eventually, I was on my way to engineering.....

THE ~~ENGINEERING~~

I buried the dream of becoming a cricketer and covered it with the soil of compromise.

Many students might have a dream of getting admitted into the college which I got as a result of a misfortune. My journey, thus, in the largest engineering college of Noida spanning across 50 thousand square feet, began.

At the right side of the main entrance of the college stood a huge three tier building shaped like a gigantic ship. It was called the 'Titanic block'. The main road led to the hostel blocks.

The boy's hostel block on the left and girls hostel on the right, named 'Bhaskar block' and 'Sarojini block' respectively. The two hostels were separated by a 2 feet thick wall.

Following that straight road, adjoining the Titanic block led to another four tier building where the engineering classes were held.

On the other side of this road was a huge ground which particularly attracted attention as it was so well kept with lively green trimmed grass.

On one corner of the ground, there was a little kennel

of a small puppy named "Delfi".

Wrapped with nervousness and fear, I stepped inside the hostel. Aditya, a Mechanical engineering student from Lucknow welcomed me. Although he was a senior in that room, yet his frank attitude suggested that we would delightfully blend together. Deeply engrossed in my first conversation with him, I forgot that I was carrying heavy bags on my shoulder.

Putting my luggage on a 6X4 bed, we set out to explore the college campus. Exploration of the possibilities of future, opportunities for success and risks of failures. The infrastructure was pretty impressive, the crowd was young and vibrant. Few couples were hanging out in the isolated corner of the campus.

I also took a stroll to my classroom, my very first milestone of my new journey.

And then, drained and exhausted, I returned to my room that evening and crashed on my bed. As soon as I closed my eyes, tears trickled from the corner of my eyes. I tried really hard to restrain the tears but couldn't.

There was a void.

I was badly missing everybody. The loneliness was killing me. The thing which was deeply hidden in veils of love; the opportunity to be a part of the cricket team of my town.

A chance for which boys would give life for.

That super opportunity, I had abandoned.

"If this is a wrong decision?"

This thought was aching me inside.

The emptiness of the room seemed as if trying to swallow me in. Motivation to achieve anything had deserted me. I had no will to speak or meet anyone. Neither did I want to eat nor embark on this journey. I got some comfort by remembering those good old days.

But how long could that continue?

Acceptance was the need of the hour and it was essentially required to understand the things at that time.

This was a ridiculous turn of life where 'One thing' had started and an 'Important thing' had ended.

But a lot was still to come, a new beginning, a new journey, a new victory was calling. Now it was the call of time,

'The thing which was getting started; had to be made important.'

* * *

The classes commenced next morning. Little nervous, as it was the first day, I entered the classroom and sat on the last bench of the class. Even though I was scared and sad, I still scanned the room and realized there were 12 girls altogether.

Yes, I had one God in my heart yet I was a saint in nature.

But this was all fake fun fact.

Hoping somehow Jahnavi would find my number, I kept checking my phone every now and then.

Even when failure was on my tail continuously, hope was the only thing that kept me moving.

Now I didn't want to compromise with studies. Rest remained with God on how and howsoever wanted it.

Seniors had advised me to select mechanical branch as it was an evergreen branch with respect to jobs. There were innumerable opportunities in the government sector. Though the college placements were more concentrated in the software companies, I took up mechanical stream. What seniors didn't tell was about the rigorous laboratory sessions over four years which would take a toll on our bodies.

Now the train had started on fresh rails having fuel of

hope in it.

Those days ragging was regular phenomena in engineering colleges. Since our classes were held on the fourth floor, we were ragged by seniors from all years starting with 4th years to, 3rd years to 2nd years as we took the flight of stairs to reach our class. Thankfully ground floor had staff rooms for the teachers. Ragging in college was just a teaser.

The actual film was played in the hostel. After completing eight hours classes in college, once we reached the hostel, ragging sessions would begin. One by one every senior would give us some tasks and we had to do it without any question. These sessions were probably hilarious for them but for us, it was a ruthless activity of killing one's pride.

One senior leaves, another comes in. Till it was the time for dinner, the show used to go on. The door of the room had become a bell of a temple that kept on ringing continuously. Either seniors or friends from first year itself would come in the room. Someone would come to rag us or some to find ways to avoid ragging.

There were one more species having a blend of seniors and first-year students, "The Gods of juniors", who would inspire first-year students to fight against ragging. Studies had become a secondary concern in all this chaos of ragging going on.

As the time was passing, I was making new friends, getting used to the new environment, getting busy with studies. The new college life had come with its own perks. The disappointment and sadness were slowly beginning to disappear.

This is a true saying that time heals everything. The story of my life was confirming this reality. Everything was changing and I was getting back to normal. I was not that sad but I still had that hope of a call from Jahnavi

24×7.

In classes, my one eye would be on the board and another eye on the phone under my desk. I was even thrown out of the class many times for the misconduct. If an unknown number blinked on the mobile screen, I would immediately get goosebumps.

The days went by and serious studies kicked off in classes. Ragging was almost over. Juniors and seniors were all gelled up now.

Fresher's party preparation had begun. Studious boys had assumed senior batch's toppers to be their path-illuminators and loafers had started to worship the gangster type students of the college as their godfathers.

For me, apart from Aditya, warden Chacha was my best friend. Actually, Tukman chacha was a regular gatekeeper for the main entrance of the college yet we used to call him "warden chacha". He was conferred the title of 'The Lord of the kings' as he always helped us to break the rules and regulations such as bringing beer inside the hostel or coming back late from parties beyond the set time.

His fee was just 'a packet of beedi', whenever we felt like breaking the rules.

There was one more creature faourite of us all. Little puppy Delfi, loved by all, Often found loitering in the premises of the college, we had sometimes found him attending classes of Mechanics, Thermal, Metadata, Oops etc.

* * *

It was the night of 15ᵗʰ August. My room was crowded with all the young hostellers.

3 cakes, 20-30 beer bottles were brought to celebrate my birthday. The festivity had commenced.

Everyone was waiting the clock to strike midnight. Sufi -music usually emanated from my room but that night it was the cigarette smoke.

I too got forced to take a puff or two with the patent dialogue,

"Just smoke it man. Nothing will happen, feel the magic buddy."

I kept on fighting and didn't even touch that.

I was warned that the revenge for the insult would be taken at 12.

As soon as the needles of the clock struck 12, I was crushed under the weight of 10 boys. That was a weird celebration. I was whipped and lashed in the name of birthday bumps. My back had turned red and my legs weren't responding properly.

I was screaming, "At least cut the cake rascals, it's enough, leave me, it's not my birthday, I have not even taken birth, I am an illusion, please leave me guys."

After an hour or so, the cake cutting took place. Out of the three cakes, one was used to smear my face with cream and other two were used to feed entire the hostel.

That celebration, not celebration, drama, that drama kept ongoing up to 4 am and it was 5 am when we all went to sleep.

It was a nap which I had because at six I received a call for blessings from home.

Papa- "Happy birthday beta. What are you up to?"

I - "Thank you papa. Just preparing for yoga."

Papa- "But you sound like you were sleeping."

I - "No..no papa, I just finished meditation. Probably it's effect is there in the voice."

Papa - "Great my child. Mom wants to speak to you now."

Ma -"Happy b'day beta. Stay blessed and party hard. No kanjoosi!!"

I - "Yes Ma, my friends won't allow me to!"

Ma - "Hehehe.. Great, have fun."

That day in the class, my phone was continuously blinking. An unknown B.S.N.L. number kept flashing on the screen. As I was in the class, I couldn't attend the call. I didn't even pay much attention since I thought it was a call from one of the B.S.N.L. operators who keep pursuing users to enable caller tune.

The treat was hosted by me in the evening for few close friends. We were a group of 5 friends hanging out at the restaurant chit chatting and having delicious food. That was when I received a call from the same number.

I answered it.

"Hello" I said.

"Happy birthday day, Tom cruise."

"Jahnavi.... is that you?" I asked taken aback.

I started to shiver and came out of the restaurant to speak to her in private. Blank and speechless, I couldn't find words to say. I kept hearing hello, hello from the other end of the line.

I just looked up at the sky with deep gratitude and thanked God. I sighed deeply and started off with,

"Where were you? You are calling me after such a long time. I thought you had forgotten me. You have tortured me so much."

"Listen....listen.....Rahul..."

"No... Today only I will speak and you will listen."

"Ohk then go ahead, I have the entire night to spare." she said with love.

And those words were enough to shut my mouth.

"How are you?" I said very softly.

"Just like when we parted." In her Captivating voice, she said.

"Hahaha, really?" (A sigh of relief)

"Yeah!"

"Why didn't you call me on Sunday?" I asked.

"Umm.. Rahul..I just lost your number." She replied.

"Seriously!! You lost my number? See, this is the difference between a boy and a girl. If you would have given your number to me, I would have saved your number at 7 different places and would have kept them safe with me."

"Hey, Listen!" she said irritatingly.

"Then how did you get this number of mine?"

"For that, you have to listen to me very patiently as it's a long story."

Our conversation furthered as the cool breeze brushed my hair under the moonlit monsoon night sky. The clouds cleared up from the sky and from my mind as well. My world has just brightened up and the night was just young.

"So tell me your looong story as I don't have any train to catch."

"Yeah.. so ...ummm ..what was I saying, okay. So your number. I told Jyoti di that Rahul had suggested me some best M.B.A. books to prepare for. But I forgot the names so I need his number."

"Oh so lying here too!" It's been so long I teased her and made her angry.

"What to lie in that, I am really preparing for C.A.T."

"No, not that, the one that I told you about some M.B.A. books"

"Rahul (she said sullenly)- *Ek toh*, I had to work up my brain to get your number somehow."

"Ohk, ohk , so what didi said?"

"Nothing! She just took your number from aunty (my Mom) and gave it to me."

"Oh really! Hats off for this much drudgery! But Miss Jahnavi, you could have done this a lot earlier."

"I actually did! But I wanted to give you a surprise on

your birthday."

This made me the happiest guy on the planet. However, after gathering all my senses, we continued to talk seamlessly for nearly half an hour to 45 minutes. We discussed everything we missed in these past 2 months.

Suddenly, I noticed 4-5 giant dark shadows around me. It was horrifying to see those shadows in the bright moonlight. I was surrounded by them. With ill thoughts in my mind, I decided to use my mobile phone as a weapon. The moment I turned and thought to act something, I discovered, with a sense of relief that those were my 5 friends who I had invited over for dinner that special evening and left them alone on the table, as I embarked the journey of my conversation with her, my own little sojourn. The looks on my friends' eyes meant trouble!

"What kind of behaviour is this man? You brought us for dinner tonight, made us order food and got yourself busy with the phone. It's okay to be busy for 5-10 minutes but one whole hour?? Bro, we have been calling for last 1 hour but your call is so important that you are not ready to pick our call once?" Aditya howled.

Shashank – "Even the bill has been paid by Adi."

"Jahnavi I'll call you back." I said and disconnected the call, as it was more important to handle those idiots (of course they were, for not understanding the importance of the moment they just ruined), who were drunker than they should have.

"I am sorry guys; it was a call from home so it got stretched."

"But in the morning itself you got a call from home and you spoke. Don't lie!! Boys don't talk to their parents for more than 10 minutes. Tell us, who is the girl?" Shishir exclaimed, who was a self-proclaimed psychologist.

"It's already past 11, we should get going otherwise warden chacha wouldn't let us in the hostel." I said averting his question.

"You owe us another bottle! No less than Antiquity Blue." Shashank Smirked.

I had no option but to fulfil his demand so that they can move their bodies from that place.

"Alright, no worries. But tomorrow! You guys already had dinner."

Somehow everything was under control and we were on our way back to the hostel. Suddenly I got a message and it was from her.

"I won't be able to talk to you now, as I had come to the terrace. Now everyone's asleep and it wouldn't be right to do the same without their knowledge."

Smiling in my mind, I replied, "Good night"

The long wait was finally over. We met again, met again to move forward in a manner.

Talking to her from the other side of the phone somehow didn't feel distant this time. It felt as if we both were together, back at our place, in the same colony park, sitting next to each other on the same old bench, and talking for hours on end.

It is said that the true love between a girl and a boy lies in the madness of the girl and the maturity of the boy.

It was an ocean of madness in her and so to match that maxim I had to show some maturity. One small mistake could have turned the first chance into the last. Every step had to be taken with utmost care as this story was not just a Love-Story now. It was more than that, It was a story of sacrifices now.

Any mistake could put our future into darkness. But still, despite these serious facts, above everything else, we both had our personal phones now and knew each other's number too.

Yeah, a reason for excitement.

THE LOVE

I had that special feeling from the moment I woke up the very next day, a feeling of completeness, satisfaction, eternal bliss. The day felt nothing less than a perfect day, right out of a Mills and Boons novel. The special day was totally different from the rest of the college days hitherto from the Day 1. As if a line was permanently drawn on the pages of the calendar marking the days before that day as insignificant and magical to days in future.

I was feeling more confident, satisfied and happy. For the first time, instead of playing Sufi music, I was avidly listening to English songs, Tylor swift & Eminem were on top of my playlist. Filled with extreme happiness I messaged Jahnavi on the first lecture itself which seemed more boring and unbearable than usual,

"Good Morning. I hope you don't have to go to the terrace in broad daylight to talk to me."

And as if she was waiting for my messages, she instantly replied,

"Wait! Let daddy go to office and then I'll call you."

The essence of true love can only be felt when it is showered across filters of shyness and limits.

I could feel that being at home under constant surveillance, she could only talk to me when nobody was home or she would need to go somewhere outside just to talk to me. We both were playing the game of hide and seek somehow. Just the reverse way, seeking and having to hide.

"How come your father hasn't gone to office yet and at this time, why aren't you attending classes at college?" I asked trying to further the communication.

"I'll tell you everything, Wait!" she texted.

There was the exchange of total 4 messages that day and classes went on. Hands of the clock ambled from morning to the evening, and then around 7 I received a call from her. I jumped in joy from within as my exasperation of waiting took over.

"Ohh, So uncle has gone to the office now!" I said irritatingly.

"Ohh no..., he didn't go anywhere today. That's why I have come to market to talk to you."

I felt so blessed when her deep and touching voice mixed with her emotions kissed my ears. She desperately waited for her father to leave the house so that she could talk to me. Now she had come to market just to talk to me. It was indeed a very special feeling.

I asked her everything from starting to the end and gratified my soul's thirst that was dried up due to redundant thinking. I was feeling relaxed now. Took a long sigh of relief.

"Do you have any idea what I went through during those Sundays starting my day with a hope of your call and ending the both (the day and the hope) in the night with immense pain." I said.

"Despite having your number, I had to wait until your birthday to call you and just to give you a birthday surprise. Can you imagine how tormenting it was to wait for so long, and not to call you?"

Here she won the war of words from me, again." B y the way, don't you go to college?" I changed the topic.

"Ohh! Come on dude, Arts students don't go to college regularly. And if we go, we only go for attendance and that too for 2 days in a week. That's more than enough."

(The tone started to lower.)

"Great! Creative people don't need to go to college."

"Haha..! Exactly."

"Jahnavi..." I stopped her between all seemingly irrelevant talks.

"Yeah" amidst the race of words, she too stopped.

"I don't believe it."

"What?" she asked perplexed.

"That you are mine now" I said very confidently.

"This is a very big thing Rahul. It's not easy to get someone, not that quickly."

"Still, I am talking to you on the phone like we've never before, isn't that a special thing?"

"This is a new beginning Rahul. Tread carefully. If we go wrong somewhere, it will hurt both of us."

I remained speechless but she was oozing out very deep thoughts continuously.

I looked at the watch; it was already 8:30 pm.

"Jahnavi, you should leave now. Your family might worry about you."

"Hmm. Okay, I should return now. Listen..."

"Yea?"

"Ahhh….I Love You!"

I controlled my happiness from rolling down my eyes. "I Love You Too." I just said, trying to hide my brimming excitement.

And from that day onwards I was being counted amongst the committed young engineering students, a rare specimen. I was feeling fantastic.

So far what I had seen people doing in colleges, in metro cities, in Punjabi video songs, now I would also do the same. And I hope the winds and the background music do their parts too.

But ...,

If it wasn't for a damn mobile, we wouldn't have been connected in the first place. Our next personal meetings were not certain. This was a long distance relationship and neither of us knew when, where and how will we meet next.

But anyhow, I was very happy.

I felt like screaming and shouting and making an announcement about who and how much I have loved. I wanted to scream it out loud to the world. Our story was a typical love story which was embellished with many kids, many families and brewed over many summer holidays. Now there was no shortfall, there was no misery, but instead, there was a new reason for living with double the will to make it beautiful.

This is indeed the power of true love; when you feel it you gotta know its strength and then you can move mountains. The idea is to harness that strength to make your LIFE's Story successful and not just 'The Love'.

Those days B.S.N.L. had a bug where if the message centre number in mobiles was changed, you can get access to all India unlimited free messages. I had bought one Reliance SIM and another B.S.N.L. So I had to buy two phones for two SIM cards. One phone for calling and another for messaging.

However, it was not possible for her to keep two phones as she lived with her family but somehow she managed to keep two phones, that too ethically and honestly. She told me that she had taken parents' permission for keeping 2 phones and two SIM cards.

Now you can guess how adorable the girls really are to their parents.

A new era had begun! An era of phone calls.

We started talking to each other daily, messaging each other day and night. But we both tried staying within a certain limit to enjoy the feeling of wanting more. We both had this understanding that some things are good only when done in limits and when limits are crossed, things which make us feel good starts troubling us.

* * *

Love was growing day by day just the way our conversations did. And there were these despicable 1st-semester exams hovering right around the corner. The gap given to prepare for the exams was very restricted. Diwali festival was nearing but the university had done such arrangements that neither we could live nor we could die. Meaning that Diwali was lying between internal and external exams.

Such was the situation that neither we could celebrate it appropriately nor could we study properly. This was the way in which the university was playing with our emotions. Slowly, the things started changing.

Now boys could be seen holding books instead of holding their girlfriends' hands and gifts for them. Instead of hubbubs, there was an eerie silence in the college throughout the day. Hymns could be heard whole night in the college hostels. A Shiva temple which was in the middle of the college campus became surrounded by devotees. Classes were closed. It was almost the end of October. Students whose attendance was less than what was required to sit in the internal exams had started attending extra classes. I also started preparing with utmost fervour.

Jahnavi's words kept me inspired in between. Yes, the great wisdom of parents and holy phrases of evolved personalities can't inspire people as much as a lover's discourse. Once a gal says even a small inspirational thing to her lover, the guy will be all set to bring the moon down leaving the stars terrified, that they're next!

To pass the examinations, students had left no stone unturned. Amidst all the tensions, we started discussing what to do with the Diwali holidays. Should we go home or should we stay? So there were different opinions and different logics. Everyone wished to go home but there was only one week's gap between the Diwali festival and the final semester exams. And it had been more than 5 months since people had visited their homes. Now students were missing their homes more than their girlfriends.

Internal exams disappeared in this conundrum. None of us took those exams seriously.

The main issue was "External exams".

On the last internal exam, a final meeting held to discuss whether we should go home or not. The main issue here was not 'Celebration of festival at home'.

No, Not at all.

The quandary was, everyone thinking "If he goes home and celebrates Diwali, buried in the festivities, burning crackers, eating sweets and having the fun of his life. What if his classmates stayed back in the hostel and completed one chapter after another, he would fall way behind in the race."

But with just one superb dialogue of my room-mate, everyone started packing his bags happily without any tension. When Adi was asked about his opinion, very poetically he said,

"Main semester ka paper chhod sakta hun, mere ghar pahuchane wali kal savere ki train nahin."

("I can skip the semester exams but can't miss the first train to home tomorrow morning.")

Everyone started celebrating with claps and dance. People were going home after six months. The joy of going home was ravishing. Students had this intense desire to go home but the fear of failing in exams was ceasing them to listen their heart. But now with one spark of excitement, all the fear vanished into thin air. Students were so excited that they were gliding with the joy.

"We will study for 12 hrs instead of 6 hrs."- One of them declared.

"We have to go home. Everyone is waiting there."

Emotions were oozing out. Everyone started drinking.

I also dialed my home in excitement.

"Ma, I am coming home!"

"Come Betu. We all are waiting here. A plate of Rajma-Chawal would be ready in your room."

"Thank you Mom. Bye"

Everyone was so happy to see their homes.

Then all of us tried to make the last night a memorable one before leaving for homes. When we went to mess to have dinner, even the movie being played was "Kabhi Khushi Kabhie Gham", the most loved family movie ever.

Finally, boys had tears in their eyes. Everyone started missing their homes badly. To be honest, I too was missing my home and more than that I was missing her. I felt like talking about her. Talking to her was a different thing but talking about her was a feeling, altogether different on its own.

It was 11 o'clock in the night. Calling her so late didn't seem right but that day I wanted to be little selfish. I dialed her number,

"Hello, were you sleeping?" I asked softly.

"Yeah.., I just slept. You tell, where are you?" She replied in a very sweet voice.

"I am going home tomorrow."

"Really?"

"Yes!"

"I also want to come."

"So come naa!!"

"Huh? Ummm !", There was something lacking in her voice.

"So from tomorrow onwards, you will play without me."

"No..No, not just that, we will burn firecrackers also and then will party hard."

"How manner-less and rude you are!"

"How weak you are ! If you wish you could come."

"It's not that easy for me, Rahul."

"Why? What happened?"

She had a habit of turning a romantic mood into a serious one.

"You will not understand. Leave it!"

Before I could ask further, she continued.....

"You enjoy to the fullest. Keep informing me about your games at park and children's playful naughtiness. I have to go now, Mom-Dad are asleep."

"Cool, Good Night."

"Good Night."

I kept waiting for her to hang up and she, for me.

"Hang up", I said.

"You hang up", she said.

Meanwhile, someone came from behind and snatched my phone and hung up.

In the middle of the college field, the stage was all set. Delfi, our favourite pet was happier than us all. With it's various acrobatics, it kept entertaining us. By lifting both his legs and dangling the tongue out, it was playing with everyone. Wagging his tail, he was jumping here and there. I was awaited. There were only boys, no girl. Girls were not invited so that there can be no impediments to the excitement we all have had. Boys were dipped in fascination.

Under the clear open sky, beneath the shining stars, lit by the smiling and blushing moon, Mattress of the green grass appealed to us and we all sat on the ground. On that night, warden chacha also joined us with his packet of beedi and next to him sat our dear Delfi. It was the month of November and some chill breeze was blowing.

Sumit, a second-year student, who was a drunkard and never attended college, was the first one to start the narration of his story,

"She used to attend Math's tuition with me in 8th standard and would sit on the first bench.

I had a habit of always coming late to the class. Every day when the teacher used to scold me, she irresistibly used to stare at me. Then the distance from the classroom door to the last bench would get travelled by her beautiful eyes and me together. The moment teacher used to get up to write something on the board, she would turn back and look at me. I would just smile and gesture her to look at the board.

She was good at multitasking, studying as well as

keeping me under her spell."

"Then?" I asked.

Sumit -"Then what, this continued for the next two years and soon her father got transferred.

I couldn't muster up enough courage to tell her about my feelings."

"Arey yaar ! Did you find out her whereabouts?" (Shashank was desperate to know their future.)

"Yes bro, I did, but got nothing."

"Damn!"

Likewise, many untold, unheard love stories that were kept buried in hearts away from the whole world, continued to lighten up that night and mood.

It felt as if we all were a part of this evergreen song from the movie Border, "Ki ghar kab aaoge". That moment was making history in the diary of time, I never thought that these sturdy, tough, rude, loafer and what not kind of guys, can also be the emotional types too.

"Chacha aap bhi jawani ki kuchh kahaniyan bataiye, vada karte hain chachi ko kuchh nahi batayenge."

I insisted warden chacha to reveal his untold love tale.

"Haha! Beta Rahul! Arey hum kaha..n, hamari bas ki naahi hai ee sab cheeje."

"Toh chacha Bebas ki hi bata do."

"Re beedi jala re chacha ke liye !!"

(Boys lit a beedi for chacha)

"Hamaar gav me rahi ek, sarkari nal se paani bharan jaati rahi, ooka piche piche hum bhi paani bharan jate."

"Fir chacha?", boys were getting engrossed.

"Chalat raha kayi saalo tak nain-matakka. Hamar samne se nikal ke jaati, ghunghat uthati, Balti hilati. Hum samajh gaye ee zalim ka isara hai, humse milan ko ...."

"Ariii chacha matlab Romantic. Phir ? Phir ??"

"Phir ka, uske vyah ki baat hamau pata chali."

"Oho chacha, tumhare saath bhi ! So sad!"

"Arey naahi naahi."

"Hum ooka bhaga liye. Aaj wahi tumhari chachi hai."

"Hain..?? Arey chacha dil khush kar diya tumne to!"

With such a happy ending to his story, everybody wished to become warden chacha instead of Einstein or Tendulkar!

Everyone started jumping and hugging each other, the celebration started as if India had won the world cup. There were tears of joy in the eyes. Naagin dance stole the night and there was this surge of energy in the body, a ray of hope that someday all will be well.

I hugged him and said, "Chacha tum toh hero ho."

"Main ghar jaa raha hu."

"Main tujhse pehle pahuchunga."

"Koi mujhe phone mat karna, main ek hafte tak college ke baare me kuch sunna nahi chahta."

"Meri waali toh station pe milegi."

"Me to apni wali ke saath hi jaaraha hun"

I looked at the sky and sighed to myself, "Meri waali to mere saath hi hai."

"Chalo ghar chalen."

"Happy Diwali to all."

THE FIRST MEET-OUT

"I am done now, go and trouble your Captain Rahul.", Jahnavi said pushing the children away, who were surrounding her.

"What happened kids? Why are you troubling Jahnavi di?"

"See bhaiya, she snatched and ate all the puffs." said Kittu crying.

"Really? Puffs from kids? You didn't spare them too."

"So what!! Is there any age bar mentioned on it's wrapper?" She said solemnly.

"God damn Jahnavi. So childish behaviour?"

"Yes! I am still a child. Do you mind?"

"Get up brother, get up. You have reached Moradabad, your destination." Said the bus conductor pulling me out from the heaven of dreams.

"What man! I was having such a fantastic dream!" I screamed in my head.

"Anyway, thank you."

After leaving your own town, when you step back for the first time after months, your soul thanks you. Lost in the past memories, I took an auto-rickshaw to my home. I didn't realize when the auto rickshaw stopped in front of my house.

"Hey Rahul, where are you looking at? Here bachche, here." Said Mom taunting me because I was still looking at Jahnavi's house.

"Arey Namaste Maa! Where is papa?"

"Office !! Where else?", like I mentioned Mom's headache.

"Freshen up beta. Let me set the lunch for you."

"Great Maa."

In Evening I stepped out of my home with the dabbed foot. Kids have already assembled in the ground at 6 pm.

"Hey! Rahul bhaiyaaaa, when did you come?"

Luv asked happily.

"This afternoon itself."

All the kids surrounded me and started cheering up. As I loved all the children and everyone loved me. Now it was the time for reliving the moments of dumb-charades and Antakshari.

"Our team's captain Jahnavi Di hasn't come yet. We can't play without her?" Kittu said.

"No worries Kittu. When didi would be here, she would play from your side. Until then let us all play." I said pulling his chubby cheeks.

Then at 8 pm, I received a call from her. I can never forget that call. I took a corner to talk in such a huge park.

"How is everyone over there?" she asked excitedly.

"Everyone's good. Where are you?" I replied.

"On the house's terrace obviously!" (She took a deep breath)

"And your parents?"

"Went to market."

"Why didn't you go?" I said teasingly.

"Will you stop asking such questions or shall I ask didi to program Kittu to take good care of you?"

"Alright. Alright. Fine."

"Better"

"Come yaar, your team is badly missing you." I sighed.

"I too want to come!"

"If you try you can come here for one or two days."

"Okay I'll come but then I can't come for 2 months in summers. Tell me, what do you want? Whatever you say?"

"What kind of deal is this?"

"Yes, this is it." As she had put her problems like an open book in front of me.

"Alright, then you come in summers only. It is not feasible to kill the golden egg poultry."

"Ohh come on dude. It's really illogical to mention this idiom here."

"Ohk Ohk Alright! My bad."

We both chuckled, followed by a pause and silence.

"Rahul, do you have guts?"

(What kind of irrelevant question it was.)

"Any doubt?"

"So, why don't you come to Agra someday?"

"Will this prove my grit to you?"

"Yeah. Of course!"

"Alright, then you will have to make me stay at your home."

"No no, this is IMPOSSIBLE. This cannot happen. Not at all."

"Why not? Don't play the one sided game."

"Yaar Rahul please try to understand. I belong to a typical Indian orthodox family. I seldom go out of the house. If my parents come to know about us, they will kill us."

"Haha of course. I know everyone in your family. And they too like me."

I thought she was kidding.

"They like you, that's alright. And that is altogether a different thing. They do not like this type of stuff."

I was not able to get her completely as she was getting way too serious.

"This type of stuff means? What kind of stuff?"

"You just leave it man, It's Diwali tomorrow, let's just talk about the good things."

There was stillness in her voice. As if there was something holding her back. It was like a small innocent girl has been subdued under the burden of stupid traditions. It seemed as if she was suffocated with these conventions.

"Yes, It's Diwali. But what were you saying … They do not like this type of stuff?"

"Did you buy firecrackers or not? Has Tom Cruise's colony been decorated with lights or not?"

I understood, she was too mature.

"Arey what to talk about crackers, I feel like laughing at Mom's behaviour."

"Why? What happened?" She inquired anxiously.

"Son comes home after 5 months. Good delicious food is served and he enjoys. He gets proper rest. And in the evening after serving a hot cup of delicious tea, Maa tells her son to dust all the furniture and almirah of the drawing room."

"Hahahahaha. Son thought that visiting home after

such a long span of time will increase his value and he'll be treated like a guest. But Maa proved that her son will always be the same Rahul for her. Thank God she didn't send you to buy dhaniya-mirchi."

"Haha! Yes lol"

I was bit relieved listening to her laughter.

"Listen, I'll come to meet you definitely."

I wrote a phrase.

"I'll wait for you." She announced our victory.

"Bring your friends along."

"No ..No"

"Ahhh.. I didn't mean that. Don't take me wrong. You just don't come alone."

"You don't worry about that. I'll make some plans. You just come first."

"I'll come. I'll definitely come."

She rushed into, "Alright it's late now. Will meet soon."

"For Sure. Happy Diwali."

"Happy Diwali to you too Tom Cruise."

"Good night Jahan"

"Hehe, Good Night."

That day we talked about some really serious stuff. She was a little bit upset. Being the youngest, she was burdened with everyone's expectations forcing her to live a life of false happiness. Even her laughter was also unnatural. She was hiding behind the mask of social and traditional norms.

That was the first time I felt something like this talking to her over the phone. When I met her in summer vacations, she seemed normal.

I never felt that she was suffocating this much from

within. I always considered her family as an open minded and modern. But the reality was something else. Apparently, they were way too strict with her.

That Diwali, I had kind of mixed feelings. There was happiness and there was no doubt about it. Diwali is such a feel-good festival; it feels like we have reached the zenith of happiness. Aah! The smell of fresh paints. Colourful lights flickering like a firefly and lightning up the atmosphere.

A cool breeze carrying the fragrance of cardamom. And the smell of the wet soil is something beyond expression. Even good perfumes are incompetent against the fragrance of desi mitti. There is different kind of liveliness in the markets.

All old friends used to meet on this auspicious day and we would play all the games we used to play and enjoy. This has been an unwritten tradition since childhood days. We adorn new clothes.

The festival of love and the festival to show the power of love.

My soul was contented with this simple and joyous thought.

But to be honest, there was something missing. It was her, her presence, her fragrance, the feeling of her belongingness to me.

Her childishness, that would coerce her to grab and eat puffs from 6 year old kid, was missing.

"I love her. I am thankful for each and everything which made me come close to her."

I knew I had to do the next big thing, "To meet her!"

Yeah! This was not such a big thing but neither a thing which could be ignored. After all, everything that involved her became big for me. That's the way it was, it always had been.

"But when should I go?? Exams are on us now. Maybe during winter vacations, in January. Or I can go and give her a surprise on the occasion of Valentine's Day in February. Yes, that would be superb." I thought.

After Diwali, having these thoughts in my mind, I was on my way back to the hostel.

I stepped back in that infernal college with this thought of meeting her in Feb. It was infernal no doubt but the truth was, the road to my destination went through that college itself.

I really needed to work hard. I had to get a good job or maybe something better than that to further our chances of getting together, to make a future for us.

This is the difference between your birthplace and workplace. Former reminds you of your past while the latter prepares you for your future. There is nothing good or bad in it, this is just a truth. A Truth which is beyond all the whims and fancies of this world. A Truth which never changes, which is eternal.

And that day's truth was,

"We had 1st semester's exams after three days."

"Now I should prepare myself for the exams. It's time to come out of the reminiscence of home and love."

On this note, I started preparing hard for exams.

* * *

The exam mode was ON. The whole atmosphere was engulfed in the silence of exams- preparations. Post dinner chitchat routines got transformed into late night studies.

Exams in the daytime, group studies in the night. This showed the willpower of the students, the will of steel. Those students, who would party late on Friday nights and would only wake up on Sunday afternoons, guys who had not seen Saturdays for ages, were now making do with barely three or four hours of sleep per day.

It was proven that in tough times even enemies become friends. Due to time constraint and vast syllabus, enemies and friends came together and distributed portions of syllabus amongst each other to finish in time, leaving behind the differences.

There were two kinds of boys in college; one who were committed and others sturdy, tough, rowdy types, in short, single guys without feminine indulgences. College couples had their own family routine; from attending classes to eating food, preparing for the exams, discussing question papers after exams and many such things these lovebirds would do everything together.

And other poor, underprivileged, single guys used to do anything and everything with a tight-knit group of 10-15 other boys. My case was somewhat special as my bird was living some 200 KMs away and was studying an entirely different course than mine.

So I couldn't make my own "Love Bird" team but was happily a part of poor guys' group who used to share things with 10-15 other guys.

So, exams went on like this with the bright hope that someday it will be over soon just like a nightmare filled pitch dark night.

It was a wintry month of December. Due to extreme cold, hands were stiff and it was really difficult for a person to write the exams even if he knew everything. Copying was a common phenomenon in exams.

After all, we had a truce to pass the exams together.

Teachers had given us a very crucial piece of advice to not keep the answer sheet blank for questions we didn't know the answers of. Rather fill it up with something or the other resembling some technical jargons we could gather in our heads.

All of us preferred this technique, after all, who wouldn't need desperate measures for desperate times.

And finally, exams were over. It felt like a big mountain had been crossed.

'Phewww, Such Relief..'

'OM Shanti, Athah Shanti!'

The drunkards in the bars, lovers in lush green gardens or theatres and simple innocent singles like me lost in the dreams, were to be found that day.

Doesn't matter if someone is a believer or atheist, pandit or priest, everyone is a fan of sweets in the name of prasad. In a similar manner, it doesn't matter if anyone had studied or not, attended classes or not, still he or she was fully entitled to celebrate.

As everyone was tortured for at least 15 hours of one's life in the examination hall for 5 question papers.

* * *

There were less than 40 days left for Valentine's Day. She used to call and ask me on regular basis as to when I would come to visit her and I kept telling her that I would come soon, not to let the surprise out.

I had already planned everything regarding this Agra tour during the winter vacations at home. Now, the next step was to set the budget up.

Papa used to give me 2000 Rs as a monthly pocket money which I wouldn't get in January as I was not in the hostel but at my home on the occasion of semester-break.

Now when I was going to a complete stranger city where I didn't have any acquaintances, it was obvious that I would need sufficient money to look after my needs. And going without any gift would surely hamper my impression.

Love bible says, "If you are officially committed and you're planning to meet your soul mate then you must carry a gift for him or her, whether it's small or big, costly or cheap."

So in totality, including travelling, boarding, lodging, food, gift and other expenses, I needed 5000 Rs at least.

Now the question was how to ask for money from parents. What would I say to convince them? I was really perplexed.

'I got to realize that a boy belonging to the middle class family can't even afford to love!'

Anyway, I had already decided to go and it was the time to stay firm on it.

Good thing was that my childhood friends also came home in these post-semester vacations. I was pretty sure if no one else, my school friends will definitely help me out in this situation.

I organized a get together for school friends. We met eternities after passing out of the school. "How is everyone? What are they doing? Who is where?" We discussed these kinds of stuff and shared some laughter. Most of us were pursuing engineering. Many got admissions in farther places like Bangalore and Chennai.

These many people didn't even meet on Diwali holidays. The party was getting over and it was the time for me to get to the point. Everyone started moving after having their dinner.

I stopped Jassi, Nimit, Rehan and Aryan, my besties.

"Bro...Shall we also leave for home? It's already 10 O' clock. We are not in the hostel here, we have to reach home on time. Have you forgotten that?" Aryan said laughingly.

"Yea. I know. Wait, I need to talk about something important." I said.

I told them the whole story and asked them for money.

"Forget about money, you got the girl and you didn't even tell us?" Nimit fired.

"To which place she belongs to?", now Rehan.

"Do you have her picture right now?", Aryan couldn't stop himself.

"Guys,guys, I'll introduce you all to her after sometime, but now I have to meet her and for that I need money.", I said.

"How much do you want?" Everyone asked in unison.

"My budget is 5000 Rs. but you guys give me any amount you can afford. Do one thing, you all give me 500 Rs each."

Nimit: "Here take these 500 Rs of my share."

Rehan: "My share of 500 Rs."

Aryan : "My share of 500 Rs."

Jassi : "Someone give on my behalf, I'll return it tomorrow."

"No worries dude. Give it to me, tomorrow. No one is running anywhere, neither you nor I.", I said.

My voice got little heavy, the emotions were almost there at the brim of my eyes.

"It is unbelievable that once upon a time we used to fight with each other to get 1st position in the class and now after all these years, here we are executing a plan together."

"This creep Jassi , Jassi used to fight." Nimit tried to lighten up the atmosphere.

Jassi : "Ohhh , shut up...! You were the one who used to study all the time. Bookworm!"

Rehan : "Maaro saalo ko. Because of them we also had to study."

(We all chuckled)

Aryan: (Keeping his hand on my shoulder)

"Bro, be careful, you are going to a stranger city alone."

"I'll take care buddy." I said.

Rehan : "So guys, let's go. Will play cricket tomorrow morning."

"Yes guys let's go. Good Night."

Everyone started walking.

"Rahul …." Aryan turned and said.

"Yeah…."

"It may be costly but instead of money, we need Bhabhi's handmade cup of tea."

"Haha..Get lost!"

So, half of the fund was arranged.

Now the next resort was Dad. Yes, I was a little afraid to ask for money from him but everything is fair in love and war. I got the next month's pocket money in advance stating that in February I have a plan to visit Agra with my friends.

Rest of the money could be arranged by asking a loan from hostel mates. This is how I arranged the finance for the trip.

* * *

Finally, winter vacations came to an end and February came knocking at the door. I booked a 13th Feb night's train ticket which would reach Agra on 14th Feb morning. I was not able to wait anymore.

She used to say, "Love doesn't mean giving presents every day, roaming the city on a bike together or dining in big restaurants. But for me love is praying for you, remembering you and being remembered by you. I get to chatter with you for just 10 minutes every day, it's the biggest gift for me."

She said such heart-felt things during the Valentines week.

I considered myself the luckiest person in the world. Such innocent, cute, sweet, lovely girl was the love of my life. If I would have been of age, I would have married her right away.

But marriage is the thing of distant future. This was only the beginning.

You see, the basic necessity "The money" too wasn't easily arranged. The main challenge was still afoot, that was to reach Agra, make good memories and return safely.

Time felt like it was frozen. Days didn't pass and my wait didn't seem to end. Life had come to a standstill and everything that was happening around me felt like distant fading noises.

As painful as it was, waiting was the only option I had. Days were long and restless but nights somehow were pleasant after I used to get her calls in the evenings. This easily could have been the slowest I have seen time traverse and the most impatient I had ever been.

Then there came the day that I had been waiting for. For longer than it actually was. That morning when I woke up, I felt a chill run through my body starting right from my feet up till my head. Even my hair and nails felt the tingle, I could swear.

I just knew that we were a day and one train journey apart. Strangely, that day passed rather quickly than the days before that. I was hyperventilating for the most part. Inexplicable nervousness hit me as the day passed. Finally, the moment had come, the evening of departure.

Before leaving I had explained everything to my roommate Aditya that in case I encounter any problem or if there is any change of plan, he would be the first person

I would contact.

I could say my worries and nervousness could be clearly seen on my face.

"Are you afraid?" I was just lifting up my bag when this question came from Adi.

"Yes! A little bit."

"Don't be afraid my friend. You have come so far. You will get until the end."

"Yeah, well, that's the intention and I will see to it." I replied with firm gumption.

We hugged each other. He wished me luck and I started the journey; Journey of a Love-Story.

* * *

It was 8 O'clock in the evening, slightly chilly and heavy rush at New Delhi Railway station. I was eagerly waiting for my train. Due to heavy fog, many trains were running behind the schedule which was a good thing for me. Arrival time at Agra was scheduled at 3:00 AM. Reaching Agra in such early hours wasn't helping me anyway.

I thought waiting there while I sip the Masala Tea, was more comfortable and safer than waiting at an unknown station at that time of the night which barely deemed safe for girls and boys alike. So anxious wait continued for a few more hours.

The crowd all around was rushing towards their destinations or have just arrived at one, displayed all kinds of faces. Say happy, strange, eager, anxious, lost, and a few indifferent too. I felt as if all these expressions had left a mixed impression on my face too, which clearly had an amalgam of all these expressions by now.

Trains kept coming and going, announcements on the big station speakers filled the air with a sense of certain urgency. Amidst all these noises, I could hear certain stillness, reciting the hymn of our soon to be union.

Little cute kids, unaware of the woes of the world were playing nearby, semmingly celebrating the happiness with me.

On one hand, I held hopes and on the other I had fate. Held prayers on my lips and carried that crazy girl with me in my heart and my soul. It was almost magical; how that one girl touched my life in ways no one had ever touched, how she transformed me from a nobody into everyone I wished to be now.

Three hours after the scheduled time, amidst a cool breeze and fog, tooting train touching a musical chord birthed at platform number 18 in front of me.

I had already been standing there for quite some time as my excitement wasn't letting me sit peacefully. Adrenalin probably dried out of rushing many times over that last couple of hours.

I was standing there numb footed, feeling the vibration of the platform with the advent of train and beating in rhythm with my heart beats. Train windows welcomed me with a round of applause and doors were singing the welcome song.

I boarded the train to embark upon my first eternally memorable journey with hopes of a great tomorrow while holding hands of the memories from the good old days of our meetings.

I penned down every single moment that I spent with her in my diary that night with a hope to make this tale a Love-Epic somewhere someday in future.

* * *

6:00 AM, in a chilled February morning, tearing through the dense fog cloud, the train reached Agra terminal. I was welcomed with a "Kullhar wali chai" and "Garma garam Samose" by the "City of Love".

Oh Yes! Agra, The place which is the greatest quintessence of love. The place where Love's pride Taj-Mahal stands tall, the wonder of the world. The Place where the wind itself was doused with the fragrance of love. Right at 10:00 AM for the first time, I was standing in front of a girls' college.

Jahnavi was still unaware of my Agra plan. After all, it was a surprise. And yes, there were more devotees in front of that college than any temple.

As per my calculation, probably strength of girls in the college must have been less than the boys standing outside. Boys, which I was also a part of now. This gave me a little confidence. At least I wasn't the only one standing there looking like a complete idiot.

Anyway, I called Jahnavi and she hung up.

"Now what is this?"

She didn't receive my calls, 5times over.

"I am in class. I'll call you once I get free." She messaged.

I was told in past by this "scholar woman" that she seldom used to go to college. In Arts, only attendance matters. And guess what; today madam is attending classes diligently.

Suddenly she called.

"Hi, how are you?" she asked.

"I am good. Happy Valentine's day!" I just wished.

"Umm, same to you. You believe in it?"

"Till when are you going be in the college today ?" I avoided time consuming discussion.

"I had to attend only one lecture. Now leaving for home."

A crowd came out of the college. I thought some class got over and she might be among the crowd. So immediately I hid behind a tree and kept looking at the college gate.

"How did you call me today in the morning, missing me haan?"

"No..no, nothing like that. All of my friends have gone to celebrate with their madams and there is a mass bunk in college. So thought of calling you."

And Yes, There she was. In a cream colour suit which might be the college uniform. The epitome of beauty was coming out with her friend carrying a book in one hand and the phone in the other.

I was able to manage everything i.e. talking on the phone and checking her entry from college to my world of dreams. I placed myself behind in the crowd and started walking with the dabbed foot.

"Oh, so the entire college has gone. You should have also taken someone with you. You're smart, handsome, funny and Moradabad's Tom Cruise after all."

I tapped her shoulder from behind and..,

"Main zaroorat ke hisab se bhagwan nahin badalta ! Happy Valentine's Day sweetheart."

As if the flowing time had frozen right around us at that moment. I could feel as if everything and everyone around us became silent.

In that very moment, I felt no one existed other than the two of us and the feeling I had just by looking at her couldn't be explained in any form of communication. Just like in the 70's movies, everything around us went in a slow motion. One moment or should I say she took few nano seconds to recognize me and to believe that Yes that was me! Rahul, her Rahul.

She had no word. She was dumbstruck.

She smiled and laughed in awe.

"Rahul, you're here!"

She just jumped in excitement and before I could think of anything or had said anything,

I was in her embrace. She had hugged me in the middle of the entire crowd without having a care for the world around us. I couldn't have felt more proud of anything. I hugged her back. Tighter than she did.

It was in that moment I felt I had everything. My whole world in my embrace. I couldn't have had asked for more. I was happier than I have ever been in my life. I could feel our hearts beating in unison.

It is one such moment when you wouldn't think of anything in the world. Just an utter calm and divine happiness is what you feel.

"I knew you would come. Such a pleasant surprise, I Love You."

"I Love You too Jahan. Are we going to stand here like this all day or shall we get something to eat? I am surviving on tea since morning and trust me, now tea must be flowing through my blood veins."

"Hehehe, Okay okay Tum nahi sudhroge nalayak !"

She said punching me in my stomach. and I acted as if it had hurt. Love makes you stupid, doesn't it!

We 3 went to a nearby restaurant, me, Jahnavi and her friend whose name was still unknown to me.

While going to the restaurant from college, her friend remained in utter shock staring at the two of us, mouth agape.

As soon as I noticed that, I immediately said,

"Jahnavi madam, make her believe that we will tell her everything in a few moments. Otherwise, her stomach would be filled with questions and she wouldn't eat anything."

"Hey Kajal, he is Rahul. I had told you everything about him naa." With utter confidence, She said.

"You didn't tell me that he could do such surprising things."

"Haha! I too didn't know that he is capable of doing such things."

After hearing this sentence, all my efforts felt successful.

I had to tell her everything from planning to execution except one thing i.e. "loan from friends". She was really really happy.

"Now that we are sitting here like this, Would 'What if someone sees us?' be an Issue for you?", I asked cautiously.

"Yes, a little bit I guess. But since you have come this far for me, I wouldn't mind a little thrill of being here with you." she said playfully.

"Think about it! I would hate for us to be in any trouble in pursuit of such thrill." I tried to be funny.

It paid off, and we all broke into laughter.

"We will see whatever happens." she said confidently.

I smiled a little and said to myself, "I have fallen in love with you for the umpteenth time after hearing this line."

"Hello,Mr Cruise, where you lost?" she snapped.

I came out of my dreamy world. Kajal was ready to leave. Jahnavi whispered something to her and dropped her till exit.

"What's the plan now?" she rolled the ball in my court.

"You say, it's your city madam." I bounced back.

"I mean you have come here with so much planning so you must have planned something about Agra excursion too!"

There was a moment of silence now. With a pause...... holding her hand in my hand, looking deep into her hazel brown eyes,

I whispered, "No"

She smiled, nodded her head and said, "Let's go to Taj Mahal."

"I can see a rickshaw there." I had lifted my bag by that moment.

While catching the rickshaw I could notice a sincere happiness on her face.

Out of curiosity, I asked her, "Are you scared?"

"Scared? Of what?" She asked surprisingly.

"I mean there are a lot of rules, regulations and restrictions at your home. You seldom go out with friends. It almost feels like you are caged in your own home. What if someone sees you here with me?" I said.

"For the first time in my life, I am doing something daring, something different. Let's cross that bridge when we get to it. And from today onwards, everything is going to be daring.

It's going to be naa Rahul?" She said with love.

I wrapped my hands around her shoulder, pulling her towards me I said, "Everything will happen smoothly. You'll see."

"Yeah," with a smile she blinked her eyes.

Don't know how many people had come to see the reflection of their love in Taj Mahal and have taken pride in themselves. People were busy in taking pictures all around, trying to capture the timeless serene beauty of Taj.

And I was standing there in the middle of the crowd, watching Taj and Jahnavi, wondering who's more beautiful. Strangely, standing before the most beautiful monument in the world, I still couldn't take my eyes off of her. It's almost like my heart has already decided who was more beautiful.

The atmosphere there was majestic. There was something in that air around that place that would make the most phlegmatic person fall in love. Such was the aura and ambience of the place.

Ergo, instead of wasting the time in capturing those moments in a camera, we invested our time in relishing them.

We had less conversation, just held each other's hand, looked ahead at Taj and then looked at each other with nothing but just love.

This was how our Taj-darshan was going on. Then I thought to myself, "What am I doing? Have I really come here to see Taj Mahal? Half the day has already gone and I only had this day with her. After this, I do not know when and how would I be able to meet her again like this. I cannot let this day pass like the way it is going. This day has turned out to be very expensive; it took a lot of wait, small struggle, friends' help and blessing, a big hope and a beginning to have happened."

I almost rushed into saying this to her,

"Jahnavi, do you see that tree? Let's sit underneath it."

It was necessary now.

"Yeah, that place is good.", Like she was also not much interested in Taj.

We sat down on the grass lying back on the tree. That place was quiet away from the sea of the crowd around the Taj. We could still see the Taj from there and we were still holding hands. We sat there bashing under the warm beams of sunlight slipping through the leaves of the Tree.

I made a gesture from my eyebrows towards her. She blinked her eyes and smiled.

"Jahnavi, we are not sitting in our park at Moradabad. There is no need of conversing in sign language here."

"Hehe, definitely. By the way, when are you leaving?"

"Tomorrow early morning at four."

"So what are you doing tonight?"

"What do you have in mind?", I said winking at her.

"Oho, where are you staying tonight? Prick!" (Hitting me)

"At your home of course."

"HaHa. Very funny! Tell no."

"I have come to meet you, so will stay at your home. This should be counted in your hospitality."

Her eyes got filled with tears.

"Rahul, few things are out of my control."

"Hey Jahnavi, Relax! I have come to see you happy. I was just kidding. I have already booked a room in hotel. Come here."

I pulled her closer towards me and wrapped my arms around her. She rested her head on my chest. After a little hesitation, I planted a kiss on her forehead and we lay there in that posture for a few minutes. She seemed comfortable in my arms and I felt complete.

It was around 4 o' clock in the evening.

"Jahnavi, since morning you are out of the home. Don't you think your parents would be worried?"

"I have told Kajal to tell them that I have viva in the evening so I would be late."

"Shall we go now?" She said looking at me with her eyes shouting out unwillingness.

"I don't feel like going but what can we do? Let's go. But now what and where? And till when are you going to stay with me?"

"Forever" She turned and said.

"Arey amma, I am talking about this evening?"

We both laughed.

"Let's get you jaunting."

Meanwhile, she made me eat 2 Kgs of Petha (a sweet dish made from condensed milk). There was some gleamy 'Sadar Bazaar' and just as I thought, in that market, she took me to some "Maheshwari Chaat`s stall to eat "Gol gappe."

"I frequently come here bunking food at home to eat golgappe. I always wanted our park's gang to come here and enjoy this delicacy."

Listening to her felt so good that I wished her voice to continue spinning magic on me for the rest of my life. She finally received a call from home while enjoying the chaat and she said that she had just finished the class and would go to Kajal's house before returning home.

"So generally you stay out for so long?" I asked.

"Not generally, but sometimes it's okay."

"Are you sure? If you want, you can go home right away. I will manage."

"What manage yaar? You just follow me."

"Are you sure?"

She grabbed my hand and took me to the rickshaw, told some strange address to the puller and I was again riding the rickshaw for the 4th time in last 10 hours.

"It's 7:30 PM now Jahnavi. It's already dark."

"*Picture abhi baaki hai mere dost!* Don't be afraid."

"I am unable to understand am I the boy or you are? You certainly are more of a swashbuckler than I am right now. What's going on?", now I was scared.

The place where we reached was a 3 tier building and the balconies of all 3 floors were packed with girls.

Truly. When God gives, he bestows upon us unexpectedly large fortunes.

Now I was really scared. I was truly in trouble.

"Where have you brought me?" I asked.

"Arey Kajal stays here, you come." She replied.

"How is this Kajal everywhere? She definitely isn't smudge-free." I thought.

Two arm chairs were kept on the terrace. There was attractive decoration all around. The whole environment was different. But amidst those many girls, I was feeling a bit uncomfortable.

"Anyway, how did you manage to do all this?" I asked her, infused with surprise and happiness.

"Little bit I told Kajal when she was coming back from the restaurant and half of the work through messages."

"You are one sly little creature."

"Thank you, thank you."

We sat in the arm chairs. We were too tired with all day long strolls and over exhaustion of all the hormones that triggers excitement, happiness and Love. I didn't even sleep last night out of happiness.

But only a few moments were left. I was with Jahnavi and I was trying my level best to give my 100% and why shouldn't have I? She was my love. She was also trying hard since morning to give her 100%.

"Are you feeling tired?" I asked as I held her hand in mine, tightly.

Now everything was quiet. There was no movement or sound on the terrace. Beneath the vast dark sky, there were just I and her. And gazing at us were the millions of twinkling stars.

As I laid back on the chair and looked at the sky, I could have sworn that I had never seen such beautiful sky in my entire lifetime. Watching the crescent moon hiding behind the clouds and coming smiling back at us again.

A few nights away from becoming a perfect, beautiful full Moon. Just like our love, almost perfect, almost beautiful but not there just yet. I knew that we had miles to go and we had just begun our journey. Our love was just like the crescent moon.

Although it was cold there in the open and yet the atmosphere had become warm as our remaining time together was burning out faster than usual.

"Yeah, a little bit." She moaned.

"Do you know when I saw you for the first time I thought you are Luv's distant cousin who must be studying in 4th or 5th std." I recalled the days.

"And that time I appeared for the 10th boards and you were about to take 9th's final exams."

"Haha... Yes! Time flies. We will enter into the 4th year of knowing each other this May."

"Yeah, truly said. And was it on Diwali or Luv's birthday? Right!! Luv's birthday, when you picked up the phone. That was the first time we talked."

"Yeah, how can I forget that call? That was a moment of a lifetime."

"I thought who is this nonsense using didi's home phone."

"Hahahaha, really?"

"Yes! But trust me Jyoti di considers you a nice lad and always advises Luv and Kush to become like you."

"That's the problem."

"Hmm! Our greatest quality itself becomes our weakness."

"Not weakness Jahnavi. Who knows they might even approve of our marriage one day."

"Marriage? You have thought about us till there?" She stood up suddenly.

"Yes, why not?"

"Will you be able to stand by it?"

"I don't build castle in the air. I know just one thing that I love you and I love you very much. As this is the age of making a career, I have this much confidence in me that the day I shall pass out from college, I'll be able to paddle my own canoe and will be worthy for you. I shall definitely be able to keep myself as well as you happy."

"Rahul…. I Love you!"

She just hugged me tightly and this was how I wanted to spend the whole night; in her arms.

"This is for you Jahan, take this as your Valentine's gift or something else. This is just for you." I slipped a gift in her hands.

"Aww, you are so sweet Rahul. I love you so much!"

"I love you too sweetheart, my love, my Jahan."

When she was opening the gift, I wanted to box and take away those tears from her eyes, the quiver of her lips and happiness on her face as a return gift for me.

I wanted to shout and tell the world that look I have earned this!

But this moment had to meet an end. It was getting very dark.

"Jahnavi, shall we go? It's 9:30 PM already."

"Yeah, we must leave now. I'll never forget this day."

"I'll live in the memories of today, every day."

We both smiled and left that place.

I found all the girls on the stairs. Perhaps they were listening to our conversation. They greeted me with all respect, and Kajal who was bringing water, tea, coffee and snacks for us on the terrace in between, was a little emotional with my farewell.

And from there itself she proceeded to her home and I went to my hotel. This was the day when my childhood love, took a moment's shelter in the inn of my life.

We sat in different rickshaws going in different directions, hoping to meet again someday.

A memorable journey of a lifetime.

Yes! Indeed it was. I recorded its soul in my diary, the stories, and the moments.

Tomorrow, when I will gather the pieces of this journey and narrate it to Jahnavi or my friends or myself, the aroma of this memory will definitely touch the strings of old childhood memories and make the coming days more beautiful.

Like this, many unsaid and unheard stories were forever treasured in my heart.

On this very note, I started my journey from Agra to Delhi.

During Taj Darshan, when Jahnavi and I were sitting under the tree, I got a message from Adi that I have topped in 1st-semester exams.

I was not a bit excited about the news. Who would be when your whole life is with you? Trivial things like these wouldn't matter.

I didn't feel like discussing this amongst us. This was nothing for me but just a mere formality.

THE CAREER

When the high tides of poverty are at their peak, it usually rip apart the weak homes of love at the shore of life.

I was aware of this fact but wasn't really worried. I was rather very inspired by this law of nature.

Just like a common desi boy, I too had a dream of becoming a cricketer, which ultimately blew off with the gust of engineering. I invested all my energy in becoming an engineer which I had stored otherwise for becoming a cricketer. I was working very hard. I am not boasting but I had seen a dream, a dream of a future for the two of us, Jahnavi and me.

Looking at the situation, I could reckon that I was left with a very little amount of time. I constantly had this strange fear. It was as if I had the capability of booking and travelling on a flight but I wouldn't be able to reach on time and would miss it.

She was two years elder to me. I was of 19 and she was 21 yrs old.

I had taken admission in engineering graduation school and she was about to pass out the benchmark in coming July. In the next 2 years after completing her post-graduation, she would be 23 and would be ready for marriage. A system designed by typical Indian traditions which states that a girl should get married by 23 or immediately after her education is over. And education means maximum post graduation.

At such an age when a girl should have the freedom to decide if she wants to continue further studies or decide her career, when she should have been given ample time to make a life for herself, she is forced to be tethered to the unending responsibilities of marrying and making a family of her own.

At an age when she is still young to explore the world, live her life freely, enjoy the life and what not, she is expected to have babies and take care of them. Such is our dogmatic tradition and such are its preposterous notions.

Even after 2 years, I would still be pursuing my graduation. I would be admitted to the final years and that too if I had cleared all the semesters without fail. These were very critical things which I was liable to think about.

I was ready to fight for things which were in my hands and for the things which were out of my control, I could only pray.

This was the summary of my story till now.

In the market of employment, software jobs were on the rise. And I was searching for my future in slow-paced Mechanical engineering. It was not like there was a scarcity of jobs in this branch or I had any doubt in my capabilities but it was just that I didn't want to take any risk in this matter.

So I decided to change my branch.

To switch the branch from Mechanical to Computer science or Information Technology, a merit list used to get prepared on the basis of scores of both the semesters in 1st year. It was dependent on the availability of seats.

Anyway, I had completed my work in 1ˢᵗ semester. The 2ⁿᵈ semester was yet to go.

Although I had 1st rank in my own branch but the aggregate percentage was just 77%, which was less than what actually needed. So it was imperative that I work harder for 2ⁿᵈ semester and secure better percentage.

I started the work with a whole lot of self-confidence. Everything was going with the flow. There was no problem as of then. Jahnavi and I had a regular pattern of late night calls. She would emphasize more on family and less on college in her topics on call and I was like exact opposite, more college and less family.

Many times I invited her to Delhi despite knowing the fact that this was not possible on her part. Not because she was not capable of doing something like that but because society's doctrinaire would not allow her to do so.

The way she grew up in an orthodox family and the surroundings were the reasons why she was incapable of doing much. That's why every night after talking to her; I fell deeper in love with her. Everything was going fine overall and time was running like a speedy current. 2ⁿᵈ semester's exams were nearing.

* * *

Exams were not a big deal, we had issues with the environment during the exams. University examinations were scheduled at such times of the year when the weather was at its extremes.

Odd semesters would be held in the peak winter mornings, from mid December to January beginning period, and even semesters would be held in the scorching heat of May afternoons.

Should students write an exam or should they prove that they can sit for those three weary hours in the scorching heat or chilling cold? Leave alone the despair of preparing for the exams during those peak seasons.

The writing was a problem due to numbness of hands in winters and sweating of hands in summers because in summers instead of air, the fan would generate steam. The moment students somehow adjust to the atmosphere of examination hall and start writing, teachers would get served with garam-garam Samose.

At that moment thirsty eyes of the students and lust of teachers for free snacks used to have silent conversations.

Poor students, at least for a moment, used to consider teachers as Gods in a hope that teachers would offer them Samosa.

Then seeing the questing paper and judging their own status, they would start filling sheets half-heartedly. There is a difference between filling sheets and writing answers, this fact was definitely not known to the first year students.

So, once again exam mode was ON. To step out in the scathing heat at 1 O`clock to appear in the exams and to write exams in exam hall after encountering sun strokes was an adventure of its own kind. Exams went on.

Days passed.

The wait was finally getting over.

The season of love was around the corner with last paper simply being a formality.

I had my last paper on 19th of May and Jahnavi told me that she would reach Moradabad on 25th May. I felt like leaving on the 19th night itself but the 6 days wait would have been too much to bear. But my gut was telling that I should only leave after completing my practical exams scheduled from 27th May to 30th May but I was paying no heed to my brain.

I told Jahnavi that I would reach on 20th morning.

"My train will reach on 25th night, so we will meet on

26th morning." She stated.

Meeting her in her town was one thing. But meeting her at my place, my home after one year was altogether a different thing.

After finishing my last paper, I packed my bags and left for my hometown. This time she was coming to Moradabad for the 3rd time.

Till now we used to meet like strangers or we had a peculiar shyness between us. But this time things would have been totally different and new.

The curtain of shyness had moved aside with the wind of love but things wouldn't still be as is love perceived in bigger cities. And I was glad that ours was one such tale that wasn't diluted as the modern-day love stories of the big cities. Such a relationship where there was true love and no-show off of teenage infatuation, where childhood was connected, and which grew up with many sour and sweet memories made with many cute kids. Very different from today's relationship, where physical proximity is the measure of false love.

It was not that we too could not start doing it, but respecting one's own love, respecting the lover and moreover respecting the childhood made the difference.

If you love someone truly, you would never have these kinds of thought in your mind.

Where there is respect, there is love and where there is love, there is respect and where these both exist, there is no place for dirt like this.

A good night's sleep was necessary after reaching home late at night. I woke up the next afternoon. Just like olden days, to brush I stood facing Jahnavi's home imagining about her, about yesteryear's and days to come.

Such a deep bond with that window.

Just beyond that window, there lived a comfort, by

seeing her my days would get started, who used to come over to balcony sometimes to dry her hair and sometimes to dry clothes, sometimes playing with children, glowing, blooming, blossoming, laughing, my lovely innocent Jahnavi.

"Jahnavi????" (Rubbing my eyes.)

"Have I gone into deep imagination? I was happy too. She was about to come on 25th.Is she Jahnavi?" I asked myself as I spotted her looking at me through her balcony.

She was waiving hand from there. My tooth brush got stuck in my throat out of happiness and surprise. I immediately called her but her phone was off.

Wasn't she supposed to come on 25th? But I didn't care about that anymore. I was too happy to see her.

I asked my Mom, "Maa, is Jahnavi here?"

"Yes, she came last night. She even came to our house, cooked dinner and ate with us." Mom replied.

For a mechanical engineering guy like me, who doesn't get to see a woman for months in his life, the sight of a beautiful lass who he loves at the very first sight of the morning was enough to kill him out of happiness.

My happiness was boundless. It was like I cleared the basic exams of loveship and now it was the time for the vacation of Loveology.

And finally, I received her message, "See you at park, 7:00 PM."

It was very good to visit Agra and meet her but it was more amazing to open the book of our childhood days and turn back the pages of memories at the place where it all began, at home sweet home.

It was 6:30 in the evening and kids were playing in the park. I, I was waiting for her, laying down my eyes in anticipation from the terrace to the street, where she usually used to come from.

6:45, 7:00, 7:15, the time was running and I was getting restless. We were about to meet after one year in Moradabad and after three months from February.

Dusk was gradually advancing into a dark night. Everyone was waiting. From "everyone", I mean, things which cannot speak, and things which cannot understand but the things which knew that a relationship was in making.

7:20, and then there she was. In a light yellowish suit, radiant like a lightning just struck out of dark clouds, with an innocent childish smile on her face, bringing with her the unspoken happiness, she was stepping towards me.

I didn't have any idea what was going around me. Or I can say that I didn't even care about it. Now the whole universe was divided into two, her and the rest.

"Hello, Ji."

With a big smile on her face, she shook hands and stood beside me.

"Hi Ji, so you have come. Such a big surprise."

"Do only you have the copyright of surprises? And you know what, I will try to do a little more than what I actually can do."

I was quietly standing and listening to her, fathoming what she said. Eyes were somewhat wet but everything was under control. I was trying to understand her by nodding and smiling a little bit. I was proud of my fate that day but still had an eerie feeling that something might go wrong.

Then everything around us except the Time which I wished to, stopped.

This was the time for celebration, very valuable indeed. Therefore, I chose not to get serious.

"So, let's play all the old games again with these kids."

"Rahul bhaiya on my side", "Jahnavi di on my side",

"Same teams like the old times."

"No, no, teams will be changed this time", "You'll lose again", "I am elder now", "I'll also play bhaiya", these voices were resonating in the compound of 'Decent residency's' ravishing park.

* * *

Kids kept on playing and we, I and Jahnavi were lost in a different world. Love was deepening and relationship was expanding. There was nothing but unabridged love in and things started to roll again from a new angle. The phone was only used for beckoning. Like "Today I am going shopping with di so meet me near the golgappa shop". I used to enjoy this *Chori chori chupke chupke wala* stuff.

The real fun was 10, 12 kids and us, all swarming over to the movies.

"A walk to remember", was the very first movie which Jahnavi and I watched together in a multiplex. In addition, 12 more kids with us. And in the climax, these kids were taking care of this kid named Jahnavi. She was crying terribly.

Kids - "Didi please stop crying, it's just a movie."

Like these kiddies were more matured than her and I was like, "Guys, let me also say something, *wo meri bhi kuchh lagti hai.*"

Haha, such moments they were!

We had our childhood full of experience of managing kids.

In this festivity and jubilation, May waived bye to us. It was June now, a historic and memorable time was about to end. I noted each moment, every day of such bliss in my diary which will hopefully delight me in future and touch the chords of emotion. Maybe it would make the eyes moist, an emotion which I had come to fall in love with by then.

Jahnavi used to come to my home regularly. She easily gelled up with my Mom. She really had done her homework. As if my Mom had also finalized a bride for me. Dad understood it a bit, but he was chill. There was no problem with my family at all. Nevertheless, if I talk from Jahnavi's perspective, I had doubts about her typical orthodox family. But anyway, "Will see, whatever happens," notion always helped me in this aspect.

Time was flying rapidly, so much that it felt that something was going to end. It was about 13- 14 June when I started to feel that the end is nearing, a fear of losing all of this. I knew that in a few days, she will leave which was also a bitter truth but I was not much worried about it.

I had this bizarre feeling of something ominous was about to happen. Whenever I had a chat with her I always felt as if I was going to lose her. I had been having this premonition for some time now.

A very peculiar, strange, odd kind of fear or madness troubled me every time.

Amidst of all this, the night finally came after which she would leave. We sat together to talk that night. I organized a party on terrace only for kids with the theme as singing and dancing. Rules were simple - Everyone will judge each other and award marks on the basis of which the last 2 standing will win and earn the rewards. I made this plan so that I can sit with her and talk to her comfortably for half an hour or so. Kids would be involved in their game and I would be involved in mine.

Exactly at 8:00 PM, all 12 little kids of the colony including two elder kids (us) assembled on the terrace. Since morning, Jahnavi had teary eyes. Kids started the game and we sat in a corner of the terrace.

"So leaving tomorrow?" I started the last

conversation of the season.

"Hmmm" (In subdued tone)

"Okay, we will meet soon. Now go cheerfully. You have enjoyed each and every moment till now. Don't be sad while going back. You have been crying since morning."

"It's not that thing Rahul." She was very serious.

"Then what is it?" The hallucinatory thought starts to pop up.

"This year, not even this year but next month I'll be a graduate. In next two years, I will be a postgraduate. My family will start searching for a groom for me. And I don't know if I can or even should hold them off. Mom & Dad are old now. I don't know if I am fortunate or unfortunate but because I am the youngest one at home and being a girl, nothing can be said; Groom searched in January, a groom chosen in February and marriage in March, things can happen so fast."

"So..? What is the issue then? You just tell them about me, when they start searching a boy for you."

"What will I say? That the boy is studying in 2nd year. He will be a graduate in 2 years and then he will get a job and when he will be capable enough, he will ask my hand for marriage."

"Yes. Of course?" (It seemed pretty normal to me.)

"Ohh.. No, no, you are not trying to understand what it means by being an unmarried youngest girl in the family. It's like ready to serve.

It's very tough to elucidate the family when everyone including society is hell-bent on getting you married. Yes, we do not care what society says or do but that is not how our families look at things. Even we breathe according to the rules and regulations made by this bigoted society. I am not saying that I cannot fight or I am weak to do it but what if things don't turn out to be well?"

I was dumbstruck. I did not know what to say and what not to say. I was not even in any situation to speak. My lips were quivering; I never thought about this. She had raised a bunch of unfathomable yet valid dilemmas. I was not even sure which ones to ignore and which ones to address. Should I focus on society or Jahnavi or her family or myself?

Then I clarified, "It's better to go with the flow. Time is the biggest healer. You just give me 3 years and then see what I cannot do."

She smiled "Yeah, alright let's do it, let's do it together."

"Yeah" I said, "See kids are looking at us periodically."

She laughed and said, "They all know about us."

"Haha, rightly said. That's why they are giving us this privacy, very smart."

"So when are you coming again?", I asked.

"Now you have to come."

"To meet Kajal?"

"Haha, as you wish!"

"Thank you for coming here." I said lovingly.

She tapped me on my shoulder and hugged me. Our eyes were teary and we had smiles on faces.

"Jahnavi, let's go. You are forgetting that we have phones now to talk to each other. We are moving forward."

"Yeah! Let's go."

"So kids who won?" I acted.

"Bhaiya, Luv bhaiya has cheated.", "No No bhaiya Kittu did it.", "Kush didn't give marks.", "How can this be a zero."

All the kids were making quite a show.

"I had the entire clue that their party would be an absolute waste."

"Shut up you selfish boy!" she said pinching me.

"So gang, Jahnavi is leaving tomorrow. We will sing a song for her."

"Yeee.. Pretty woman.." "No no, Ladki kyu na jane kyu." "Are didi's favourite Kabhi aar kabhi paar…" "Are english wala, smack that.." "chheee, no.., check on it by Beyonce"

Kids will always be legends. They started again.

"Lag jaa gale, ke phir ye hasin raat ho na ho, shayad phir iss janam me mulaqaat ho na ho…"

She started singing the most romantic song by Lata ji.

Under the open sky, in the bright moonlight, in the presence of million stars, amongst the lovely kids, in the silent night, in the voice of a nightingale, she sang the song. What to say, the moment was different from all the feelings of the world.

I wish the time had stopped therein, entire existence stopped existing. She was singing, crying, smiling, even the kids who had never heard this song before, started crying. She continued to sing, crying and then smiling without any pause.

'About me?' Haha, leave it…Some other day.

She was rewarded with the claps. She hugged everyone one by one. Making a promise of meeting next year at the same place.

She wished Alvida!

I didn't say any word to her after the song that night because I was not able to.

So this was the last night of that mesmerizing *"summer vacation of 2007"*.

* * *

And after that holiday, on the Lord's computer, our names got registered in the "Soul mates'." folder.

We used to talk regularly on phones. In between, I used to visit Agra to meet her. This had become a yearly affair. The arrangement of money had always been a matter of thinking and analysis but due to fewer and no useless expenditure, I used to manage and save the sufficient amount by every odd semester's end.

In summer vacations, she used to visit Moradabad for straight 2 months. We had a team; I, Jahnavi, Luv, Kush, Kittu, Bittu, Jango, Jaya amma and many other kids.

Each day of those vacations was like a lifetime. We used to play daily, went movies every Friday, went on an excursion to nearby places like Rishikesh, RamNagar, Nainital etc. We all used to enjoy a lot. No one ever stopped or questioned us. And we all were the happiest kids on the planet, especially the grownups, she and I.

We also knew that with freedom comes responsibility and discipline. That is why all of us knew our limits especially Jahnavi and I. I was slowly advancing with my Mechanical Engineering studies. I couldn't switch my branch due to unrevealed managerial reasons. She was rapidly progressing in her graduation and post graduation. She couldn't get approval for C.A.T. coaching from her family so she had to leave the idea of M.B.A.

We all were growing up. Time was changing and everything was going smoothly.

3 Years Later

THE STRUGGLE

The night just after Diwali holidays of engineering final year was unsettling.

On the fine evening of 10th December 2010, we 7-8 friends took out some time from studies and went on to have some tea and snacks just to relieve some pressure. A mug full of tea in every hand and a plate of savoury snacks in the other. Tea was the ultimate saviour from stress.

The stress of placements as well as the final semester. The discussion was ON about the companies visiting, packages being offered, contract bonds and related stuff. Suddenly I received a call, it was Jahnavi's. Saying hello, I went a little far from the group.

"Hello Rahul, where are you? Please save me from all this, I cannot tolerate this anymore."

Her voice was subdued under the sound of her crying. She seemed dejected and in pain. My heart sunk.

Worryingly, I asked, "What happened Jahan? Take a deep breath and tell me. Nothing good is gonna happen if you keep crying like this. Tell me everything properly."

In past 6 years, I had never seen her crying like that, and this terrified me to the bones with an intuition of something wrong.

She replied, "Tomorrow a family is coming to see me for their son. Mom, Dad have already seen the boy and they have informed me of everything just an hour back. Rahul, please come here. I don't even want to see his face."

Each word expelled from her mouth and the honking of passing vehicles felt like a slap on my situation and stature.

I could feel the earth under my feet slipped away and I had sunk right in where I stood. All my emotions were imploding inside me, all at once. I was unable to understand as in what to say to her and how to react.

Even though I knew this day was imminent and someday or the other this situation would come, yet I could never prepare myself to face this. And I never knew what to tell her off if anything like this happens.

Therefore, I explained her about it and told her to play along and meet the guests and added, "When your Mom, dad ask you about your decision, you tell them about me straightforward."

After a lot of pacification for about half an hour, she was finally appeased. She also understood that now she had to act wisely and take care of things very carefully. Before hanging up the phone she said,

"Listen, there is one problem!"

"What now?'

"What if the boy turns out to be smart and handsome?"

(Even in this deadly situation, she felt like mocking.)

"Don't worry! If that's the case, the boy will instantly reject you."

We both laughed. Hush! Happy ending… of a scary call.

Anyway, the matter was not so profound that couldn't

have been handled but also was not something to be ignored.

The speculum of the truth was clamouring that it will take six more months to finish the college and I didn't have any job yet. The game was ON and here I was, not having much power in my arsenal.

"No worries, I will give more than the best I ever gave." I pondered with an enlightened mind that moving forward, tugging along hope and hard work was the only way out.

* * *

Next day in the hostel, my attention was diverted to the arrange marriage drama that was about to happen in Agra. With books in front and mobile like an idol in the temple, whole day, I kept sitting on my bed. I was praying and studying simultaneously. The tension was rising with time, it turned out to be a dreadful day for me. My eyes were fixated on the phone. I was waiting for her call desperately. I was even taking the phone to the bathroom while I took the leaks.

"What's happening over there? The bottom line is, any Indian guy cannot say NO to Jahnavi. In front of her innocent face, even film stars' prominence would fade away."

These kinds of thoughts kept me on my toes.

I decided to call or message her to know the situation over there but then I stopped myself, thinking that my act could hinder her action plan.

It was 11 O'clock in the night when mustering up my courage, I dialled her number but sadly it was switched off.

I got terrified. The condition was getting worse. I didn't know anything. I was unable to presume anything. If the person knows a bit about the situation, he can reason himself by giving at least false explanations, consolations and excuses. But if things are not apparent, it becomes hard to perceive anything. All the insight is useless.

In this stressful situation, there was no news from Jahnavi. I knew nothing of anything that might have happened that night. I was going insane. "Where should I go? What should I do? Should I rush to Agra?", I was unable to find any solutions. "But solutions of what? First, I should know the problem." That night praying with pure intent, I somehow managed to sleep after hours of unrest.

I woke up in the morning and plunged towards my phone. There was a message.

"Good morning, everything is fine. I'll call you in a while."

I took a sigh of relief.

I laughed and prayed to the lord, "Keep saving me like this."

When I looked carefully towards Lord Krishna's idol, it felt like he smiled and said, "Dude! I had the same story."

Now, her call was awaited.

Approx at 11:30 AM,

"Yes, ma'am."

"How are you?"

"Forget the pleasantries and tell me everything from the beginning."

"So now listen from the very beginning."

"I'm all ears, shoot now."

"They came early in the morning, I guess at 10. All dressed up like they have already made up their mind. Mom had already filled my ears with the do's and don'ts like 100 times from the time I woke up. But I had already told Mom that it won't last even for an hour and they are going to go back.

The typical family with typical melodrama statements; "Somebody very dear to your Dad has asked these people to visit us and your Dad will feel hurt if you don't treat them well. At least for your Dad, entertain them like other guests and do not cut a sorry figure for us."

I said, 'Okay Mom...'

So, the boy and his parents sat in the dining room and the entire table was decorated with all possible sweets, snacks, and tea.

And the living room had new curtains, cushions, and flower vases, and not to forget about the room fresheners that reeked of my relentless unwillingness. Some of these decorations were even new to me when I have been living there since my childhood.

Can you imagine the level of hospitality those scumbags were getting?

And my sweet dear Mom had so much faith in my cooking skills that I was instructed NOT to even step into the kitchen or its vicinity.

Had I at least prepared the tea myself, the boy would have rejected me on the first sip (She chuckled). But no, I was only expected to dress up well and carry the tea tray or something to serve. All modern you know, we are cool people.

I was nervous but it was fun.

Dad called me out in a caring voice which I don't remember when I heard last time."

"You were wearing a suit?", Interrupting that avid narrator, I asked.

"Yes! But, how do you know?"

"Never mind, you keep going."

(You won't understand.)

"Ahh, okay, so I entered and greeted everyone. 'Hey, Guys, What's up…!' In a very casual tone, no old-style 'Namastey' and all. Before they could say anything, I offered them to eat. Just to make their mouth shut all the time, I kept offering. So much formality, (In grumping tone).

As usual, everyone started the same old routine conversation, your likes, dislikes, your hobbies, your aspirations, your preferences after marriage and all that crap. This lasted for nearly an hour. Then, it's the time for climax just like they show in Bollywood movies.

I didn't know which movie Dad got inspired from?

"Jahnavi, why don't you show your room to Vipul.", Dad said.

In my mind, I was thinking that atleast he is sitting calm over here. If he sees my room then he would immediately run away. (She chuckled for the second time)"

"Then?" I asked.

I was getting very impatient to hear the end of it and honestly, she was dragging it. Usually, I love to hear her but for some reasons hearing about her marriage proposals was unsettling.

"Vipul and I, we went in my room. He was getting nervous and I was in the mood to mischief. Relax…! Vipul. Take a chill pill, I said to him. Then his two questions and my answers to them ended everything."

"What were his questions and your answers to them?" (I was highly inquisitive).

"He asked, 'Do you smoke?', I said "I have a Marlboro for now. If you want some other brand then I can ask Kajal to bring it. Wanna take a puff? It's been a while since I too have had one." "No, no, I didn't mean that. I was just asking in general to know your choices." said Vipul with a shocked expression.

"Hahahaha. And what was his second question?" with more curiosity, I asked.

"Do you drink?"

"And what did you answer to that?"

" 'Scotch or Rum? How about a shot? Yes, I think, a shot would be perfect for the moment, will help you with the nervousness and gets you talking. Kajal….Kajal', I started calling and he interrupted.

Then he went on to his office gossips, showed me his social networking pictures and all that. I showed the least interest and he was wise enough to flip out and asked for going back to the living room.

He ran and sat between his parents and whispered some confidential shit into their ears. Then they greeted and took our leave. That's all for yesterday."

"Did it end there?" I asked in a very anxious tone.

"Ummm... Can't say, until they official communicate 'NO' to Dad."

"I rest my case." I said in a very low tone.

I think my low voice had articulated the pandemonium inside me very well to her.

"I will talk to Mom. Don't burden yourself with my worries. Now, I have understood very well by the act I did in the morning that few things can't wait. I need to take charge of them at the earliest and get them done. You please don't worry so much and take good care of yourself.", she added.

"Yeah. Let me know as soon as you hear from Vipul's parents and I will take care of the rest. You too take good care of yourself, my Jahan."

"Yeah for sure. Bye"

"Bbye.."

* * *

In totality, the final chapter of this love story had begun. She was in her final year of post-graduation and that was the right age for her to get married as per the unwritten dogma of this patriarchal society.

Here, I was working hard day and night to end up being eligible for her so that she could put a strong case before her parents. She never showed me that side of the mirror that reflected my inefficiency in being a strong independent guy.

But I could easily make out that she couldn't present them the prospect of us being together until she had answers to all the question her parents might ask.

Semester exams, P.S.U. preparation, hustling for Tech companies' job and numerous other stuffs were in progress, all at the same time. I didn't want any stone to remain unturned. I was working incessantly like a machine, albeit with emotions that fueled the efforts. In any case, I didn't have any other option too. Perhaps, that was my only chance and I could not afford to lose time. This was the time when I was battling hard for the desired life.

During that cold December, in an engineering college of Noida, we were writing our 7th semester's exams.

My priority was Jahnavi and her priority was to convince her parents which was ironically related to me grabbing a job.

One day, to my surprise we heard the news that one of the top IT big shots is going to organize a job fest for all branches in our campus very soon. I got excited and felt as if I had covered half of my way and now only a few more steps and we will be all set. This time a happy new year is really going by it's name. It is no more like the same for me.

Semester exams had almost ended and I had only two days left for the interview. For others, this interview might have been for a job only but for me it was everything.

And now, we were about to break the 1000-year-old tradition of hostel dwellers. We decided to stay at college and study even after the semester exams.

Next 48 hrs were exactly like those 70 minutes of Chak de…!

I couldn't afford to lose even a single second.

It was a war against all odds and time. A tussle with quantitative aptitude, verbal reasoning, DI, and communication skills.

As an engineering student, this was not new to me. We had always purchased our books only 24 hrs prior to exams.

I was confident but for the first time, I was nervous too. 300 to 350 eligible candidates and among them nearly 50% had this tech company on top of their wish list.

The competition was cut-throat. Limited seats had added fuel to the fire and I was way back in their choice as I was from the Mechanical branch and had no kin to software even in my dreams.

I kept practising online tests for day and night like many others. Lights of the hostel were not switched off for even a second in those 48 hours.

It was "Do or die" situation for me here on. It was all dead silence on the D-Day of the interview. I was more worried about Jahnavi.

In my case, I was not at all tensed as I had just one thought in my mind,

"Whatever is in my hands I wouldn't lack anything in

that. And which is beyond my limits, I can't do anything except pray."

Hence I was going with the flow and was confident in my mind. I was determined that whatever it took, I am ready to pay the cost. Poor Jahnavi too was relying on God and praying for my success.

* * *

10th January 2011,

Finally, the day had arrived. It was nippy, cold breeze all around in the morning. Last night it had rained for the first time in that season.

Rays of hope were struggling to bash me through the dense clouds of competition, perseverance, and commitment, yet I stayed positive. We all were dressed up so formally that it was appearing as if we all were going for some international meeting to crack a billion dollars deal in White House.

It was a tensed environment inside and outside. It was the day which everyone had been waiting for. It was a day of fruition for the 4 years of meticulous work all had put. Each and everyone of us needed the job that day and that was the dream of hundreds of students as well.

Talent scanning process started with a written test to filter out the maximum. It all started at 10 AM with perfectly ironed formal attires in different slots and rooms, and ended at 2:30 PM with greased shirts.

Lips were praying and confidence was getting lower and lower as the time went by. Results were to be sent to the placement coordinator's e-mail. It was a very long day. The result of the written test was still not out and it was dark already.

To ease ourselves and release some burden we started a walk after dinner.

All of a sudden people started clamouring and I was

sure that it was the result time. I ran at full pace towards the placement coordinator's room.

On my way, I bumped into Adi.

"Rahul, our names are on the list." , Adi shouted with utmost happiness.

We both started jumping and smashing things around us out of extreme happiness. We were so into the flow that we were about to cry.

We immediately took a hold of ourselves as we noticed some girls passing by us.

"Adi, Adi wait bro, we are halfway done yet. We still have the interview to crack and we have only next 12 hours to prepare. Thereafter we may echo the golden words to our parents.", I said.

"And you have two sets of parents bro, to break the news.", Adi teased.

"Hahahaha, shut up and let's go, prepare for the last toss."

We started preparing for our last phase of the war with studies of programming, quantitative, P.D., and reasoning. Every book was well spread across the length and breadth of the bed. We were evaluating every possible question ever asked in the technical round of interviews happened in our college over the time.

All computer programs, each and every topic was covered. It seemed as if we had completed the entire 4 years of software engineering in just 8 hours. We were excited, anxious and nervous. An amalgam of numerous strange feelings we had in our hearts at that time.

I was doing meditation in between to relax and calm myself down. Finally, at 4 in the morning, we closed our books and went to bed to catch some sleep.

After few hours, we all dressed up again like the government agents in spy movies. At around 11 in the morning, I was sitting outside the interview rooms, jittery blood was still running through my veins.

I was struggling to calm myself down. My name was next in the line for technical evaluation. Standing outside that room, I could easily make out the tension inside the room.

Finally, the long-awaited moment was there. I was in front of the interviewer. Contrary to my expectations, the interviewer just asked me to rectify the programs written by other candidates and brief him about that, which I did. I left the Interview table in less than 15 minutes with a little grin on my face.

I knew I did well.

Next, we all were sitting in the common area and were waiting for the results. Then there was that beautiful H.R. who stepped in and started announcing names over the microphone.

Names of the students who had to leave for the day.

It was not at all pleasing as it should have been at the sight of a beautiful lady. Seeing your friends leave having their dreams shattered in the palm of her hand, wasn't a nice sight. It was very saddening.

Aarav Sharma and Rahul were called together for a Managerial round.

"What the hell is this "Managerial" round?", we both looked at each other and said.

That was something new and abrupt which we weren't prepared for. The moment I entered the room for the next round, I was told that either one of us would get selected for H.R. round.

Which meant a direct competition with *"Sharma ji ka Beta"*.

Interviewer - "One question and one answer. Either you or Aarav would get the pass."

"Bring it on, sir" (I was ready to face it.)

"Being a mechanical engineering student, why IT company?" He asked.

And this was it.

The triumphant moment that I was waiting and hoping for. I had been preparing this very question for ages and that answer would be used over and over in coming centuries by every mechanical engineer while interviewing for an IT Company.

After my unique answer, those golden words which I was yearning for.

"Welcome Rahul!!", the interviewer said.

The end formalities of H.R. round lasted till 9 in the evening and I was completely exhausted.

Meanwhile, I got to know that Adi and Aarav both couldn't make it this time.

This was not at all good news because Aarav's elimination happened directly because of me and Adi, Adi was more than a brother to me. I was feeling very dejected.

In my case, official confirmation was still awaited and I was longing once again to see my name in the inbox of coordinator's e-mail.

* * *

12th January 2011, 2 PM approximately,

The placement coordinator was passing the tickets to numerous candidates for their journey to the corporate world. I was watching the scene from my balcony and it seemed like herds of people were trying to snatch away the list from him. New blood, very evident by the impatience in the air around.

My favourite Delfi too was very excited to share happiness with his mates. I think he sensed our feelings.

He was standing first in the queue even before girls to see the names. I was standing afar in a poised manner. "Few more seconds to go and I will rest my 4 years of backbreaking hardship". The list contained 56 names in total and somehow I managed to get in to scan the list.

On 12th row, it was written, "Rahul" in capitals.

I took a deep breath, raised my head towards the sky and thanked God for everything.

Now, it was the time for that special call which you make only once in your entire lifetime.

A call to make your parents feel proud, a call to make them feel the happiness that they desired and deserved, a call that they had the rights to get first before anyone in this whole wide world.

"Hello, Papa...!"

"Hey, Rahul, what's up beta ?"

(I took a deep breath, followed by a silence for fraction of a second.)

" I...,. I got the job!"

"Superb...! Waaaow. Excellent. Congrats beta!! May God grant you lots of success and happiness. I am very proud of you! Your Mom had been waiting eagerly to hear from you. Give her the good news yourself."

"Maa…! I got the job. God has answered your prayers and investment with me."

She almost cried and could only say this, "Come home now. Let's celebrate."

"Maa, carrot pudding, I just want that. I am coming tomorrow."

"For sure, just come fast."

Mom and Dad were extremely happy. It's difficult to pen down those moments of ecstasy, those feelings were inexplicable.

Now, it was the time for me to call the second home.

"Hey, Jahnavi…! Rahul this side."

"Yeah I know, I haven't deleted your no. yet, Hehe."

"I got the job in Adobe."

"What…? Really …?"

"Yes, just got the official confirmation."

"You didn't even tell me about the company's visit."

"Yeah…! I was planning to surprise you."

"Amazing….Love you…! One more thing to celebrate. Vipul's parents called up this morning and they said that Vipul wants to go for his M.B.A. first."

"Wohoooo…! This really calls for a party."

"Hey, did you tell uncle and aunty ? What was their reaction?"

"Yes, of course! They were extremely happy and said it's time to get a girl now (: wink)"

"Hehehehe! Okay, let me call you back as I get free. Now your work is done and mine has started." she said with utmost confidence.

With those two calls, I ended up with my celebration. When she said that my work was done and her's had started, it was not entirely true. The work which was mine, I solely held the responsibility of that but I owned the accountability in her assignment as well.

What I mean here is that MY work had ended but OUR work had started. I had a job now but we still had a mammoth of a task to convince each other's parents and let them talk and decide. This sounded very normal but in fact, it was the most difficult part.

At this moment I was still worried about my career. Adobe was just the first step. It was just to secure a job. My goal was to get into a P.S.U. through G.A.T.E.

Whatever I said in the interview was not exactly what

I wanted. Being a mechanical engineer, I really wanted to do mechanical stuff, not the software. But I had to secure a job to be able to make it work with Jahnavi.

Her parents had already started looking for a groom for her. She had prepared an entire case to present in front of her family covering all the possible scenarios, numerous examples, and evidences, positives and negatives, no scope left for any mistake. I was confident that she will make it through.

In the meantime, I left for my home to celebrate with my parents.

We decided that while I would be at home, she will talk to her parents. So that in case if anything goes south, I will introduce my parents into the equation and could try to ease things out. Vipul's case had already rested and it made complete sense to talk to her parents and present a compelling argument.

* * *

That day I was playing counter strike in my childhood day's study room when Mom brought me my phone from another room.

Mom: "Some Jahan is calling. You and your gaming craze. It is pissing me off again. To hell with counter-strike."

"Maa...Chill. Will try not to play from tomorrow."

So it was Jahnavi with good news. She had a word with her mother. Her mother was not at all expecting anything like that from her. She was kind of shocked and she was more worried about presenting this to Jahnavi's father. Anyhow, we needed to tell this to her father as well, but "How" was the real question.

We were happy because at least we moved forward one more step.

After talking to her mother, Jahnavi felt very relieved

as it gave an impression that she too had joined our team and now we three were together in the game now.

She had asked a couple of questions to her which Jahnavi had already prepared for and at last, she said, "Yes", with her magical words, "If you are happy, then I am happy".

Now, it was the time for her father to ponder on the idea.

For an Indian father, when anything like this comes into play then he follows his mind more than his heart. He needs to balance his daughter's happiness and the societal bindings, satisfying both.

And as I was expecting, next day that fear came to reality over a call from Jahnavi.

Jahnavi's Dad shut the discussion without even listening to the entire story. He was fuming out on the entire thing.

But the way Jahnavi narrated the entire scene to me over the phone, it seemed that her father discarded the whole idea without even listening to her part. As if some notions of some imperceptible cobwebs were pulling him out. He was sounding more like a rudimentary thinker than rational.

At this point, I had formed an opinion that all fathers were like that. He was not in a state of listening to the idea, let alone considering it for a discussion. Perhaps he had lost the power of argument and counter-argument, or the interest to do so.

Anyway, her mother was with her and that was a sigh of great relief. With half the battle won, I had to leave for college next day.

* * *

It was 20th Jan 2011, which I precisely remember. I had plenty of remaining vacations and my entire life was on a crucial verge, spanning over the next three months. I had to win the remaining battle anyhow. Considering the criticality of that time, I needed to clear the entrance of P.S.U. (G.A.T.E.), as well as the final semester of engineering to acquire the title that I had been labouring for the past 4 years: "Engineer".

I wanted to describe the entire story to my parents as well but I was waiting for the right time, perhaps stillness at that moment seemed more convincing.

That last evening at home was very different, very uneasy.

I was packing for hostel disheartened and dejected. Nothing was in my mind except one thing,

"How to convince her Dad?"

Suddenly I noticed Mom sneaking in and out of my room.

It was like she was playing "Hide and Seek", where she was seeking the stories I hid within myself. It was a little scary scene. She was just looking in and would suddenly move to the kitchen. This went on for almost 30 minutes.

"What happened Mom?", I irresistibly asked.

"Nothing. Just like that!", She just deflected.

She said nothing to me and stepped into the kitchen quietly. After sometime she came to my room and handed me a box of sweets with tears in her eyes.

"What happened, Mom? I am not going for the first time."

"No. It's not like that. My eyes were having irritation so your Dad brought some medicines and this is just because of that."

"And you want me to believe that? Come on! It's only a few days now. I am surely coming back for Holi and it's just a few months to that."

"It's Okay beta! Even I don't know why it's happening today! Shall I pack anything else?"

"Yes. Pack my care for you and keep it with you at all times."

"Sure.. God bless you bete!"

At that moment I was thinking to tell everything to Mom. Perhaps that would have helped me in getting some way out of this debacle but couldn't utter a word.

That day realization dawned on me that if I am not able to tell my Mom then how I would tell this to the entire world.

I was back in the hostel and winters were almost bidding adieu. Still, it felt very cold inside. I was wobbling through infinite thoughts and possibilities to convince Jahnavi's Dad. My brain was perplexed like a 12 year old's trying to solve Rubik's cube.

On the other hand, G.A.T.E. was counter striking on 13th Feb.

I was trying very hard to separate my personal life out from the career but I was failing miserably every time. Jahnavi was petrified to debate again on the same topic with her Dad.

* * *

Like any other day, we four or five friends were sitting in the hostel's room and blabbering, when somebody out of nowhere asked about the strongest, deepest and most honest relationship. I was not listening to their tame conversation as I was processing something else.

Suddenly, I heard somebody saying 'sister-to-sister'.

I jumped in with all ears to the conversation.

"Two sisters are always carbon copy of one another. They always stand for each other and understand each other very well. They are like mothers to them, best friends and also act as the pathfinders when required."

That was my cue. I sneaked out of the conversation and immediately dialled Jahnavi's number.

"Jahnavi…! How is the weather inside?"

"Dad is not even speaking to me since that day. Mom has tried various means to convince him but he is ignoring it all. Last time Dad ended the conversation by saying that 'I have no problem with the guy but society surely has'."

"Okay. Now listen."

"Yes, tell me."

"Do one thing, ask Jyoti didi to come down home or call her. Take her into the confidence and let her talk to Dad. Just make sure that Dad and didi should be face to face while discussing this. Physical presence augments your arguments."

"But do you really think that this will work because when Dad is not even listening to Mom then how could he listen to didi."

"This is the last thing that we can try. When there is no choice, there is no confusion. Let's get this going and cross our fingers."

"Okay. Let me try and get a hold of her. Hey...! You used to call her aunty. How come didi now."

"Yeah…! I know. That was way long back. Now, I should call her didi otherwise she'll feel offended. Anyway, some buttering never harms."

"Hehe", she chuckled.

And her smile was a sigh of relief for my arid soul.

Everything was now dangling between two points.

"One is to convince didi and other is to convince her Dad eventually."

I was worried what will happen if we fail at the very first step because the second step was entirely dependent on the first. Although chances of denial were very little knowing the state of affairs with her sister, still I was very sceptic.

That was one of those moments when everything inside and outside me was divided into two separate units. Three more months and everything would be changed. I was super excited and enthusiastic about the upcoming life.

* * *

I got a message from Jahnavi,

"Jyoti di is happy to hear about us, but she is worried about convincing Dad."

Me: "Not again! Same rudimentary thoughts."

But the first level had been cleared. Jyoti di was convinced.

Now she should be our messenger and delegate for convincing Dad.

To delegate a message not only of love but also of welcoming a new thinking against all persistent social stigma that has rooted deep within all of us, a thinking of reasons than a prejudice of rudiments.

I was not against our traditions but I was against the traditions which we have moulded as and when suited us.

Traditions these days are more of a weapon of destruction of social prosperity than being the harbinger of good faith. Ethnicity is no longer accepted whole heartedly. Instead it has become a burden. Social diversity is no longer a matter of pride but a reason to divide. Such beliefs are forced down the throat of our generation and instead of somebody explaining us, reason us with such erratic social notions or debate the ungrateful presence of such stigma, we have been forced, brain-washed and slaughtered many times.

Traditions, festivals, religion or rules are made for the happiness of the people, for the prosperity of mankind.

These things are made by the people and for the people. People are not made for them. I am not against any rule or religion. On the contrary, I respect all but my foremost belief is in truth.

The truth which has no versions and is one, and only one.

All I needed was Jyoti di to convince her Dad in whatever language he understands, to show her polemical skills and way us out. Many a time these so called elderly people lose their ability to reason, think rationally and question or even listen. They put their rituals in between and slaughter our dreams with the sword of their egos.

I knew that this was something that was happening with us then and I was going to be the victim this time.

Now, it was the time for elder daughter to take a stand and fight for the right thing. After doing the entire math, she decided to visit home on the Holi break and talk about us to her father. I was feeling a tad relieved after hearing this. After all, the elder children always have their ways with the parents. Funny thing about me being relieved was that my parents were completely oblivious to this entire love story. I was thinking to narrate the entire thing to them on Holi this time. I was very confident on my parent's part that they won't have any problem regarding this relationship.

Rather they would be quite happy to hear this. I had obliterated the other side of the coin, the side that cast doubts on my family end.

But if in case that side would exist then I would be in a huge trouble.

On the flip side of my life, I appeared at the G.A.T.E. entrance exam with full confidence and preparation. I made sure that my personal life and its problems had the least impact on my G.A.T.E. preparations, or at least I had tried.

I was so concerned about my plans for Jahnavi that I wrote my exam in 2 hours and started pondering over the plan in the 3rd hour. I only wanted to hear good news from Jahnavi's home. All I wanted to hear was,

"Her Dad has no problem with this relation".

I had an entire month to chill out and relax. I had a job and I had nailed G.A.T.E. as well, I hoped. Final examinations were due in the month of May and it would not take more than 15 days to revisit the entire course as I had already covered more than that during my stint for G.A.T.E. preparation.

I was only due for my final year's project work.

'Life had changed a lot. I was just a kid a few years back, playing cricket on streets having a dream of becoming a cricketer someday like the maestro Sachin Tendulkar. And now I am playing with thermodynamics, endothermic-exothermic reactions, 2-stroke, 4-stroke engines, year end project submissions, G.A.T.E. exams and the odds of winning the love of my life.'

I was thinking all this while resting on a chair and staring at ceiling fan of the examination hall and then in a blink of an eye I was dragged down to the ground reality by that clamouring bell announcing the exam was over.

It couldn't help a thought crossing my mind at that very moment.

"Understanding the time on time is the biggest learning of the time."

THE TWIST

It was the festival of Holi after two days and almost everyone up to 3rd year hostellers had already left for their hometown but the scene was different for the 4th year folks this time. There was a slight possibility that 'Oracle' would visit our college for offering jobs in IT.

And the offer was open to all the grads without any restriction of the branch.

That was the last hope for on-campus recruitment for many.

Although I had nothing to do with recruitment this time but everything to do with Aditya, my roommate. He was more than a brother to me. He was my family.

I decided if we got the confirmation of the arrival of Oracle then I would stay and prepare with him the same way we did for 'Adobe'.

Some of the unemployed grads had already decided that they were not going home anyway. All of them were saying, "In two months we will be kicked out of the hostel and we still don't have any job. How shall we go home and what shall we say to them?"

This was a perfect depiction of victory of compulsion

over love.

On the other hand, a few bags were packed. If the news gets confirmed then they would stay otherwise they would leave.

I guess this set of people were more practical. I liked this approach.

Placement cell had asked us to wait till 5 in the evening to get any confirmation. There were many guys and gals like me who were roaming in and around, arranging notes, garnering information for their dear friends.

1600 hours' 15th March 2011, we got notified that 'Oracle' would visit the college on 19th March.

Can't tell how many packed bags were unpacked and a ray of hope was again sprouted in many dejected hearts.

This was probably the first time when people were happy when not visiting their homes on a festival.

I also felt nice but....

If I had to speak my heart then I was more tempted to go home.

It was not the festivity that was dragging me to home but my love for Jahnavi. I needed to break the news about Jahnavi to my parents. This was a very good opportunity as the ambience of the home would be festive and I could have had squeezed in my love story in between.

But something inside me was stopping me and asking me to not be so selfish. And.... It was 'Friendship'.

It was late evening when I started unpacking my bag in despair.

"Dude, what are you doing? Go home!" Aditya interrupted.

"This cannot happen, Adi. You battling here and I am celebrating there." I stated.

"Do not start any melodrama" and he hugged me.

"Once you get the job, we will celebrate together and anyway this is just a matter of few days. I am sure you'll get this one." I said in a firm voice.

"Yeah, hope so ... Let's start then."

"Sure ...Mate."

* * *

On the other hand, the stage was all set. It was Holi, the festival of colors. Jyoti di had reached her home and I informed my parents why I was not coming home.

Didn't know why but while I was talking to Mom her same face was flashing when I was leaving for hostel last time. Dejected face, tears in the eyes. Dad had understood the cause but Moms are very different creatures on this planet.

No one is like a mother.

She was trying to cajole me by suggesting different measures,

"Don't stay, explain him on a call. He will do it. At least come for a day and then leave the next morning, etc."

Somehow, I convinced her by saying, "I will come in 2-3 days and we shall go shopping. I will buy you a gold pendant from my savings."

"Okay! Meanwhile, I'll select the best shop. And now when you are not coming then do take care of Adi. Study hard and help him in getting the job."

"Cent percent Mom. You please take care of yourself."

"You too bete"

This was the conversation between a son and his Mom that day.

And 'The conversation' was taking place 200 KMs away, in Agra.

A new chapter of this 7-year-old story was being written. From the day, Jahnavi had a word about us with her Dad, our routine calls got highly messed up. No late-night calls or long calls. Only small and crisp chats.

Because,

"If you want to reach your destination with full honour, then you have to adjust your steps in accordance with the road leading the way."

Our calls were getting short and stress was piling up. We knew we couldn't afford to make a single mistake until we were in the negotiation phase. On the eve of Holi, we had a sensitive, little chat over the phone for 5-10 minutes.

I was forced by my inner conflict to drop her an important message, which I felt after talking to her.

"Don't be in the same room when Jyoti Di talks to Dad."

I specifically put this point because I didn't want her to jump in the conversation with the same arguments and get back to the square one all over again and again.

Anyway, when we had called people from overseas to play forward, then I didn't want to take any risk by making my injured player take the lead. We were over with our tasks and now it was Jyoti Di's turn to take us forward.

In her last call, Jahnavi mentioned that Jyoti Di would leave early morning on the following day of Holi or may be late in the night.

Jyoti di's conversation could either embark a new chapter in our story or close the book on an unaccomplished love.

There in the hostel, we were playing an unenthusiastic Holi. Career was at stake. Nobody was staying for more than an hour on the ground.

Everybody was looking exactly the opposite of what they looked on the interview day.

Messy hair, unshaved beard, coloured old clothes, doubtful looks, tensed gaze and foreheads shouting out huge pressure. Every hour was slipping through the palm of our hands like quicksand.

I was discussing Java programs with Adi in our room. I had kept my phone and books with pictures of my deities near my bed. It was like I was praying to God to make my cell ring to good news and books to enlighten a brighter career path for my bro.

Everyone associated with me in my life was living in one world, but I was getting crushed between two worlds. Two worlds like two walls, Nevertheless, I was the one who chose this path and I didn't regret this a bit. I was the one who was responsible for the current situation.

But above all, I was confident that I would be in equilibrium one day and will cherish this situation in my memories.

I had never let my feelings go out of my heart, only my diary has it all. I had found someone who would always be the ears to all my emotions, who would always be the shoulder to my worried head, and who would always be my home.

Only a very few had access to my heart which Adi topped but he too had a microscopic view of everything. He always felt the need to dissect everything and know everything from the cellular level.

I had always ignored his questions about me and Jahnavi but he was well aware of my secret diary which even he wasn't privy to.

Many times he got pissed off because of my closed nature in matters like this and he was the only one whom I assured that my story will one day become an "Upanyaas": An Epic Tale of Love.

I always tried to cajole him saying, he would be the

first to read it.

* * *

Even on the day of Holi, we didn't have any long chat or conversation, just 2-3 messages and greetings. I knew with all the guests in her house and tautness in her heart, love will be the last thing on her mind. I was praying for easing out of her worries and mine too.

I knew that the day after was going to be the D-day and some inexplicable fear had made its permanent home inside me. Throat was drying up way too often and I was feeling hot and cold at the same time. I probably never had such jitters in my entire life. The biggest result of my life was going to be revealed the day after.

Closing my eyes and praying to the God almighty seemed to be the only way out of such precarious feeling.

Next day, it was lunchtime and I was heading for the mess when Jahnavi called up.

I quickly ran back to my room and locked the door behind me, plugged in my ear-phones and sat on my bed in rapt attention. I could feel my blood rushing down my legs and my heart pounding in my ears.

I gave out a long deep breath and muttered,

"Hello", I had my figures crossed.

"Hi, How are you?" she asked.

"I am good. How about you?"

"I am fine as well. Jyoti di went back today morning."

"So...! What's the latest in our case?"

"Reason for Dad's denial is not what we were thinking."

"What?? What do you mean by that?"

"Papa said that he had no problem with our relationship going forward and us getting married. He would be very happy to welcome you as his son in law. He even said that he was very sure of me that whomsoever I'll choose would really be a nice guy and he has faith in my choice.", she said in a muffled tone.

"Then, where is the BUT clause here ?"

"But"

"Oh come on! I really hate this BUT now."

"But Tau ji, my uncle, who is a potential candidate for M.L.A. in coming elections, is the root of this but."

"WTH…!"

"Dad had a chat with him regarding us, and he said that his entire base of the election was minority exploitation. Commencing an inter-caste marriage in his own family would ruin his entire life's struggle and his only chance to win the election.

Dad tried his level best to convince him but he was so obstinate on his stand that he even reprimanded Dad by saying, if he as much as thinks of crossing him then that would be very perilous for him and his family. Dad knows very well how he is, and was. He knows in and out of everything uncle did, does or can and will do.

When tau ji used so harsh words and language with an adamant voice, Dad backed off. Dad is more concerned about life than love."

I could feel the quiver in her voice and could sense the tears that rolled down her cheeks.

"So, now what are we supposed to do?", I asked.

"When even Dad failed to convince uncle, then I cannot even think of Jyoti di speaking to him and making him change his mind. Rahul, I really love you so much. I can't take this. Please, I beg of you, please do something."

She started sobbing like a 2-year-old kid. She was begging for her life.

I wanted to hold her tight in my arms and take away

her pain, her fear, and her feebleness. But I was helpless. I felt miserable to hear her cry and beg and see her helpless from afar and not being able to do a thing about it. It is in situations like these, I felt I could go through any pain, any struggle but to see Jahnavi in the tiniest bit of pain tore me apart.

"Heyyyy..! Please don't cry. I am with you and I am sure we will do something. We will convince your uncle. We will beg him to give us our life. I am sure nobody in this world can be so hard-hearted. There must be a way. There has to be a way. Please don't cry." I tried to convince her with all my might but even the words were unwilling to leave my mouth. I was shaken too.

"Please come here. I want to see you right now. Please come." She begged.

"I want to meet you more than you can imagine but compulsions always supersede love. Please stop crying and we will meet soon. Let me think of a way out of this situation. Please, take care my Jahan."

"You will have to take care of this situation, please handle it."

"Everything has two sides. Even the moon has a dark side. And everything gets balanced out eventually. If there is any problem in this world then it has a solution too. Easy or tough doesn't matter. We will get that. Love is the most powerful weapon in this world. I am confident that we will make it happen."

"Yeah...!" Said Jahnavi in a very low tone, like she was completely traumatized.

"Your smile is world's demand and you should fulfil that. We want justice. We want justice."

"Hmm...! Hehe ..." (wiping off her tears.)

"Take care. Bye Jahan."

"Bbye. You too take care."

Somehow, she managed to smile a bit and we closed our call. This was a U-turn in our love story. The road ahead seemed to be a dead end. Somewhere deep down I was having a premonition that something bad was going to happen.

How can a love story be so easy? Without a villain?

That was the only time in my life when I was feeling like getting defeated.

I realized that day that to achieve the things which you desire the most are the ones which are hardest to get and invariably you end up paying a lot more than you had fathomed to achieve.

Things did move a bit and gave us hope but seemed like this was the dead end.

I had only two options then, either to compromise with this or make my own way out through this dead end to the other side.

I voted for the second option.

The worse that could have happened was I would have been lost while finding a way home. But not trying and giving up wouldn't have helped too.

And at least this way I wouldn't blame myself the whole life for not giving it a try.

I knew the destination I needed to reach. Just that now I needed a guide to underscore my optimized path. I didn't have much time to spare thinking of an approach. I needed to act and act fast.

I was finding it difficult to find my escort: Mom, Dad or any friend. Mom, Dad at this point in time didn't seem like an appropriate choice. This could have had raised their concern for my safety from her uncle and could have worsened the entire situation.

My CPU was again under heavy load. Melancholy shades were all over in my cabinet- music, food, clothing, thoughts, and conversations.

* * *

It was 8 or 8:30 in the evening, once again the notice board was serving hundreds of eyes. Oracle's result was out. Once again happy and sad faces filled the college campus. I was worried about Adi.

Meanwhile, I was scanning the mob around the notice board, I saw Adi sprinting towards me and within the next couple of seconds he lifted me up on his shoulders and started running around the ground.

I knew the good news from above his shoulders yet I wanted to hear it from him.

"Hey man...! What's the news?" I formally asked.

"I got the job in Oracle bro."

"Superb bro. Burrrrrrraahhhh.... It's time to party."

"Name the place. We will kill it on the dance floor."

"I am glad, at least somewhere something is happening well."

"What the hell do you mean by that? Where is it wrong?"

"Let's leave it for today. It's party time bro."

"Oh! Come on, dude. Speak up."

"Okay.. But keep it up to you only." I said.

I thought I had found my navigator. So I went on narrating the entire drama. We sat till 4 in the morning and wrote all the pros and cons of this situation on a piece of paper, more cons fewer pros. We evaluated meticulously that entire night and after all our brainstorming, we finally reached to an L.C.M. (conclusion) that Jahnavi would have had to step up.

"What would be your role in this entire situation?", I asked Adi.

"I..., I can go there and can talk personally to Jahnavi's

uncle if you allow me."

"Haha…! Leave it. Let me ask her to talk to her uncle."

* * *

Before I had stepped into this new game, I needed to understand and master the rules of the game which is known as politics.

Politics - the activities associated with the governance of a country or other area, especially the debate or conflict among individuals or parties having or hoping to achieve power. This is what politics is in books but in actuality, it only means any means to achieve power.

One topic that has no religion, no ethics, no morals, no emotions, nothing. Only one thing- greed to achieve the power, by hook or by crook. Power to rule and not to serve, the power to control and not to direct, the power to suppress and no to elevate, the power to gain more power.

This was, where I was the weakest. I hated this topic like a hell. This was never on my list. But now this was my need, my obligation.

In a state like U.P., a maxim is very prominent- *'Don't cast a vote, vote your caste.'*

Every time political parties would make minorities their agenda and would fool the commoners. They made a hell lot of promises to them in the name of social upheaval and kept none. The only thing they kept time and again was their greed for power and money.

Every time the common man had suffered and these stupid crabs kept on becoming the kings.

It was not just that bad as I had thought. In actuality, it had worsened far more and beyond my imagination. No other word can define the filth of politics other than the very word itself- POLITICS.

Politics, in my opinion, was something like rust. If it

catches the foundation of our society and prosperity, then no matter how strong the rods of the foundation are, it will destroy them. And the character that Jahnavi had portrayed of her uncle was only steering me to think that our hearts will meet but outside our bodies.

Now, if I had decided to jump in, I had to finish it, having faith in God and in my love.

* * *

It was a week past Holi and she was much tensed. Her voice which was once chirpy and enthralling had turned into a grave silence. I had no way for her to be like before other than asking her to stay calm and hold herself strong. I needed her by my side while I fought through all the odds. Elections were in July and anytime party could have had announced the names of the candidates.

Everything was quiet, maybe it was a premonition of something bad and I was right about it.

I don't know why I struggled to sleep throughout that night. I heard phone vibrating near my head besides the pillow.

It was nearly 3:00 in the morning when I saw Jahnavi's name flashing on the screen.

I got scared.

"Hello", I started the conversation.

"Sorry to call you up so late, but I am really very excited and everybody just went off to sleep. I couldn't resist myself so, I called you."

"Excited for what?", A sigh of relief ran down my body.

"Tau ji wants to see you."

"Hain??"

I jumped out of my bed, splashed some cold water over my face and pinched myself to wake myself up completely from the state of trance I was in because of lying down sleepless for hours in the bed. Just wanted to make sure I was not dreaming.

"Hello. You there?"

"Give me a sec."

When I realized that this is reality and not any kind of dream or hallucination, I asked her,

"What happened? How did he get convinced to meet me after all that happened last week?"

"Listen Carefully, I was preparing for my exams this evening when he came home.

He said, 'Hey Lado (dear), what are you doing these days? It's been a long time since we had any party. Are you doing okay ?'

I said 'Yeah! Doing perfectly fine Tau ji just busy in exams.'

'Are you sure?', he said. I said, 'Yes, Tau ji'

He continued, 'Are you a cent percent sure lado? You know that you are dearer to me than you are to your father and I can never see you unhappy or low. If you had someone in your mind then you could have directly approached me.'

I was feeling slightly uncomfortable and was trying to avoid this conversation when he asked me that so politely.

Then he said,' Call him. I want to meet him. I want to evaluate him whether he can get my best or not?'

I just hugged him and thanked him. While leaving he said 'okay, so now tomorrow's party is on you.' I said, 'For sure. Done, Tau ji.'

'God Bless You beta…!', he said and he went back."

I jumped in and said, "Hold on, hold on... these are golden words for me. I need my time to digest. You never told me that your uncle was so close to you. I had never thought that this would be so simple. You should have talked to him in the first place."

"Yeah..Yeah but I was confused. He has no progeny. In an unfortunate incident, he lost his only child when he was very young. And, I am the youngest in the family, so am most loved. He has always treated me like his own child.", She replied.

"Then, what was the problem in approaching him first. Oh Madam...! You are so adorably naive."

"I thought he might get hurt. I cannot see him in distress because of me."

"Lol.., okay leave it now. Come to the point. So can I assume that the road for us is clear now ?"

"Of course it is, you idiot! Tell me now, when are you coming?", She chuckled.

"Whenever you say, my love."

"Okay, let me check with Uncle."

"Sounds great."

"Okay, listen."

"Yup"

"Were you sleeping?"

"No..no, Not at all. It's almost sunrise no, so I was preparing breakfast for the entire hostel. You wanna join?"

"Hehe, no. no am fine with my coffee here. Good Night!"

"You too should sleep now. Good Night!"

And now, I wasn't in a damn mood to sleep.

I told her that I was going to sleep so she wouldn't worry but I knew deep down that this news won't let me asleep.

How could a happy, relieved and excited soul could have slept after having felt such ecstasy? It was the time to celebrate, the celebration of triumph. My life was about to change.

I jumped out of the bed, jumped into my shoes and stepped out.

Sometimes out of presumptions we make certain images of some people we don't even know that well, only to realize later that we were terribly wrong about them. That's one hell of a guilty feeling. I presumed so many dreadful things about her uncle as a politician. Never mind, it was now time to start a fresh inning. I was about to meet our last predicament and to her entire family as well. I must admit that I was about to be the first person in my entire immediate and extended family who would have met his in-laws without any inkling to his parents. It was scary at first to even think about it but I think I was, by then, used to having such scared feelings.

Everything was almost done, only the last and most vital interview of my life was pending.

I was very happy even at the thought of it. I was having goosebumps and the feeling of those old butterflies all over again.

* * *

The weather was changing inside and outside. Outside, it was sunny with the cool breeze and inside it was exciting and pleasing and full of hopes and mirth. Around 11:00 in morning, I was in the attic, watching the passing by the crowd. It was a religious fest week of Navratras and the temple of our college was overcrowded.

A second-year couple of my branch was passing by the ground, hands in hands, grin on face bashing under the light of love. I sensed a sudden calmness in my heart. That couple and I exchanged smiles.

I couldn't control myself and probably for the first

time in a very long time, I called her up first.

"I was dialling you myself.", She spoke first.

"Ahh...Great! I called up because something made me remember our first ever call. I guess, 7 years back."

"Yeah…! I can recall it. Best phone call ever that had ended very weirdly. Listen, Tau ji was asking for this weekend or next for you to come and meet him."

"Oh … Let's keep that topic aside for some time."

I continued, "How amazing were those days. Whenever I stop and look back in time I realize how much things have changed. Those summer vacations when we used to meet at park and roam around. I never thought that we will be at this stage ever. I really don't know when our friendship and compassion for each other turned into affection and love. It is an amazing feeling but I really cherish those days. And as odd as it may sound now, I miss them too.

Jahan! We have grown up. Days have gone by. And sometimes I don't like this adulthood. How good would it be if we could go back to those days when we used to meet without anyone's knowledge? Those stolen glances we exchanged amidst all and those secret long night calls. Remember our first evening in Agra where we sat in the chairs looked at the night sky and were thinking about, well thinking about this particular day when we would be just a step closer to being together like the moon and the stars that night!"

"This is what meant to be. This is what we aspired for, dreamed of. One day we will be together. No more distances from one another. No more excuses to anyone for a meeting, no more waiting for summer vacations or festivals. Everything would be together. No more you and me, just us."

"What do you think this was good or bad? Whatever

had happened in the past, especially the roller coaster of a journey we have had."

"Everything cannot be categorized in good or bad, Rahul! There are things which are beyond the convention of good or bad. Some things aren't good or bad, easy or hard. They are just special."

"Yeah…! You are right. So, when shall I come to meet your uncle or shall I say, meet your entire family?"

"(Grinning) Now you're coming to the point. So, this weekend or next. You decide and let me know."

"This meeting would really be very interesting and historic for our love story."

"Yes, indeed. Please be prepared and I will do my homework too."

"What kind of homework now?"

"Oho... You and my parents both are going to be under the same roof for the very first time. I better be prepared for anything and everything. Don't be surprised if you see a Daddy's girl that day. (Chuckles)."

"Oh..that 'homework' for sure. Yeah, you know your parents best. I have to rush to college now. Take care. Love you Jahan!"

"Love you more..bbyee !"

It was the right time now. We had stepped into a new age of our lives. An age where we were going to ensure our futures, where we were going to vow to each togetherness in thick and thin, where we were to vow to our parents to make them proud and happy, inculcate their teachings to future generations and would always strive to continue their legacy and raise it.

I was on the verge of the entrance of that world. Only a few more formalities and I would be there. I was tensed and excited at the same time.

On the other hand, my trip to home got postponed

again. Mom's face once again flashed before my eyes. She was very sad that day and she would be bereaved this time too.

First, it was because of Adi, and now because of Jahnavi. In actuality, it was because of me only. It was me, getting more submissive to the greed and need every time and postponed the trip twice.

* * *

It is Friday evening [22nd Apr 2011] when I am gearing up for Agra.

I am going on a bus tonight.

This time it is not going to be any surprise, but it is exciting nevertheless, the excitement of meeting her, excitement for seeing the happiness on her face, excitement for being close to her and feel our souls getting inter-tangled for eternity.

In the meantime, something strange happened today.

Adi, who had always been an introvert, came to me and said,

"Hey, Rahul! Let's go for some tea. I really want to discuss something with you."

"At this time? It's lunchtime dude.", I said.

"Let's go. You can have lunch later as well.", He insisted.

" Ohk bro! Let's go, " I said.

Throughout the entire way from our room to the tea stall and back,he didn't utter a single word about the 'Important Discussion' he wanted to have and brought me to have tea for. After pushing a lot he said he just wanted to have tea and he was good now. This felt like a premonition of something unusual, he was looking very tensed and scared too. Somehow, he was trying to suppress his emotions but was not much successful in that.

THE PHONE CALL

I had heard of such phone calls and had seen people receiving such calls but never expected that I would ever get one.

It was early morning on 24th April, 2011(Sunday). I precisely remember that it was 3:00 in the morning when that call woke me up. What I heard was something I still remember, and I still feel the same chill run down my spine thinking about it even after all these years.

It was a sudden gush of sweat from my entire body; I was shaken from the roots of my very nerves. And what happened after that was something which shook many lives.

"Hello" (sleepy me)

"Am I talking to Aditya?" (A frightened voice)

"Yeah! Who is it?"

"Please rush to Agra as soon as possible. I will message you the address."

"Agra? Why? Who are you? Hello... Hello! You there?"

And the phone got disconnected.

The very next moment I received an address of some

hospital in Agra from that unknown number.

I tried calling the number back, but it was out of reach. I even tried Rahul's cell, but that too was switched off.

I knew that Rahul had gone to Agra two days ago.

I googled the address, and it was a valid address. I even tried to call that number from another cell but the number was still unreachable. I tried that number on truecaller but didn't find a match. Now I was more petrified. It was not a prank call for sure.

I was unable to understand what was happening, but one thing hammering in my head like an emergency alarm was,

"There is something wrong."

I took a deep breath and walked towards the window. It was a grave silence outside and very dark. A malfunctioning tube light which was getting on and off simultaneously on the basketball court, that's chrrr... chrrr.... scary scratching sound could be heard from my room. Except for that eerie sound, the entire hostel was quiet.

At the entrance of the college, there was warden chacha who was resting in his old armchair and near to him was Delfi, who was supposed to be sleeping at such late night hours, was alert, wagging his tail.

Everything was placid. An aghast stillness was all around; soothing winds started stinging suddenly.

There was little heaviness in my eyes, and a strange fear started making a lump in my throat, I was feeling petrified.

Like a bolt of lightning had struck me and I had no Idea what to do next. Like, I wanted to scream, Scream like anything. Heavy breaths and negative thoughts had already started their business in my mind and heart.

I turned around.

There was a photograph of Rahul in a checkered shirt and me together on the wall, seeing which I could not control but gave out a smile.

I again tried both the numbers but the status was still same.

It was the longest night.

The time between that scary night and the morning was getting elongated, as if someone had prevented even the sun from rising.

The sleep and restlessness were making me weak, and I could feel the tight slaps of all sorts of cranky questions on my red face.

This was the moment when I was standing clueless between the skies 'wrapped in clouds of danger' and the grounds of 'questions and uncertainties.'

Rahul had told me that I would be the first person to be contacted in case of an emergency. It's just that I never thought that it would ever come to be a reality. It was a deciding moment for me and I thought I had decided just after the call itself what I needed to do but was just trying to gather myself and move. The fear inside me was holding me back, terrified to discover the worst.

I draped myself and started for Agra. I remember, I had only Rs. 3000 in my pocket.

Bus stand was roughly a mile from the hostel. I started walking as it was very early in the morning so I wasn't expecting any auto-rickshaw or anything at that hour.

I saw Delfi tailing me. I tried to get away but he didn't want to leave me. He dropped me at the bus stop. This just added to my fear as I could feel that Delfi had sensed something wrong.

The first bus for Agra was at 5:30 am, I reached well before the time and occupied a seat at the back. I was still trying both the cells but both were inaccessible. I was just praying,

"May this all be a prank"

The bus started and gradually gained the speed. My pulse rate started rising with the increasing speed of the bus. As the bus moved faster, I laid back on the seat and closed my eyes.

Before I could have run numerous bad thoughts through my head, I went to sleep.

After nearly an hour I woke up to the irritating ring tone of my cell. I was glad to see that the number which had called me in the middle of last night, It was the same unknown number.

Me: "Hello"

Unknown voice: "Hello Aditya?"

Me: "Yeah! Please be a little bit louder, I am on the bus to Agra."

Unknown voice: "Where have you reached?"

Me: "I am on my way. It will take me nearly two, three hours to reach."

Unknown voice : "Okay. Call me as soon as you reach the hospital. I will meet you at the reception area."

Me : "Sure, but please let me know who you are and what exactly happened?"

Unknown voice : "I am Jahnavi's friend. You just get in as soon as possible."

Me : "Hello… helloo…"

And she hung up again before giving proper information.

Her words and voice again flooded my mind with all sort of bad thoughts. I would have been a little bit relaxed if she would have told me what had happened. At least I could have controlled the "Tsunami of Thoughts" and concentrated on one single thought.

It felt like the Clock had broken down, speed had reduced and roads had stretched a bit too far. Anyhow, I just wanted to reach the hospital as soon as possible.

It was a very beautiful morning, calm and soothing. The air was cleaner than usual and very less traffic on roads, yet everything was feeling dreadful. There was a pandemonium inside of me which was insulating me from every pleasing thing around. I was very concerned for Rahul's well-being.

To calm down and gather my strength, I closed my eyes and started meditating.

"Meditation is conscious sleep and sleep is an unconscious meditation", I always find this very helpful.

Somehow that ordeal ended as my bus neared Agra bus stop. I had inquired about the address from a co-passenger and it was a couple of miles from the bus stand. I hopped on in an auto-rickshaw and reached the hospital at around 10:00 am.

I called the girl who had introduced herself as Jahnavi's friend in her last call to me.

After 10 minutes, I saw a girl walking towards me with a poly-bag which was full of drips, medicines, and injections. She was looking very tired, having messed up dry hair and sunken eyes.

She was trying not to show any fears in her expressions. It seemed that she had not slept for a couple of nights. The condition she was wearing and the one she was trying to conceal on her face, was screaming bad news.

"Aditya?", she asked.

"Yeah", I said.

"I am Kajal, Jahnavi's friend."

"Where is Rahul? How is he? What happened to him?

Is he doing okay?"

"Rahul...Rahul is in I.C.U."

"Whatttt ??"

I had my mouth wide open. I thought of many possibilities but none of them zeroed down on ICU.

"Rahul is in ICU and Jahnavi too."

"Are you even serious? Oh my God. What happened? Please take me to the I.C.U.", I spoke mustering all the strength I had.

She started moving and I followed her dragging myself.

She didn't answer my question, so I asked again, "What has happened?"

"Doctors have detected a case of poisoning."

"Case of poisoning?? But how? How can that be even possible? He left happily for Jahnavi's home. He was very excited to meet her entire family. How did that come to this?"

And she again walked silently without answering my question.

That was bed no. 19 in I.C.U. where my friend, my brother was lying down like a dead body. Eyes closed, with some mask on his face, drip on his wrist and surrounded by numerous machines, beeping spectral sounds. Nobody was allowed inside, NOBODY.

I was looking him from outside through a very small glass window. Just next to him was Jahnavi on the bed no. 20. For the first time, I saw them together and had never imagined in my worst nightmare that I would ever see them together like that. That needed lots of courage to face such situation and I clearly didn't have any at that time.

Outside the I.C.U., there were two more people who

were Jahnavi's parents. They were introduced to me by the same girl who had shaken my world by just a phone call the night before.

"How did this happen?", After composing myself, I asked her, again.

The story which she narrated was unbelievable, unimaginable.

I felt like the ground slipped beneath my feet after listening to what she said next,

"Rahul came fine on Saturday morning. He was our special guest. Special arrangements were made to please him and make his stay comfortable. To make sure of all the arrangements and support Jahnavi, I was also called. We all enjoyed a lot that evening. The entire family went shopping too. Everything was working very smooth, frictionless. Everything was looking well planned and going by the same. Rahul and Jahnavi had prepared a very good script in advance.

All their coordination and actions were matching.

It was around late evening that day when Tau ji (Jahnavi's Uncle), Jahnavi's dad and Rahul walked into a room for some private conversation. While me, Jahnavi and her mother stepped in for cooking dinner.

They were talking so loud that we could hear them in the kitchen as well. Loud voices belonged to Tau ji and it was Rahul who was laughing.

We got little scared.

It felt like a class was going on and a strict teacher was scolding a naughty student. Jahnavi was most worried among us. We were almost done with our cooking but they were still having the chit-chat. None of us was courageous enough to knock the door and break the momentum. One hour had stretched to two. Then finally, Jahnavi gathered herself some courage and knocked at the door.

Tau ji came first and said, "Serve the food and we will be there in a while."

Surprisingly after 15-20 minutes, they all came out with smiling faces.

Aunty said, "What sort of official meeting was that huh. You people got us scared!!"

Tau ji seemed very happy. He said, "This boy is very mischievous. His stories reminded me of my childhood days. I really like this boy. Let us call his parents right away and finalize their wedding. May God bless my child Jahnavi!"

Everybody was very happy after this. Then we all started having our dinner. Then...All of a sudden…"

"Then? Then what? Speak up Kajal."

Albeit I was listening to Kajal my eyes were on a continuous watch over Rahul and Jahnavi. Both of them were still lying motionless. No movement at all.

Kajal continued, "Uncle called Rahul to his home after dinner. His house is on the next floor to Jahnavi's home. He asked Jahnavi to come along as well, stating, "Lado come, now onwards you two have to walk together forever." "I guess it was 10 in the night when they all started for uncle's place. We all were very pleased to witness that scene. I and aunty started our remaining work of cleaning utensils and other preparations for the next day's breakfast. After nearly half an hour, I heard repeated ringing on Rahul's cell.

Noticing the cell ringing continuously, I checked it and guessed it was from his home as on screen it was prompting "Mom Calling". I thought it could be important so I took his cell and left for Uncle's place.

And there… I saw........"

Kajal stopped speaking and now the storm of tears

was breaking out from her eyes. She was trying to collect the words and power to speak further.

"What? What did you see there? Please tell me. I can't hold it now."

"Both were laying down unconscious. Foam oozing out of both of their mouths. I screamed my lungs out. Jahnavi's parents rushed in immediately and tau ji was nowhere to be found. Jahnavi and Rahul both were unconscious. We tried splashing water drops on them but nothing happened. We immediately rushed to the nearest hospital."

"Oh....God! Please help. Please save them. What did the doctors say? And where is her uncle?", I exclaimed.

"No clue about her uncle. All the phones are switched off. Not even his office phones are working. We found him nowhere. Neither in his office nor at his home or any other possible place where he could be.

For now, their state is stable and doctors have kept them under observation for the next 48 hours."

"Oh, God ! Oh, God ! This can't be true. no... No.", I panted cluelessly.

"This is it, and here we are in this situation.", she ended it.

* * *

24-Apr-2011 (Sun) 3 pm

There was no movement in Rahul and Jahnavi. Jahnavi's parents were sitting on a bench like lifeless stones. I could sense the pain they were going through at that moment. I requested Jahnavi's parents to take some rest and leave for home but they refused, as was expected.

I spoke to the doctor who was on duty at that time and she said that Rahul and Jahnavi are stable now but no sign of improvement in past hours.

We all were worried and 'no sign of improvement' was

not at all a good sign. We all four were sitting outside the I.C.U. staring at each other's faces in search of some hope and courage.

I was looking at the bed on which Rahul was laying down like a breathing cadaver, and I was playing all the memories we made in my mind. That person who was laying just a few yards away from me was my best friend, my brother, my family for the better part of my life; and yet I wasn't able to do anything for him but staring at his still body from afar.

My eyes were frequently rolling from Rahul's bed to Jahnavi's bed and then to the monitor screens that were hooked to their bodies. And the moment I used to get weak and felt mortified at this sight, I was trying to search for some positivity in the eyes of others sitting beside me.

Periodically, nurses were asking for medicines and Kajal was taking care of all that.

I had a much greater responsibility at that time, "To inform Rahul's parents."

I was waiting to get a positive response from the doctors before calling Rahul's parents but all hopes were gradually weakening as the hours were passing by.

Rahul's parents knew me very well as they used to come regularly to meet Rahul at the hostel and often uncle used to call on my number when Rahul's phone was inaccessible.

It was almost impossible for me to hide anything from them but I knew I had to talk to them.

I was very scared to lie to them and I knew I shouldn't at that time. Somehow I convinced myself and mustered up some courage to break the news to them. It was tough but it got me going, I finally rang them up,

"Hello. Namaste Uncle!"

"Namaste beta. How are you, Aditya?"

"I am a good. Rahul is not doing good uncle and he is in a hospital. Can you please come over to Agra?"

"What?? What happened to him? And how come Agra?"

"Uncle, few of us friends had come to Agra for a small trip and suddenly in the night Rahul complaint about the stomach ache. We tried painkillers and antacids suspecting it might have been because of change in food but when we saw no improvement in his health even after waiting for a few hours, we rushed to the nearest hospital. Doctors diagnosed stones in the kidney and have hospitalized him because of continuous pain."

"Strange!! He never mentioned anything about Agra in any of his recent calls. We even called him last night but he didn't answer. This felt very strange because for the first time in past many years he had missed to call us for an entire day. Things are murky here. Please tell me what's going on, Adi bete? Put Rahul on call. I want to talk to him."

"Sorry uncle. Doctors have given him some sedatives and he is sleeping now.", I tried to manage one lie with another.

"Beta, message me the address now. We will leave immediately."

"Yes, uncle will do it right away. Bye."

I hung up as I was out of air to breath. I was about to break when I pressed the end call button. I was lying to someone who had the paramount right to know the truth; what had really happened to his only child.

I think Jahnavi's Dad heard me talking to Rahul's Dad. He hugged me with all the composure and started crying over my shoulder.

I controlled my tears somehow.

"What had Rahul done to your brother? He is such a

naive person. He could have never harmed or hurt anybody.", I had to ask Jahnavi's Dad this question which I had been keeping stoppered within for a while.

He was very ashamed because of the act his brother did on one hand and was equally shocked on the other. He was equally mad at him as we all were. His daughter too was laying in I.C.U., motionless. How could someone who is family, poison one of his own? How could he do that to those two innocent souls?

* * *

24-Apr-2011 (Sun) 7pm

Doctors came for another round of periodic checkup. A ray of hope shone upon our hearts and chants of prayers donned our lips. We all started looking through that small door glass. Doctors came outside after their checkup and said,

"We see some improvements in Rahul. He might come to his senses in a few hours. Let's just be hopeful."

"And Jahnavi ?", Kajal asked.

The eldest and the most experienced in the team Dr. Jayant just shook his head and went by without saying anything about Jahnavi.

Kajal was standing there motionless and Jahnavi's parents started crying out loud holding one another. And I was standing there clueless about who to hold. I just held on to hopes and prayers.

"Oh… Lord. Please shed some mercy on them." I just prayed.

One thing that I learned very well at that moment, "World's biggest court and holiest temple lay under the same roof, the roof of a hospital, in a split of a second one may get life or death here."

Here a doctor always strives to save lives of everybody irrespective of any discrimination based on race, religion, creed, or gender but death anyhow steals its way through at times.

But something that binds every soul in a hospital is the prayers on their lips and the loves for their near ones lying on those beds.

World's most pristine prayers are recited here and the most heart-wrenching cries could be heard here. Among those crying eyes sitting outside the I.C.U. that day, there were the begging eyes of Jahnavi's Mom. She was perhaps the one who was going through the toughest among us.

She was the one looking at her child, a piece of her heart in that worst condition for last 24 hours. Jahnavi's dad had held himself very well, perhaps he knew to hide his emotions better than any of us. He knew that he can't be emotional in that situation.

He was feeling so miserable and helpless that he said to me,

"Adi, you people are very lucky. At least you can cry. I am not even that lucky. I am that unfortunate father who is looking at his baby girl lying on the bed struggling between life and death. And I am an ashamed brother who will have to face the wrath of the entire world because of what his own brother did to satiate his infernal greed for power."

* * *

24-Apr-2011 (Sun) 10 pm

Jahnavi's elder sister and her husband arrived. There was a dead silence among all of us and this just added to the horror of the whole situation. For many hours nobody said anything.

We were watching the passing by doctors, looking through that small glass window to capture a glimpse of that unlucky couple and then were looking at one another's pale faces.

We were all sitting in a hope of some good news from routine doctors. I once again requested Jahnavi's parents to go home and take a nap. I and Deepak, their son in law offered to stay behind in the hospital in case of an emergency and tried to convince them in every way possible.

Finally, they got convinced. Jahnavi's parents and Jyoti didi headed towards home without forgetting to mention to be back at first light the next morning.

Rahul's parents had stepped in as soon as Jahnavi's parents left. It was entirely out of my limits to narrate them the exact true story.

But as the time demanded, each of us was doing exactly what was beyond our normal bounds and limits, doctors with their doctoral abilities, Rahul and Jahnavi with their will powers and their parents with their strengths. And past few hours had already stretched my limits.

I started with what I knew and Jyoti didi added to it over the phone. None of us knew the entire story. It was wretchedly sad that the thing which Rahul had been preparing for a very long time to tell his Mom and Dad, the whats, the hows, the whens of his relationship with Jahnavi. That special thing had to be narrated by me to his parents in a situation when Rahul was just a few feet away from me laying there in all silence.

This was a situation where I couldn't hide anything from them and to be honest I didn't want to hide anything from them. They were witnessing their only child lying lifelessly in a hospital bed hundreds of miles away from home. The least they deserved was to know the truth.

After listening to the entire story, none of Rahul's parents spoke anything. They just stood with tears in their eyes and went over to the small glass window to see their struggling son.

It was because of me only that social worker of our hostel, Rahul didn't go home for Holi holidays and this all happened. Had he gone his home, probably he would have been fine and so could Jahnavi.

This thing was pinching me a lot by then and I hadn't been able to shake it off.

Rahul's Mom wanted to see her son and was very obstinate on this but doctors had given very strict instructions that nobody could meet them.

It was very difficult to convince her.

We all could very well understand the heart of a Mom who had seen her son happy and healthy just 3 months back, was now looking at him lying inside the I.C.U.

We all wanted her to meet her poor son but for dear doctors, their professionalism and rules were way above any attachments.

The agony of that heart was very apparent but doctors are supposed to be next to the God. We couldn't ignore their directives.

It was 1 AM when I requested Rahul's parents to go to Jahnavi's place and take some rest.

I knew that my request would be futile and indeed it was.

There were many reasons for their denial of going to Jahnavi's home.

Their only son in I.C.U. fighting with an uncertain death was "only one of them."

* * *

While resting on a hospital bench, I fell asleep for a little bit and suddenly it broke due to some unpleasant noise. It was raining cats and dogs. It was not at all an expected one.

Avery dark night, pitch black and incessant rain. It got scary, very very scary.

I walked down the corridor for some water and thought of asking others if they needed, but when I saw Rahul's parents leaning on each other's shoulder and sleeping, I stopped myself.

It was a very compulsive sleep, must be what we call as human limitations.

As it was 2:30 AM the entire hospital was silent, no more commotion, no more doctors or nurses running around, no more horrifying rush, just much more terrorizing silence.

Only a very few doctors and nurses were seen sitting in their respective places, seemingly composed and at peace with that ghastly ambience. Rest of the staff in the emergency ward and everywhere else was half-past slept.

I could hear the roar of lighting and the heavy rain very clearly as it was very quiet inside. I walked down towards the entrance of the hospital. A cool breeze was blowing. Water started logging on the roads.

The wind felt pleasant. I sat down on a bench near the entrance of the hospital.

I noticed one girl and a boy jumping into water puddles. They were playing something in that dark, splashing water over one another. Few more kids joined them and formed teams.

Cute, innocent and very natural smiles donned their faces, as they were playing mirthfully.

"Oh no Rahul. Please stop it now. Water is very cold and is dirty too. Please don't toss it over me."

"If you are so scared of it, then why did you start it? And Aditya what happened to you mate. Come on. It's raining in April, it's a bliss. Kittu, Luv, Kush, Jiyansh. Let's pull Adi bhaiya here."

"Hehe.. hehe ....Let's go Adi bhaiya.... yipeeee......let's play."

"Hey ya ! Jahnavi. Stop it haan ! This is not Holi, from where did you get those blood red colours?"

"Why are you scared now, Rahul ? Hahaha.. come ..come .. I am not going to leave you this time."

"Adi, stop her, please. Hey Adi, stop her.... Stop Jahnavi, Adi... "

"Adi.. aadii ... hey Adi "

"Adi.. aadii ... "

"Umm... h.. hey.... look there, Deepak sir."

"Why are you sleeping outside, in such a cold weather? Let's go fast, it's an emergency."

I was woken up by Jahnavi's brother-in-law in a haste. We rushed back to the I.C.U.

I saw Dr. Jayant and 4,5 nurses shifting Jahnavi to some other room from I.C.U.

"Doc, what happened?", I asked with fear, my throat was already choking.

"Renal failure !", Dr. replied.

"What ??"

"We must shift her to a dialysis unit and perform a renal transplant as soon as possible."

"Oh.. God !"

* * *

As it was 4 AM, we thought to wait till the sunrise before informing Jahnavi's parents. Doctors were doing their best. These were trying times. The longer they were to be unconscious, the complicated the situation would have become; and more difficult it would become to save them. We were racing against the time and against all odds. Hands were held in prayers and eyes had already dried of all tears.

Rahul had shown some signs of improvement in the daytime but Jahnavi's condition was getting worse with each passing moment. We kept talking to doctors for mining some hope out of the barren lands of fear, but they too had started ignoring us now, probably tired of giving the same answer over and over again.

We were much tensed because of the word we heard, 'Transplant'. We didn't know why and what had happened and now hearing this, we couldn't stop our minds from making the worst of the assumptions. No one was giving us any answers, but just one assurance that they were trying their best. And, they actually were. None of them had taken any rest through the night, and looked as tired and drained out of energy as we were. No one was giving up, neither the doctors with their medical ways nor us with our spiritual ways.

It was very loud outside because of the lightning and heavy rain. And it was very silent inside the hospital at the early hours. It was very frightening as we were trapped between the loud and the silent. On the contradiction, we were numb on the outside, but inside there was so much commotion of emotions flooding through every nerves triggering fear in every corner of our body. Our eyes were wet and hands were folded, begging God for some positive news. Rain didn't stop and Jahnavi's parents and sister rushed in anyway at 5 in the morning. Guess, they couldn't sleep the night despite our attempts of sending them back home. And how could they, a piece of their life was sleeping midway between life and death. They could use all the support and prayers, and we did our best.

They were completely drenched and were shivering, unsure if it's because of getting wet or out of fear of the unknown. They all came amidst that dark and rainy night for a ray of hope.

But fate came up with an unexpected reply to their

hopes.

I didn't have the courage to face them after I broke the news to them. So I ran towards the room where Jahnavi was taken. Doctors' and nurses' rounds were getting more frequent by the time around Jahnavi. I started to get a strange feeling in my gut, something similar to what I had felt when Rahul was leaving for Agra to meet Jahnavi's family. I was trying to close the ears to my gut calls but I wasn't able to. I started pacing through the corridor to clear the head and find more hopes, but everything seemed very difficult at the moment. I thought getting some answers from the doctors would help.

They all were rushing in and out of her room. We tried to excuse them for some detail but they blatantly rejected our request saying nothing could be said at that point. Adding to our misfortune this room didn't even have any window to peep in. All this had been happening for the past two hours. And I was getting restless with every passing moment.

The doctors who were making rounds of Jahnavi's ward, all seemed very worried and tired. They were using big jargons while discussing among themselves and we didn't have a clue of what they were talking about. This was further adding to our fears, we just needed to hear that everything will be alright; yet no one seemed to be giving that to us. There was just Dr. Jayant who was looking towards us with a smile in between their discussions, giving us some hopes that things will be fine.

But …..for the last 30 minutes,

I sensed that he too was ignoring our poor faces. My gut started kicking harder to the fear side of me.

Jahnavi's parents were sitting outside the ward in high hopes, they didn't see what we had experienced throughout that fateful night. They were begging God for Jahnavi's life. I wished their prayers were heard. We couldn't handle that situation, and we didn't know how. How to give hope to someone else, when you yourself are grasping at the straw of hope. Looking at their helpless faces, I was feeling lifeless and powerless for not being able to do anything. This test that life was giving us, wasn't like all those college tests that we would clear somehow, all on hopes. My body was numb, and my soul was tired.

It was 7:30 in the morning when Dr. Jayant who was leading the team of doctors came out of the ward, where Jahnavi's family and we were sitting. It was after many hours that he came to us with news. I prayed to god that he came up bearing good news.

"Who is patient's father ?" Dr. Jayant asked.

"Yes, Doctor ! It's me. Jahnavi's father."

"Sir... I am so sorry. Jahnavi...... has left us."

* * *

एहसास सारे धरे के धरे रह गए,
कितने किस्से थे जो अनकहे रह गए,
मंज़िलें चल पड़ीं ख़ुद-ब-ख़ुद,
रास्ते बेचारे देखते रह गए।

सोच रहे थे सहर साथ होगी,
दिल से दिल की फिर वही बात होगी,
और तुम थे कि शाम से ही खामोश रह गए,
करके एक दौर खत्म ख़ुद को निर्दोष कह गए।

एहसास सारे धरे के धरे रह गए,
कितने किस्से थे जो अनकहे रह गए।

ओस की बूँदें उनको भिगोने वाली थीं,
चाँदनी हसरतों को सँजोने वाली थीं,

पर ये क्या हुआ मैंने कुछ न सुना,
और तुम सब कुछ कह गए,
जुगनू अपनी ही आग में जलकर रह गए।

एहसास सारे धरे के धरे रह गए
कितने किस्से थे जो अनकहे रह गए।

हाथ में हाथ लिए कल मुस्कुरा ही रहे थे
हँसी से अपनी आसमानों को जला ही रहे थे,
क्या हुआ आज ये सारी दुनिया बोल रही,
पर तुम आँखें बंद किये बिन बोले रह गए।

मंज़िलें चल पड़ीं ख़ुद-ब-ख़ुद,
रास्ते बेचारे देखते रह गए,
एहसास सारे धरे के धरे रह गए,
कितने किस्से थे जो अनकहे रह गए।

A dreaded silence followed what the doctor just told. My legs were cemented to the ground I was holding, the world around me felt like it would implode all on me. I didn't know where was I looking but I couldn't see anything but just a blur of white. My eyes were filled with tears, my body was struck with shock and my mouth was so wide open that I could feel my throat drying. I could see two people standing like stones before me, no movement rock steady stance, they were Jahnavi's parents. A few seconds later, which felt like hours, Jahnavi's Mom lost her conscious and fell down on the ground.

I rushed to help her and I could still see Jahnavi's father standing in shock as he stood for the last minute. He didn't move. Did not even flinch at the sight of his wife dropping on the ground. Their son-in-law grabbed the bottle of water from a bag and started sprinkling water over Jahnavi's mother but no one said a word.

A few splatters later, she got back her consciousness and the first word that skipped her mouth that had broken that long cold silence was "Jahnaviiiii". It was a cry of pain, a scream of helplessness and a melancholy of loss. She cried with so much pain, the kind I had never seen in my life before.

What broke my heart into pieces was the sight of Jahnavi's father breaking down in tears. Watching a man cry must be the most painful sight. He sat down beside her, held her tight and both cried helplessly at the loss of their world, at the loss of an innocent soul whose only mistake was to love truly.

Those innocent eyes had been shut forever.

She had left the world of agony and ecstasy suffrage forever. It was impossible for us to console her parents. Rahul's parents were trying to console those unfortunate parents but they too were going through a very tough situation. The news of Jahnavi's death had heightened their fears and worries for Rahul. And I was standing there and witnessing a victory of bogus honour over an innocent and true love.

Life is the biggest teacher and each day is a new lesson.

Her eyes were forever closed but it was her parents' eyes which were going to be forever dead hereafter. Entire hospital was expressing their grief and condolences.

Whoever came to know about the incident visited the ward and shed their share of care for the ones that were left behind to cry and blessings for the one that had left us. An unimaginable and unbelievable thing had happened and no amount of cursing and abuses for the person who was responsible for this seemed enough at that moment.

* * *

On the other hand, from the I.C.U., news came that Rahul had opened his eyes. We were asked to meet him with a clear instruction that we should not break this piece of emotional news to him. He was conscious then but not out of danger.

He was still very fragile. Rahul's dad came out to me with the tough request.

He pleaded, "Aditya. You go and talk to him. He would be open to you more than anyone else and would also take it easy."

With tears in my eyes, I gave a glance at Rahul's Mom, shook my head for her consent, took blessings from the ill-fated parents of Jahnavi and started walking towards a guy whose entire world had been toppled in the last 24 hrs.

Rahul's bed was a mere 10 steps away from the doors of the I.C.U., the same door that I had developed a deep relationship with, the door that had the window to peep through, the window through which I had seen Rahul and Jahnavi together for the last time. I knew that I had those 10 steps to traverse before I prepare myself to meet Rahul.

He was lying in his bed facing up towards the roof. His face was seemingly pale and his eyes looked sunken. There was a chair adjacent to his bed. I had to sit in that chair next to him, hold his palms in my hands, look him in the eyes and lie to him.

I knew I had to 'Act', Act as if the world was still the same, he last saw a couple of days back.

The bones inside my body were cracking out of the pain I had experienced in these people in the last two days and after what had just happened, the first sight of Rahul as his eyes met mine ran a chill through my spine.

Somehow I composed myself, tried to put the best

positive face I could manage at that time and I touched his shoulder gently,

"Rahul.. !", I said.

He slowly turned towards me and murmured something but I couldn't understand anything so sitting in that chair I leaned forward.

"Dude, please ask someone to remove this mask", Rahul said moving his eyes towards his oxygen mask."

"Okay..."

I requested the on duty nurse to remove the mask for some time but as expected she blatantly rejected that. She said that it was supposed to stay on, and I had no other way but to agree with what she said.

I looked back at Rahul and before I could have convinced him to keep the mask on, he had already removed it on his own.

"What the hell are you doing?", I yelled.

"Oho. Don't worry. I am not gonna die."

Rahul said in a very timid tone.

"You are crazy man ..!"

"Where is Jahnavi and how is she doing?", came the question I dreaded the most.

"Jahnavi...,Jahnavi.. !! She is at home and she is doing good."

"Call her I want to see her, right now."

"I mean she has been discharged but doctors have recommended her bed rest."

"Oh, God!! Thanks a ton. Where are Mom and Dad? Are they here ?"

"They are out, shall I call them in?"

"Oh, no man. They will scold me like hell."

(We started chuckling)

After a pause, he continued,

"Adi..I am not able to speak properly, neither I am able to feel my legs. I want to turn my back but I am not able to."

"Don't worry brother, you will recover soon."

He clutched my hand, like it was taking him a lot of efforts to speak.

"I am sure, you have the background of this entire happening." He spoke out again.

"Yeah"

"You know, what is the first thing you see as you enter Jahnavi's uncle house?"

"What"

"A very big sculpture of God and Goddess Radha-Krishna."

I was trying to make him go out of everything which had happened over the past few hours. It was getting very difficult for me to hold myself.

"He told us that he had organized a feast in the temple for our affluence and togetherness. And then while having the offerings, we both......" He continued.

"Oh Man. Leave it. Jahnavi is at home, and you too will be home by tomorrow. Everything will be alright man. You wanna hear something good?"

"Of course buddy. It's been a long time."

"Your parents and her parents are out and glad to meet each other. They are very happy for you people. Shall I call an astrologer and get a date fixed?"

"Hahahaha !! Really?"

He smiled. This time he was smiling for real. That despicable nurse came back again.

Nurse- "Please leave him now. It's time for his injection and who removed his mask?"

"Sister, please! Just for two more minutes."

Rahul requested her with his hands folded and this time she didn't refuse.

"Listen, Adi... If anything happens to me..."

"Just shut up..,. Sister! Please give him injections."

"Oh. No... Man.. Listen and promise me that you will do it (Rahul held my palm tightly).

It's time to face the reality. And in this condition, anything can happen to me. Promise me that you will do it."

"Hmm...", I just shook my head in agreement.

"You remember that diary that I always keep on writing?"

"Yes. I do."

"I want you to complete it and get it to its destination."

With heavy heart and tears in my eyes, I shook my head and committed him to complete that.

"And something more important than this. And that is; when you will go to my home for returning my stuff from the hostel, then grab all the snacks from my travel bag. I used to eat those secretly."

"What?? used to eat those secretly ??"

(We both chuckled)

"Sometimes I have shared with you as well. You are forgetting!"

"Ghanta.. ! Never !"

"Adi, Mom had made that all with great love."

"Shut up. We will share that. Don't you dare think about leaving us like that? Take some rest now. We have exams from next week and entire branch is waiting for you at college."

"Hahaha.. Take care of Mom and Dad. And listen, you

have to do these things if something really happens to me. Before that, you dare not touch anything."

We both laughed. That nurse came back with another injection in her hand and put the oxygen mask back on and asked me to leave in a ferocious voice.

"Thank you so much, sister!" , we together tried to appease her.

I left the I.C.U. with a good feeling after sharing a few laughs with Rahul.

"How is he??" Rahul's parents asked me.

"He is fine now. Don't worry Uncle, aunty ! He was cracking jokes inside."

Rahul's parents smiled a bit after so long.

But....

That was not the truth, not the whole one at least.

The 'Truth' was, "Rahul was in I.C.U. for more than 36 hours and he had just gained his consciousness back for few minutes in the name of improvement and even doctors had not declared him out of danger yet."

But a little hope did shine upon us, and for all of us who had been through a lot in the past days, this little was much for us.

There, Jahnavi's parents had left for her funeral. This was a state of restlessness. We didn't know where to go. It was a dreadful time. Jahnavi's final rites were about to take place but none of us wanted to leave Rahul's side even for a moment. Someone mentioned if one of us could go there but no one wanted to leave Rahul in this critical condition.

One positive thing was; Rahul's parents had no resentment or any bitterness against Jahnavi's family. Rather there was no time for that sort of negativity. They had lost their baby girl. If anyone had paid the most for that atrocity, it was them. Those poor parents.

I had met Rahul around 10 o'clock in the morning and it was about the afternoon. He laid asleep with heavy doses of injections. He hadn't had a morsel of food. Even liquid diet wasn't prescribed.

Kajal and Deepak sir kept calling me to inquire about the situation in the hospital and Rahul's condition. He also informed me about the state of affairs at Jahnavi's house.

A weird anxiety had overwhelmed me. I had lost the power to reason. My body was swamped with a strange numbness out of intense grief. I felt heavy and irritable.

I wanted to weep, but I could not. Neither I couldn't bear the sight of Rahul's parents haggard in helplessness, nor could I imagine the insurmountable grief Jahnavi's parents were going through.

The cruel time was like a fierce and a vicious storm in which we were tossed and turned by the violent winds. The atmosphere dropped into heavy eerie silence.

* * *

25-Apr-2011 (Mon) 3 pm

Rahul's Mom and Dad were still silent. Their hopeful eyes were permanently fixated at the I.C.U. door. They hadn't eaten and slept since they had arrived.

"Uncle, aunty, Tea!", I offered them some tea from a stall outside.

"Thank you, Adi bete !"

And aunty lovingly brushed her hand over my head. Uncle, Aunty and I, started to talk. To lighten the mood I started to share some of the funny incidents that happened in the hostel. I managed to bring a smile on the worn out faces of despair and felt a mini triumph in my heart.

To be able to reap flowers of smiles on those drought-stricken barren faces of grief was a big achievement.

Around 4 or 5 in the evening, Dr. Jayant approached us with another bad news.

"Rahul is suffering from Septicemia. We have to shift him on the ventilator."

"But his condition had improved in the morning.", Rahul's Dad said.

Dr. Jayant put his hand on uncle's shoulder and said slowly, "Rahul just got conscious. Keep praying, he would improve too."

We were terrified after listening to this statement.

I said with jitters down my spine, "I met him in the morning and he was talking to me. I think his condition was improving."

"Yes beta! We also saw a ray of hope in the morning. But now the vitals are dropping. Rahul is going through minor attacks, in common language 'shocks', which is due to septicemia. This all leads to blood infection."

Septicemia, which meant Infection and Infection meant more danger.

This was injustice, injustice to our hopes. It felt like the storm which was slowly subsiding, had regained its strength in the form of a tsunami wave.

Uncle stood strong like a blade of grass which survived the violent winds of the storm even when strong trees got uprooted. He was the source of courage for both aunty and me, when we were just losing our strengths to bear that unendurable spell.

He said in a firm tone,

"We shouldn't give up and must hold on to the faintest ray of hope and make it stronger by our will. Apprehension is a characteristic in situations like these, however, I know my son is a strong boy. He has fought with difficult situations many times and has emerged out of it victorious and stronger. He will win today as well. And yes, make sure that our minds and hearts are in prayerful reverence, no fear. No fear at all."

Uncle was trying really hard for us to hold on to hope that was sinking at the speed of a dying tornado. The fact that Jahnavi's conditions had deteriorated in the exact same manner, was bothering us further more. I passed on the wretched news to Jahnavi's home. Deepak sir joined us soon after.

Since there was an urgent requirement for two units of blood, I and Deepak sir donated it.

We needed Jahnavi's family's support and help in that strange unknown city away from home. Doctors had informed us that since it was a case of blood infection, there would be a regular need of blood donors every now and then. Thankfully Jahnavi's family was up for any kind of assistance in these troubled times.

As excruciating as the time it was when a daughter's final journey's bier bearers were offering their blood for Rahul's survival. Time is a heinous dictator and we are it's slaves.

How Jahnavi's parents would be explaining the entire scenario to their relatives, how would they be convincing them for blood donation and facing useless inquiries from insensitive people, this thought was killing me inside.

It was almost 10 in the night, four units of blood were already transfused. Still, however, there was no sign of improvement.

And this fateful merciless day had started with the first rays of the sun which had brought with it the woe of Jahnavi's departure.

* * *

It was 11.30 in the night when uncle, aunty, Deepak sir and I were sitting outside the ICU.

Dr. Jayant hurried towards us and said, "Rahul's condition is worsening. Immediately we need these injections.", and forwarded a slip in our direction.

Before Uncle could act, I immediately grabbed the slip from his hand and ran to the pharmacy.

I was fourth in the queue. Waiting was filling me with anxiousness and it was getting on my nerves. The events were despicable. Every moment was about an hour. I was screaming at the deplorably slow staff at the counter. My state was comparable to a demented person. In one hand I had a phone and in the other the prescription slip. My eyes were filled with tears but I wasn't crying.

I was unusually stuttering and locking - unlocking my phone out of restlessness. That is when I noticed the Google shortcut on my phone's home screen. I immediately searched for the injections mentioned on the slip.

"NORADRENALINE, DOPAMINE
AND CALCIUM GLUCONATE."

The link read that it is used when chances of survival are slim. I couldn't finish reading the page as I got my turn at the counter. I grabbed the injections and rushed to the ICU. I handed over the injections to Dr. Jayant, and like a hapless mendicant, I implored upon him and said, "Save him at any cost."

A few moments later suddenly a nurse came and handed me another prescription for another set of medicines which were needed immediately. I was fourth in the line again. Even though it was so late in the night, the pharmacy was still crowded. I didn't want to wait. I even thought of jumping the queue and buy the medicines first since I wanted to be as close to Rahul as I could. However, it was not a ticket counter of the movies or trains. Just like me other were also standing there to buy a few 'breaths' and 'an ounce of hope' for their loved ones.

"Yes, what do you want?" The person at the counter asked me.

That's when my phone started to ring. Rahul's Dad, flashed on the screen. I immediately picked up his call assuming he might need some more medicines and hence I shifted a little away from the queue to take the call.

"Yes uncle. Tell me, is there anything else required apart from those medicines?" I inquired.

"Medicines....!"

A deep silence followed.

"Yes uncle, I am right at the counter, tell me fast."

My heart sunk, I felt a strange feeling in my heart. In that moment I closed my eyes and begged to god miserable. "God, please no. Please let it not be that, please please save him."

Tears started flowing from my eyes, my throat was choked in pain.

"Bete! Leave it! Medicines are not required now." his voice muffled and he hung up.

I ran towards the ICU, I didn't feel where I was or who and what I passed by, everything just blurred around me, every sound silenced, everything vanished. I just see a blank in front me and I was running into abyss sucking in all the air around me, I was restless. Suddenly, my feet stopped near the ICU where Rahul was moved into. I was panting heavily, like the soul was leaving my body. I looked around hurriedly but I didn't see anyone.

I didn't see uncle or aunty or anyone outside the ICU. I peeped inside the I.C.U. window.

Everything was over.....Everything was gone, taken away from me. From all of us!

Rahul was no more…

Our Rahul, was no more.

Two lives were gone in one day. Love was dead.

My soul had left my body. I was standing inside a dead body, I was feeling nothing. I crawled towards the wall and crumbled in pain, and cried loudly. He was gone, I needed him, I needed to see him; he couldn't go. He has to stay, god make him stay.

Uncle was crying. Aunty just sat in one corner staring at Rahul's face. She was dumbstruck with shock and grief. She hadn't blinked or uttered a word. Rahul's dad tried to pull her back from the shock. He wanted her to weep but all in vain as she was standing like a lifeless statue. Rahul's bed was surrounded by grieving people now. They were weeping at the death of innocence. I couldn't believe that this had really happened.

Among the inconsolable cries of the loved ones, I heard a doctor say "Prepare to shift the body".

A cheerful boy who used to make everybody laugh was reduced to a still body now.

He didn't have a name now and he didn't mean anything to them but a body occupying a bed.

The game of time which Rahul lost this time had vanquished with no fault of his.

He only did the right thing in the wrong world.

And he paid for it with his life and the life of his one true love.

Thus they left behind a sea of people to suffer behind them.

क्यूँ चीख बनकर आवाज़ जमीर की आज सताने लगी,
मुनासिब नहीं कि काफ़िर हूँ फिर क्यूँ ये आजमाने लगी?
वक़्त आ गया शायद अब चलने का
मौत महबूब बनकर बुलाने लगी।
ए मौत जरा ठहर!
मुझे मेरे बचपन से मिलने दे,

इसे आख़िरी ख़्वाहिश समझ
और कुछ पल खेलने दे!
पर ये आख़िरी बाजी भी मैं हार गया हूँ,
इसी 'सच' के साथ,
आख़िरी साँस भी साथ छोड़ जाने लगी
रूह बनकर मेरी एक अनकहा किस्सा,
इन फ़िज़ाओं में समाने लगी
आजाद हो रहा है सदियों से कैद एक परिंदा,
हसरतें आज यूँ गुनगुनाने लगीं
हो गई है शाम सूरज थक गया है अब,
मौज साहिल से मिल चैन की नींद सो जाने लगी
चिथड़े-चिथड़े हुआ वजूद रंगमंच का,
चिथड़े-चिथड़े हुआ वजूद रंगमंच का,
कहानी ख़ुद किरदार को दफ़्न कर ज़श्न मनाने लगी!

26-Apr-2011 (Tue) 6:30 am

I didn't know what had happened and how it all happened, but whatever happened, at least had brought some closure to Rahul and Jahnavi's love.

Their last rites were performed together. And if not in life, they were together in death.

I didn't have the guts to ask uncle when he conversed with Jahnavi's family for cremating their bodies together, perhaps it was not necessary to talk about that.

Rahul's parents would have never thought that they will lose the apple of their eyes in a city not known to them.

Neither Jahnavi' parents would have envisioned such a fate for their daughter. Not even in their worst nightmares. The eldest of the house would do such contemptible thing, who would have imagined?

Something which was not accomplished while they

lived, was happening after their death. Rahul and Jahnavi had finally bid adieu to this world, together.

This eternal love of 7 years was getting their final farewell, to be remembered forever on the earth and celebrated hereafter in the heavens.

From being in love, they became love, the definition of love.

The Agni (fire) which could have bound them together into a married life was now going to decimate their physical existence only to bind them together for the eternity in a world far beyond our perception, free from all the prejudices and dogmas.

There was an eerie silence in the atmosphere.

The fears in our hearts were finally gone, went unto becoming a reality. The one that had thrashed many worlds in a matter of just two days.

We all returned home after attending the funeral.

And this was how for personal profit, for name and fame once again politics killed them.

This accident was a proof of the fact that to what extent the human race can fall for its ego. The mentality here has become numb and the pain is asleep. This scandal was not done on any particular section, person or any society.

It was done on the whole system governed by this scholar mankind.

No one else is responsible for all this, the credit goes to our own "Mentality" which has just become pretense and a perfect evening show of a spectacle.

This is not painful because somewhere you can even delineate pain and quantify it.

But this incident is something beyond human definitions. This is a subject; which we should think about before taking the very next breath.

The storm had passed, but not before taking a serious toll on our lives, a permanent damage had been done, an irreversible void had been created. People were mourning the loss.

Many had several baffling and unanswered questions, but for some of us, the only thing that was going in our heads was to bring the culprit to the dark alleys of the law.

Rahul's family had registered an F.I.R. against Jahnavi's uncle who was responsible for such heinous act and deserved nothing less than facing justice.

If it were up to me, I would have killed him at the first sight for the inhuman act he committed. That man didn't deserve any respect or kindness.

In fact, he was not worthy of any human relationships.

Even bringing his name unto lips felt like a bad omen.

Now since everything that we all feared had come to pass and the worst had already happened, I had a moment to cry and comprehend what had happened, how could someone not have the faintest amount of compassion for such innocent souls.

This felt surreal, a hysterical reality which has struck all our lives like thousands of Volts of lightning, but didn't kill us and left us only to suffer.

It was very hard for me to ascertain how cruel someone can be. How far someone could go to keep his own wishes afloat. How could someone stoop down to such a level of inhumanity where he could poison his own family in cold blood!

It was the death of humanity, a death of compassion, and a murder of true love.

What was their mistake? Why did they deserve this fate and several such questions were pounding inside my brain and I couldn't wish less than the worst fate for her uncle.

Like the thousands of other youth in the country, I too didn't have any trust in our judicial system. Especially knowing the political connection of Jahnavi's uncle.

But I had a certain grit inside me which made me make a promise to self that I would go to any lengths and breadths to ensure that he got the worst form of punishment.

I knew nothing could have brought Jahnavi and Rahul back, but human emotions are so complicated, and rightly so. It would get a certain closure when it sees justice being served.

And in my opinion, he deserved much worse than what he did to those poor souls. Every bit of it, in every possible painful way.

THE TIME

10-May-2011

Very less time was left for the 8th semester's examinations. My family, my friends and college staff; everyone recommended me to change my room. Each one of them was suggesting me to stay away from the room that I shared with Rahul and from the memories that were attached to it, to stay away from any harness to the glorious times I spent with him. Those times were my treasure to cherish for a lifetime. Those were a part of my existence now, my very own shadow!

Poor people, they were not wise enough to understand that you could only run away from your own shadow but you could never hide from it, not until the rays of memories and love were still shining. It was a foolish idea.

Moreover, who wants to get rid of the shadow which had always been your glimmer in the darkness?

No one, right!

Now after the most horrifying episode of my life, whenever I sat for studies, it felt as if he was studying with me, he was turning pages, like.. like he and I were having a competition to finish the chapters first. As I turned pages, I saw him laughing at me. At the same time, I felt we both were having serious discussions and conversations on said topics. It was all in my head, but it wasn't any less than the reality I wished to be living in, again!

And ... the truth was, "I felt his absence badly."

Probably, this was my brain's way of coping up with the void.

Rahul, who used to fight every morning to take bath first, was not there anymore and there were no more morning rush or petty fights. Without him, everything seemed so incomplete.

With him gone, I felt fragmental. Talking about anything under the sun was just his thing, lying in the bed blabbering about nothing useful, I missed that the most. Now that he was gone, I realized his pointless blabbering was my lifeline. Oh, I missed him so much. Now I had to go alone at the tea point. No more Sufi music was played in the room. Pulling people's legs and mischievous talks were a thing of past now. Cricket matches still happened in the college, but the guy who used to make everyone play, Rahul, he wasn't there.

Our local hero, who used to pull off a filmy dialogue at every other thing, was now quiet forever. No more jokes were made on mundane topics, no more poems were written on crumbled papers, no more giggles were heard in those barren corridors, and no more love was inspired.

That year, no farewell party was conducted in the college. The whole college was in the aftershock of the incident.

As I was his closest friend, everyone enquired about my condition and took antecedents of the incident. It was painful to be conscious of it every time.

There was a fake smile on my face in an attempt to live

through the hard times. There was an insurmountable amount of sadness in my heart, yet sometimes I broke out laughing remembering his jokes.

He was the saviour of many students in semester exams and had inspired many of us to get through the miseries and stand on our own feet. And now that he was gone, we all went forward with life. We carried with us the inspiration he had filled us with, as he embarked on his last journey.

I must have had called Jahnavi's house some 2-3 times and they half-heatedly proclaimed to be alright.

And it was a daily routine for me to call Rahul's parents to check up on them and made sure they were alright. I had a plan to visit Rahul's house after exams to fulfil his last wish, I guess.

* * *

Exams had started. Every time I went to write the exams, the moment I bend to lock the hostel room, I couldn't help but think of what he used to say,

"Adi, agar mjhe Jahnavi nahi mili hoti na to main tujhse shaadi kar leta, saare ghar ke kaam kitne achchhe se karta hai tu."

(Adi, if I had not met Jahnavi I would have married you. How well you manage everything like a perfect house maker.)

We used to go together for exams singing all trashy bollywood songs. Our daily routine was almost similar but he was ahead of me in almost everything. He used to guide me like a mentor and support me like a big brother. But now there was no one to lead and no one to guide, just me and his memories.

He had worked very hard for 8th semester exams, only to get closer to the most beautiful thing in his life.

Neither he had left any stone unturned and nor did he

had any lacuna in his personality, nor was his love any less than sheer divinity. He deserved to live with the love of his life.

Now I had also developed a fear of the ways and means of this imperious society. So far I had only heard of the Heer-Ranjha, Romeo-Juliet, Laila-Majnu and Shahjahan-Mumtaj of various eras, but now I had experienced it through my own eyes in the form of Rahul and Jahnavi.

"Musafiro ko zindagi me kaha..n aaram mila hai,
Sacchi mohabbat ko yaha..n maut hi anjaam mila hai."

* * *

After finishing my exams, I was on my way to visit Rahul's home. I had to do the toughest job of returning his belongings back to where it belonged, safely.

For the 1st time I was going for the visit to his home. I took a bus on 10[th]June, 2011. Eccentric thoughts of things he often used to say troubled me.

His habit of witticism, commenting on narrow lanes and small buses leading to smaller towns, as a pretext to his regular invitations -

"Jab tu mere ghar chalega na bhai…"

(Bro..the day you will come along to my place …..)

It was around 8 in the evening when I stepped down in that small murky town. Uncle had come to receive me at the bus stand. The moment I touched his feet, he hugged me tightly like a father mourning to embrace his son. I could feel it in his eyes and the warmth of his hug. We both were trying to hide our grief.

He was trying hard to ask me about my journey but he just couldn't.

His voice was breaking and he was unable to hide his bereavement. Somehow I managed to look at Uncle's face and have my eyes meet his, but to look at aunty was not possible for me.

I could feel her pain just by being close to her and I didn't wish to cry or make her cry, so I avoided eye contact with her. I didn't have the courage to look at her dreadful condition. I knew that both uncle and aunty would see Rahul in me.

The toughest part was to take out Rahul's belongings and give them back to his parents.

But anyhow, I had to do that.

I handed them the bag which had Rahul's belongings in it and I took their excuse to go out for a walk. I knew that they would have cried holding his stuff, close to their hearts and they had all the rights to. I just wished to give them their space to mourn for their dear child.

That night at dinner, aunty had decorated the table and food on plates in the same way as she would have had done for Rahul. I kept on thinking, how she would have been thinking of Rahul while she prepared all the food as if Rahul was coming home. And every knock of reality would have had made her cry. It felt as if the food had Rahul's name written on it which eventually got erased by the tears of reality that his mother must have had shed.

We let silence take over that fateful night with nothing left to talk about.

I was given Rahul's room to rest that night.

That room was sobbing, there was a kind of heaviness in it as if every corner of that room was carrying a deep pain. The walls were filled with screeching cries, the ceiling had wept, and the doors creaked of pain.

I was not able to sleep that night, kept on changing postures the whole night, but not a single wink of sleep. I could feel his childhood memories entrapped in that room forever, and somewhere along with those memories, a part of his soul. I got up and checked up a few of his things.

There were a few pictures adjacent to his study table that included Sachin Tendulkar, Rahul Dravid and Einstein. There were lots of trophies and certificates on the shelf. His room reflected every bit of his hard work while he was growing up. There was a smile on my face while seeing all his stuff as if I were a part of his childhood now.

He was so fond of stickers. Stickers of Pokémon, Spiderman, Batman, the whole team of Marvel. They were seen pasted on his notebooks, boxes, rewards and what not.

It was 2 AM and I was feeling tired by then.

I reclined back on the chair and started dozing off.

And then suddenly my eyes caught the glimpse of his slam book, The slam from his school.

Less than words, it had faces on stick figures made by coloured pens. More than a slam book it looked like an art book. It was getting funnier. I started to get lost in it.

I was feeling relaxed now.

Calm and Peaceful….

Very caaaaalm …......

"Adi will be in my team. You keep quiet Jahnavi."

"Listen Rahul... I am a guest. Adi is also a guest and all guests will be in one team."

"Alright! So we will play cricket."

"No... no...Rahul! You know that I don't have any idea about cricket."

"It's okay, still you play. Adi and you will be openers, Kittu will bowl."

"Please, please, please play anything but not cricket. People will laugh at me."

"Hehe... you know ….I want that.. I wanna see people appreciating your cricketing skills."

"Why are you fighting Rahul, Oh come on yaar, let's play dumb charades no."

"See Rahul, even Adi is saying now."

"Kar diya saale aaj apne bhai ko paraya tune, Chalo jaise 'Mehemano' ki marzi."

("et tu, Adi ! You switched sides with her now, we're brothers, man. Anyway, 'as the guests please'.")

Saying this Rahul came close to me and said,

"Hey Adi, Thanks for coming brother. You did a good thing coming home. Mom, Dad must have felt good.

Adi, it wasn't like I didn't fathom my ending at Jahnavi's home that evening, but in those remaining moments, I just wanted to live that 'Life' which perhaps GOD hadn't had written in my fate.

Anyways,

Give my love to Mom ..And tell dad to forgive me this time.

Adi, I too miss everything...

I too want to stay here but ….

Some other time. I'll take your leave now.

Hey...Jahnavi, let's go."

Rahul rested his hand on my shoulder with his eyes wet.

I tried to speak further but couldn't.

Rahul and Jahnavi held each other's hand and started fading into a light. It was so bright that I failed to look into it.

I was soaking wet in sweat and the sun rays were falling on my face slipping through the window pane.

It was 6:30 in the morning and uncle was reading

newspaper sitting next to me. I had slumbered on the chair itself.

"Adi bete, you slept on the chair?", Uncle asked.

"Yeah! Good morning uncle."

"Morning bete, go get ready and have a cup of tea."

"Sure uncle."

I freshened up. Uncle and aunty got busy with their usual chores.

I wanted to see all the places that Rahul had told me about. One more day to spend with uncle and aunty and that was the day when I stepped into Rahul's shoes.

My return ticket was booked for that night.

That day I had a long discourse with his parents. Uncle somehow managed his emotions but aunty kept on crying talking about Rahul.

I tried my best to console her but even I didn't know the right words to say. I was crying from inside too.

The good thing was that few kids of the locality kept coming to their house, diverting their attention from all the grief from time to time. Those were the same kids Rahul used to talk about.

He lived in a very peaceful place. It seemed he was deeply missed by the kids too.

* * *

In the evening, I was standing in the balcony overlooking the park. Kids were playing and fighting. Seeing them made me feel happy.

"These kids have been playing here for a very long time, very sweet they are. They are very close to Rahul. Without him, these kids never started their game. He was loved by all. Kids will keep on playing and the games will go on. With time, these kids will grow and the games will change. If Rahul would have been with us in these changing times, then things would have been entirely different. The void he has left, can never be filled. Rahul will be forgotten by them. He will be all but a blip in the continuum of time." said uncle joining me in the balcony standing adjacent, looking at the park. His eyes were wet, but he stood there as strong he ever were.

"Yes uncle…." I replied.

"Adi bete, eat something. You also have to catch your train."

Aunty called me from the kitchen.

"Yes aunty, coming."

I looked around one more time, all the places where Rahul ever would have been, and kept each of them inside me; as his valued memory.

It was getting over forever … FOREVER !

I bid my farewell to uncle and aunty and hugged both of them. I promised them to keep coming on every festival.

And I started off from there. I wanted to look back, but I knew she must be crying and I was afraid I would make her cry if she wasn't. My eyes were wet and I was weeping like a child, so I walked a few paces ahead of uncle who was coming to drop me off. I wiped my tears immediately before he could have seen me.

I wished to stay for some more time but…

While returning, my thoughts were going towards Jahnavi's house. I had an intention to meet her parents as well, but I guess it was not possible from all angles.

When uncle came to see me off at the station, I had this feeling that

"This was not the way I ever imagined meeting Rahul's parents in his hometown and this was not the circumstance I had imagined to be bidding my farewell to his parents. I had always imagined meeting them with Rahul under happier times and with lots of laughter to be shared."

Now, this had come to pass as well. The last couple of months had been devastating, slower at some times and faster at other.

I touched uncle's feet one last time before I boarded the train. I saw uncle standing there on the platform until my train started moving and went away.. far... very far from him.

Like the train that had rode into sunset that evening, all our lives had set into a faraway sky of despair and pain, waiting for our sunrises of frail happiness and justice.

In the meantime, months had passed. Time was doing its thing and justice was getting served.

That inhuman, who had taken two innocent lives, destroyed two families and shattered many lives, got arrested and was in jail.

The Court, the judiciary system, the police, and the law had done their job and surely will keep on doing their duties.

but .....

Two families lost their adorable children. I lost a friend who was more than a brother to me and this world had lost two lovers to the eternity.

Everyone had lost something.

This was 'L O V E' ladies and gentleman, wherein we all had lost something….and gained nothing... Nothing!

5 Years Later

~~THE PRESENT~~ DAY

23-June-2017

Everything related to Rahul and Jahnavi is gone now. The only thing which is left with us today is their Tale of eternal love.

This, a heritage of love in the form of a story which will be read, recited and sung for years.

Rahul had always told me that he would write his story to become a well-known love story in the form of an epic-book.

This is how the cookie crumbles in corridors of time; his story has become an epic tale not just as any regular love story, but as an eternal story of love that will live on after the death in form of legacy and tales.

That cursed day, while leaving from Agra, I had one question on my mind and I asked Kajal, why she preferred calling me instead of ringing Rahul's parents that night.

She answered,

"After that prolonged informal meeting held in a room among Jahnavi's Dad, Jahnavi's uncle and Rahul before the dinner, Rahul sent the same message on my number, aunty's number and Jahnavi's number and that was,

"Something surprising is going to happen tonight, call my brother (Aditya: 97********) before informing my parents to witness the surprise :-) "

I guess that night during the meeting Rahul had sensed that he was not going to meet Jahnavi in this mortal world so he knowingly opted death to meet her in some other world, far from inhibitions of this world where rights and wrongs meet halfway.

I remember, while he was leaving from the hostel for Agra on Friday evening to meet Jahnavi's family, I too had some intuitions of something bad to occur. I actually wanted him to not go right then. I mean everything he had told me, specially the hindrance of Jahnavi's uncle in his relationship, and then a sudden twist in his mood was very suspicious to me.

Not even in my worst dream, I had imagined something so appalling to happen that would change all of our lives, forever.

I wanted to stop him from going, my gut was telling me something didn't fit properly. God, why did I not stop him? I sent my friend, my brother to his own death because I chose to be silent. I couldn't stop thinking how all of it was my fault, how I wasn't the friend when he needed it the most. I was cursing myself for not telling him about my intuitions and fears. If only I was friend enough to tell him my inhibitions, had I stopped him from going that day; everything would have been different now.

And now, how much ever I wish to go back to the day to change everything; I cannot. The happiness that I had seen on his face after ages, the way his eyes brightened when he said me the news, the way he couldn't stop smiling; that's all I remember from that day before I had bid him adieu. And this was the reason; I couldn't tell him my fears, fearing to steal away his happiness that day. And I had let everything happen. And now, I knew I was going to regret this all my life; living my life blaming myself for contributing, even in a small way, for his death. It killed me to realize that, no amount of blaming would bring him back . He was gone, and I had let him. I had created my own void. I killed him.

[*Tears rolled down from my eyes, and god knows I wanted to die at that moment.*]

He was writing a diary alone, silently, hiding it from everyone by staying awake late in the nights. Jotting down his emotions in that diary, who knew one day would be the only witness to his truest deepest feelings.

He was writing a story, perhaps his own. But there was someone else who was writing his story.

Today I am working with a top software firm. Whenever I get a promotion or any success in my work, I feel as if Rahul has made me through it, just like those semester exams.

Whatever I am today, is just because of his help, his constant push and those last night studies that we did in the hostel.

Poor me, I could never find the chance to thank him properly in this mortal world. And now that he is immortal, I hope he sees me from up there and knows that I am so thankful to him.

I just close my eyes.... his laughing face appears in front of me, I smile a little and this is how we talk sometimes. He has never faded in my memory, and he never will.

It's been 5 years since that Incident has happened.

If everything had been fine, they both would have tied a knot together and I would now be holding a mini Rahul or a baby Jahnavi in my arms.

And here I am, holding this notebook in my hand which I have spent the last many years to write Rahul and Jahnavi's story, which was Rahul's last request to me.

Today, I fulfilled his last wish and I am sure that tonight a star will shine brighter in the northern sky.

Whenever I think about Rahul's story I recall few lines written by Ghalib,

"Hui muddat ki ghalib mar gaya par yaadaata hai,
wo har ik baat par kahana ki yu..n hota to kya hota."

www.ingramcontent.com/pod-product-compliance
Lightning Source LLC
La Vergne TN
LVHW040011070726
842759LV00026B/416